VIGILANTE

**Center Point
Large Print**

*Also by Stephen J. Cannell and available from
Center Point Large Print:*

The Prostitutes' Ball
The Pallbearers
On the Grind

**This Large Print Book carries the
Seal of Approval of N.A.V.H.**

STEPHEN J. CANNELL

VIGILANTE

CENTER POINT LARGE PRINT
THORNDIKE, MAINE

This Center Point Large Print edition is published
in the year 2012 by arrangement with
St. Martin's Press.

This is a work of fiction. All of the characters,
organizations, and events portrayed in this novel
are either products of the author's imagination
or are used fictitiously.

The text of this Large Print edition is unabridged.
In other aspects, this book may
vary from the original edition.
Printed in the United States of America.
Set in 16-point Times New Roman type.

ISBN: 978-1-61173-263-4

Library of Congress Cataloging-in-Publication Data

Cannell, Stephen J.
  Vigilante / Stephen J. Cannell.
  p. cm.
  ISBN 978-1-61173-263-4 (library binding : alk. paper)
  1. Scully, Shane (Fictitious character)—Fiction.
    2. Police—California—Los Angeles—Fiction.
    3. Women—Crimes against—Fiction.
    4. Television personalities—Fiction.
    5. Reality television programs—Fiction.
    6. Los Angeles (Calif.)—Fiction. 7. Large type books. I. Title.
  PS3553.A4995V54 2011b
  813′.54—dc23
                                                  2011033698

VIGILANTE

Chapter 1

The filthy rug limped along the sidewalk on swollen plastic baggie-wrapped feet, hunched against the chilly February wind. It was a Persian design with a navy and cranberry center surrounded by a stained, red and gold border. The rug was worn to the nub. I watched as it leaned against the wall of a six-story ornate rococo structure located on the corner of Broadway and Third Street in downtown L.A. A minute later a puddle of urine seeped from underneath it and spread across the sidewalk to drain into the gutter. The rug was pissing on the north wall of the magnificent Bradbury Building, built in 1893 and considered by most to be one of Los Angeles's most significant architectural landmarks.

A minute later, the rug turned, revealing that it was wrapped around the shoulders of an ageless man with a complexion like a strawberry pie that had exploded in the oven, the planes and furrows of his face made red by a landscape of sores and broken capillaries. He was one of L.A.'s street denizens. This homeless resident of downtown was on a breakfast tour of the overflowing Dumpsters that sat in the alleys behind Broadway and had paused during his 8:00 a.m. buffet for a

7

leak in plain view of a line of commuter traffic.

He deposited about a quart of dark, yellow liquid on the side of the rococo brick building, the top four floors of which currently housed the Internal Affairs Group of the LAPD.

I'm a police officer posted to Homicide Special, an elite investigations unit that is part of the LAPD Robbery-Homicide Division, and this was my first cop dilemma of the day. As a sworn badge carrier, I knew I should arrest this guy on half a dozen public nuisance ordinances, but it was chilly outside and warm in my car and I had left my overcoat back at the office, so I really didn't want to budge. Emotionally, I was sort of past this stuff. I'd given up rolling drunks years ago when I'd left Patrol.

I sat there, buffered against the crisp February wind, and tried to conjure up some pity. He was just a poor soul who had slipped through the cracks in our transient, fast-moving society. But ignoring him wasn't working, because he still had his junk out and continued to urinate in public. I reminded myself that he was pissing on a building that housed the LAPD Internal Affairs Group, an act that most cops would certainly applaud.

I was working on these excuses, while waiting in the red zone in front of the Bradbury, hoping my partner, Sumner Hitchens, would hurry up and come down from a deposition he was giving upstairs at Internal Affairs Group. If he arrived in time I could get out of here without incident and leave the homeless guy to his urine-soaked wanderings.

Detectives all drove department cars, the sole exception being Homicide Special, because of the high-profile, often covert nature of our investigations. Hitch had called me this morning to ask if I could pick him up at IA because he'd dropped his Porsche Carrera off for servicing a block away on Broadway before walking over to the Bradbury.

Hitch was giving this deposition on behalf of two patrol officers who had been accused of beating a suspect named Quadry Barnes in a Hollywood Station interrogation room. My partner had been in the adjacent holding area when the event was supposed to have happened and had witnessed everything. He told me the arresting cops never laid a hand on Quadry, who by the way had just held up a 7-Eleven, killing two teenaged clerks, casually blowing them out of their socks with Teflon Black Talon 9mm hollow points, also known as cop killers, without so much as a shrug.

There was a continually changing set of rules in the street game we all now played. This felon had committed a double murder and, stupid asshole that he was, had done the deed in full view of the store's surveillance cameras. Once confronted with the video, he abruptly cut a deal with the prosecutor and drew a "Skip Court, Pass Death Row" card, saving the court the time and expense of a lengthy trial and the state endless capital appeals, not to mention the final medical dispatch of Mr. Barnes to the lower regions of hell. As a result, this dirtbag got to keep breathing until he died of natural causes or got shanked in some prison yard brawl.

Right after making his lifesaving deal, Quadry promptly accused the arresting officers of doing a drum solo on his head in the station I-room with their PR-24 aluminum nightsticks.

The EMTs were called but couldn't find a mark. This fact was of almost no consequence. Once the charge was made, regardless of its validity, Internal Affairs was mandated to take the case. The two patrol cops were pulled from the field and put on paper-clip duty for several months until the adjudication of their IA Board of Rights hearing.

Filing a false police report was a Class C felony worth, at best, only a year in jail, which meant nothing to Quadry Barnes, who had just agreed to serve a life sentence. It was just another part of the endless cycle of BS that cops were now forced to deal with.

I watched as the Persian rug wearer turned to look at the street. He still had his equipment out and now began waving it at the passing commuter traffic. I'd been studiously trying to avoid dealing with this guy, but he'd finally crossed the line. I opened my car door and got out. As I approached him I began to pick up a raw downwind odor, which grew in intensity as I neared.

"Excuse me, sir, but you're unzipped," I said politely. "Exposing yourself in public is a violation of Criminal Statute Three-One-Four, punishable by fines and incarceration."

"You miss me wid dat, dog breath," he growled through a busted mouth with the few teeth he had spaced wide like the front grille of a '53 Buick. He waved his meat at me to make his point. "Dis here be the English Sentry. The English Sentry, he do what he do. I got no say over Lord Ding Wallace."

"Don't make me arrest you," I said. Of course we both knew jail would be a step up in his accommodations. To back my empty threat I pulled out my badge. The wind shifted, and I was suddenly treated to an overpowering mixture of ripe odors well beyond my limited powers of description.

"The fuck do I care 'bout dat?" he said, taking offense.

The exchange was starting to escalate, as it usually does with schizophrenic street people.

"You stargazing, tally-whacking piece of shit." "This here be Morning Pride. Big Boy needs his space."

I really didn't want to cuff this guy. If I put him in the Acura, I'd have to shampoo the interior when I got home. I was trying to decide my next move when my cell phone beeped with an incoming text message. I looked down and read a note from my captain, Jeb Calloway, at Homicide Special. He was asking me to call a homicide detective named Rick Laguna in Hollenbeck Division. I turned away from the Persian rug and punched in the attached number.

"Shane Scully, Homicide Special," I said when he answered. "Is this Detective Laguna?"

"Yeah, Rick Laguna," an unfamiliar voice replied. "I'm with Hollenbeck Homicide. We just picked up a fresh one-eighty-seven that you guys at Homicide Special need to process."

"Who got killed?"

"I'd rather keep that off a cell transmission. The address is 1253 North Savannah Street in the Four-A-Fifty-Nine Basic Car Area of Hollenbeck. That block is claimed by the Evergreen gang, so park in tight near curb security."

The Evergreens were a Hispanic set named after Evergreen Cemetery, which was located in Boyle Heights and was the final resting place for scores of their bullet-riddled homeboys.

"Is this gang related?" I asked.

"Who the hell knows what it is? I'll tell you this much. You ain't gonna like it. I'll fill you in when ya get here." He hung up.

I heard a splattering noise and pivoted to see the rug had moved behind me to my Acura. Lord

Ding Wallace was now dispatching a yellow stream onto my right front tire.

Just then, I spotted Hitch walking toward me from the Bradbury Building carrying a blond alligator wafer case with chunky gold fixtures that he'd once mentioned cost him over two thousand dollars. My millionaire partner was handsome, athletic, and looked tricked out this morning as usual, wearing a gray herringbone jacket with a silver pocket square over dark Armani slacks. Not that I can exactly spot an Armani cut, but I know Hitch favors that designer. His expensive wardrobe, coffee-colored complexion, and neatly trimmed moustache all contributed to his stylish *GQ* look.

My wardrobe is much closer to the ground. Off-the-rack Macy's suits that go with my battered club fighter look, broken nose, and cowlicky short black hair.

Hitch stopped short when he saw the rug urinating on my tire and made a gesture of disbelief. "You gonna just let this ragbag piss on your ride, dawg?"

"He's not pissing on my ride. He's giving my tires an acid wash," I deadpanned. "I can have him do yours later if you want."

Hitch was still frowning at the homeless man as I said, "We just caught a case from Hollenbeck Division. Let's roll."

We climbed into the car and pulled away

from the curb as the bum shouted after us.

"Go on. Run from the Purple Prince. See if I give a shit!"

I turned at the corner and headed north up Third toward the freeway and Hollenbeck Division. The fresh homicide was a perfect reason to leave the filthy rug, and Lord Ding Wallace, behind.

Chapter 2

"What are we rolling on?" Hitch asked.

"Don't know. You ever heard of a Hollenbeck dick named Rick Laguna?"

"Ricky Laguna? Yeah, we were in Southwest Patrol together. He's a good guy when he's not drinking."

"He wouldn't give me anything over his cell. Just said that I wouldn't like it."

"What's to like anymore?" Hitch grumbled, still bummed over this morning's deposition. "Damn job is getting to be less like police work and more like sewage management."

We took Broadway to the 101 Freeway, turned east, and headed toward Hollenbeck Division.

"Get my laminated division map out of the glove box and tell me where the Four-A-Fifty-Nine Basic Car Area, will you? I need a good off-ramp for North Savannah Street."

Hitch opened the glove box and reached for the map.

"I can't believe how the job has changed," he groused, leaking cynicism. "Think about how much time is being wasted on fuckheads like Quadry Barnes. That animal shoots two kids in a market and we got the killing on tape, but our patrol guys have been jacked up over it for a month. Half a dozen cops and witnesses get stuck doing depositions; then we have to waste a week next month testifying. All so this bleeding hemorrhoid can get a ride to L.A. from Soledad, sit at the advocates table in his orange prison jumpsuit, and laugh at us. Worse still, these one-eighty-one complaints are like penicillin-resistant clap. Even when they're cleared, they never get off your record."

Of course, I was in complete agreement. Hitch fell silent as he looked down at the division map.

"Best off-ramp is First Street; then go left," he advised, then dropped the map, pulled out his phone, and hit a preset number.

"Jerry, it's Hitch. When you pick this up, I forgot to tell you I sent the story option papers for *Trial by Fire* over to Ziff last night for a legal opinion. I think the second eighteen-month renewal option is okay, but it shouldn't be free. Warners should have to pay for it. Call me once you've talked to him." He clicked off.

My partner hit the jackpot when he sold a big

murder case of his to the movies a few years ago. It ended up being a box-office smash. The case was about a serial murderer Hitch caught when he was in Metro Robbery Homicide. The killer believed the only way he could stay alive was to drink his victims' blood. The film was *Mosquito* and it starred Jamie Foxx in the lead role of Detective Sumner Hitchens. The damn thing grossed over $600 million worldwide. Hitch had three back-end points, making him instantly wealthy.

The second case he sold was one we worked together last year, which he calls *The Prostitutes' Ball*. We're still in script development on that and it probably won't get shot for a year or so, if at all. I reluctantly took a piece of it, because my half of the story rights payment is rebuilding my son Chooch's garage apartment at our house in Venice, California. "Chooch" is short for "Charles." He's my only child and is in his final year at USC on a football scholarship.

Hitch has agents at United Talent Agency. The guy he just called was Jerry Eisenberg, who heads their film department. Ziff is a Hollywood power lawyer named Ken Ziffren. These guys are all at the highest levels of the Biz, and Hitch sometimes manages his movie interests from the front seat of our D-ride.

"I'm thinking we're running out of road here, dawg," Hitch complained as he holstered his cell, still marinating over his morning deposition. "You gotta have a law degree to do police work anymore. I'm thinking maybe it's time for us to jump out of this free-falling safe before it hits ground. Team up for real, make movies full-time."

It was a discussion we had at least twice a week lately. I don't want to be a movie producer—I'm a cop. I think I'd look really stupid in silk shirts and overlapping gold chains. But it seemed like Hitch was becoming more and more disenchanted with the job. I had been trying to find a way to pull him out of his funk.

When we arrived at North Savannah Street, I started picking up curb numbers, looking for 1253. In the late forties, the houses in this district were newly built postwar homes for middle-class factory workers, but the last sixty years had taken a heavy toll on the neighborhood. Now the decrepit stucco and wood-sided bungalows displayed security-barred windows, peeling paint, and graffiti as they squatted in a ragged line of weed-choked postage-stamp-sized lawns.

Throughout the seventies and eighties, these blocks had slowly been turned over to poor Hispanic families who came north to find a better life. More recently, the neighborhood had become ensnared in a dense maw of gang violence. Tagger art announced the competing sets. Varrio Nuevo Estradas claimed blocks right next to Clique Los Primos. Farther down were White Fence and

Krazy Ass Mexicans, Avenue 43's, Fickes Street Locos, and Evergreen territories. At last count there were over forty-five Hispanic gangs operating in the Boyle Heights section of Hollenbeck Division.

During the daylight hours these blocks looked forlorn but not overly dangerous. Most of the *vato* hitters worked their drug corners all night, stayed up until dawn, and slept until late afternoon. This left the streets to little kids and old women with swollen ankles who ventured out to make their morning trips to the market, pushing their stolen silver schooners from Vons or Albertsons.

After dark, as any Hollenbeck patrol officer could tell you, this hood had a whole different vibe. Lowriders full of young killers were parked on every street with the lights off, watching their turf. Heavy salsa beats rocked the tires while marijuana smoke, called *yerba*, drifted from the open windows. The nights were often interrupted by the savage rip of a MAC-10 spitting out copper-jacketed death.

It was easy to spot the crime scene. Six patrol cars were parked at the curb with a bunch of cops milling out front. Graffiti tagged the street as Evergreen turf. As we headed toward the address, we drove by a new white Ford Econoline van with a big blue *V-TV* stenciled on the side.

"Uh-oh," Hitch said as we passed the vehicle. The back door on the van was open, revealing an impressive array of large, silver-studded equipment boxes. A TV crew had set up in a yard and was interviewing a tattooed Hispanic youth, gunning off footage using two digital cameras and an elaborate lighting package.

"We're fucked," I groaned as I caught a glimpse of a familiar man conducting the interview. He was a medium-built blond-haired guy wearing a blue blazer and diagonally striped tie. It was Nixon Nash, host of *Vigilante TV*, a hot nationally syndicated TV show that was currently riding the top of the Nielsen ratings.

"That guy needs a permanent room at the asshole academy," Hitch said sourly. "Just one more example of what I was saying."

He turned around, looking out of the rear window at the receding TV van. "It's not bad enough we got wet farts like Quadry Barnes to deal with. Now we gotta also put up with this guy." Then he added, "With him here, now I'm really wondering who got murdered."

Vigilante TV had sprung to national prominence a few years back. The show billed itself as a police watchdog. Nash actually referred to himself on the air as America's number one video vigilante. *V-TV* was just beginning its third season. However, according to the show's main title, the police legacy of its host, Nix Nash, had started twenty years earlier in Miami Beach.

Most cops across America knew Nash's history

by heart, because we all watched the show like ghoulish rubberneckers checking out a freeway disaster. In the mid-nineties Nix Nash had been a patrol officer in South Florida. After just three years on the job, he'd decided to change professions and quit the police force to go to law school.

As a lawyer he found his way to L.A. and began practicing here. The majority of his clients were violent predicate felons who, by the account of most, were guilty as hell of the charges brought against them. Despite that fact, Nash did very well getting them off, usually by claiming every imaginable brand of police impropriety. His favored courtroom tactic was to put the arresting officers on trial.

From 2000 to 2006 he expanded his L.A. practice to cover civil lawsuits against cops. The word around the courthouse was he was not above buying false testimony, although, in all fairness, that claim had never been proven.

If there is such a thing as karmic payback, it made a heartfelt appearance in 2006 when one of Nash's partners turned him into our bunco squad for embezzling from his own law firm to support an over-the-top Hollywood lifestyle. Needless to say, a lot of overtime went into that investigation, but not one of the cops working it put in for even an hour. The case quickly rose to the level of divine providence.

This magnificent investigatory effort resulted in a three-year sentence for Nixon Nash at Corcoran State Prison in Central California and the stripping of his law license. However, because of "good time" served, he got out in eighteen months.

While in jail, Nash wrote a book about his adventures taking corrupt cops to court. The book was titled *Vigilante.* It won the Prison PEN Award, was published in New York, and became a national bestseller. With its success, Nash arose like a battered zombie in a George Romero film. Nash optioned the rights to *Vigilante TV* to a local TV station in his hometown of Miami and continued his crusade against local law enforcement there, only now it was playing to a much larger audience. The guy was like a fungus you couldn't kill.

The first season of *V-TV* with Nixon Nash aired on a local channel in Miami Beach. At the end of the year the show had left a trail of broken police careers in its wake but had earned a huge Nielsen share in the Miami market. That encouraged a big syndicator to pick it up and distribute it nationally.

Then *V-TV* moved on for a second highly rated season in Atlanta, this time going after two homicide detectives who had mishandled a serial murder case that took place in Piedmont Park. Because of Nash and his show, the two Atlanta detectives were humiliated on national TV and took early retirement. Two months later, under intense media scrutiny, the Atlanta police chief also resigned.

Now Nix Nash was in L.A., ripe for vengeance against the city that had cost him his license to practice law. The third season of *V-TV* was about to start, but nobody yet knew what case they were going to cover. So far the show had been riding our radio calls, and sending crews to crime scenes, where they would shoot a little test footage and leave.

"Maybe this will just be another dry run," I said hopefully, looking over at Hitch, who just grunted as he turned to look through the front windshield at the murder house we were pulling up to.

Ricky Laguna was waiting by the curb. He was a short, stocky forty-year-old Hispanic detective who wore his too-tight blue suit uncomfortably, like the costume from his high school play. He had a low forehead, lots of black hair, and tobacco-stained teeth. His garish tie was too wide and out of style. The whole ensemble screamed cop. Adding in his drinker's red nose, all that was missing was the white socks.

His partner was a tightly wrapped female detective named Pam Becker who, after we all introduced ourselves, stayed outside with Patrol, busily organizing the yellow tape detail.

We got what we needed from our briefcases, stuffed our pockets, and got out of the car. Rick

Laguna walked us up to the house. He seemed glad to see Hitch.

"I seen your movie. Good shit, homeboy." He grinned as he pulled aside some yellow crime scene tape blocking the front door, then said, "Better put on your paper booties."

Hitch and I reached into our pockets and pulled out hospital slippers to protect the crime scene from unnecessary shoe prints. We put them on and stepped inside.

The front room of the house had several bedsheets tacked up on the front windows. I wondered why. All the lights were on. We followed a premarked entrance path strung with yellow tape along the east side of the small living room that had been set up by the patrol officers. They had also taped off the murder room and marked an egress path. All of this was standard academy-taught procedure for primary responders on any murder scene. It kept the swarm of LAPD officers and crime techs from inadvertently leaving their own trace evidence near the body. I glanced around the living room. It was strewn with old Coke cans, fast-food boxes, and magazines.

"Is it okay for you to tell us now who the vic or vics are?" I asked Laguna as we paused outside the kitchen, which had a big X in yellow tape across the threshold, identifying it as the murder scene.

"One vic. Female. Looks like she got beaten first, then double-tapped in the face with a large-bore weapon."

"You got an ID on the deceased?" I asked.

"Oh yeah," he said, and rocked back on his heels like a man surveying a tall building.

"So who is it?"

"Lolita Mendez," he said.

"Shit," Hitch hissed under his breath.

"Lita Mendez lives here?" I said, looking past Laguna into the kitchen, where a woman's lifeless body was sprawled.

With the *V-TV* van parked half a block up the street I instantly knew that this was the case Nix Nash had been waiting for.

Chapter 3

Standing in the kitchen doorway, I noted that the inside of the house had a faint but pungent odor of garlic. I looked down and studied the body.

I'd never seen the deceased in person, only in an occasional newspaper photo, or once or twice on TV, but it was now easy to understand why Hollenbeck Homicide had kicked this one over to us.

Lita Mendez was one of the city's most aggressive police critics and gang activists. She'd filed over a hundred civilian complaints against Hollenbeck Division police officers on behalf of Evergreen gang members and their families. As a result, quite a few cops had lost grade and pay. Some had even lost their pensions.

I'd been in break rooms in different stations over the years when Lita's name had come up, and the hatred that poured out was genuine and overpowering. She hated us and we had returned that hatred in full measure. She'd been arrested several times by overly ambitious cops on questionable charges. None of those arrests stuck.

Her younger brother was a notorious Evergreen banger named Homer "Conejo Loco" Mendez. The Crazy Rabbit was incarcerated in Corcoran State Prison for conspiring to kill a police officer, something Lita Mendez always maintained was a trumped-up charge and another example of police harassment against her family.

I remember reading a news story once that claimed Lita had nothing more than a tenth-grade education. That hadn't slowed her down, because with natural intelligence and street guile she'd served up a lot of trouble for the LAPD.

Hitch and I took two short steps into the kitchen so we could view the crime scene but stayed well back from the body. The victim was lying on the floor and, in death, no longer seemed as formidable. She just looked shriveled and sad. It was still hard to believe she was dead.

I saw that the "Chalk Fairy" had been here. Patrol officers all carry chalk to mark the pavement during traffic investigations. Occasionally, on murder scenes, they develop the unreasonable urge to draw an outline around the body before detectives arrive. This is in violation of all the rules of a homicide investigation, starting with disturbing the crime scene and up to and including potentially leaving the patrol officer's own trace evidence on the victim, which can end up sending us on a search for a red-haired killer when the hair actually belonged to the responding officer.

At the academy, it is scrupulously explained to recruits that chalk outlines are only drawn by the medical examiner, and then only just before the body is transported. However, the Chalk Fairy still made the occasional phantom stop at various murder scenes. My guess was in Lita's case this outline was more than just helpful enthusiasm. Whoever did it was making a statement on behalf of all the cops in Hollenbeck Division.

"You find out which numb nuts chalked her out?" I asked.

"It was like that when we got here," Laguna said predictably. "Patrol is claiming it wasn't them, but you know how that goes."

She'd been such a large presence in life I was surprised by how small Lita Mendez actually was. Only about five-two and no more than a hundred pounds, she lay sprawled on her back in the center

26

of the kitchen. Her once natural gold tan complexion had turned ashen. Purple lividity colored the lowest parts of her body, indicating she'd been dead for a while. Her head had leaked blood and cerebral spinal fluid, the result of two gunshot wounds in the face.

One shot looked like a third eye, dead center in her forehead. The other was squarely in the nose, leaving nothing but a deep, nickel-sized entry wound and fragmented chips of nose cartilage. The exit wounds were massive and had taken out most of the back of her skull. I looked around but couldn't see any bullet holes in the walls or appliances.

"You see where the slugs went or find any brass?" I asked Laguna.

"Not yet."

"Maybe she was already on her back when she got tapped. I bet CSI is gonna find the slugs in the floor under her head. From the placement of those wounds, center forehead and nose, this looks execution-style."

Laguna nodded.

The victim's legs splayed awkwardly, like she'd been unconscious or even dead when she'd gone down: her arms were bent at the elbows as if signaling a touchdown. The green blowflies that find a corpse within hours of death had been at it for a while. There were maggot larvae in her open mouth and inside the two oozing bullet holes.

"Let's get an ambient room temperature to help Entomology pin down a closer time of death," I said to Hitch, who was sketching the murder scene in the expensive red leather writer's journal he used as a crime notebook.

He nodded, then took a small digital thermometer out of his pocket and set it on the nearby kitchen counter. Heat or cold has a drastic effect on the speed of fly larva gestation. The warmer it is, the faster they mature.

"I don't see any footprints near the body," Hitch said. "But we should get ERT out here to do an electrostatic dust lift for latent shoe prints."

It was a good thought, because often if a killer doesn't see that he's left footprints, he won't bother to clean up the floor. That doesn't mean his shoe prints aren't there. If present, an ESDL would find them and lift them up for us.

"You think that piece of shit, Nash, knows Lita's the vic?" Laguna asked.

"Probably," I said. "He's been cruising our radio calls. Not hard to back-finger this address, use the real estate tax records to find out who owns this house."

"Except Lita didn't own it. Just renting," Laguna said. "Matter of fact, she just moved in about a week ago. The real estate contract is on the front hall table."

"He's coming up the street with his camera crew," Hitch warned. He had moved and was now looking out the side window at the advancing group of TV people in the street.

"Okay," I said, turning back to Laguna. "Have your partner tell Patrol we're widening the crime scene area. String the yellow tape all the way down to the intersection on First Street, put a cop on it, then set up a media control area one block over and make sure Nash waits there."

Hitch and I stepped back to the kitchen doorway as Laguna went out to talk to his partner.

"We're sailing into a big storm here," Hitch said, looking down at Lita's body.

A moment later, Laguna returned and told us Detective Becker and two patrol officers would take care of Nix Nash and his TV crew.

"Let's get all the patrol officers off the property," I told Laguna. "Get hair and shoe-print samples from everybody who was inside and see if there's a house nearby we can use as a CP. I only want people on this scene who need to be here."

"Already did that," Laguna said. "There's a vacant house across the street. We're calling the owner and will get the phones turned on. I also had my supervisor call up the superior court. He's working on getting us a crime scene search warrant."

"Nice," I said. "Thanks."

Without a warrant we couldn't do anything but secure the scene and the body and do a neighborhood canvass to see if anybody saw anything. The collection of evidence had to be done on constitutionally legal grounds or it would be challenged in court. Until the search warrant arrived we could only observe the crime scene, make sketches, and note transient evidence, which included such things as smell or temperature and the fact the room lights were still on. All pattern, trace, and conditional evidence had to wait for the warrant.

"You call the crime techs yet?" Hitch asked Laguna.

"Soon as I got here. CSI, the ME, and photographers are all rolling."

"Who found the body and called it in?" Hitch continued.

"Leasing agent. Apparently there was a problem with the old tenant on some of the attached fixtures. The agent came over to work it out this morning and she found the body. The door was ajar, so she just walked in."

"Where is she?" I asked.

"Waiting in her car out front." He pointed out the side kitchen window to a blue Prius parked by the curb. "Name is Vanessa Valente."

Chapter 4

Hitch and I decided that I would question the leasing agent while he observed her demeanor. Ms. Valente looked up from the laptop she was working on when I knocked on her car window and flashed my creds. Then she opened the door and got out. She was a big-boned Hispanic woman about thirty-five, wearing a nice-looking dark business suit and conservative two-inch heels.

"Ms. Valente? I'm Detective Shane Scully. This is my partner, Sumner Hitchens. We're taking over this investigation. We understand you found Ms. Mendez's body?"

"Yes, I did."

Vanessa Valente was not fat, but she wasn't exactly thin either. A good description would be "abundant." Her features were rounded, pleasant, and ordinary. She also seemed strangely unaffected by the violence that had greeted her this morning.

"I came over because the old tenant who used to rent this duplex had a list of things that needed to be retrieved," Ms. Valente said with no trace of an accent. "Things that had been left during the move. I talked to Lita about it and we set a time to meet and go over the list first thing this morning."

"Detective Laguna said you opened the door, walked in, and found her already dead?"

"Yes. It was ajar. She was in the kitchen. Those green flies were everywhere. I touched her. I hope that was okay. I only took her pulse. When I couldn't find one I called nine-one-one."

"Were the lights all on when you got here?"

"Yes. I guess that means it was still dark when she was killed, huh?"

"Probably.

"Was her body stiff when you tried to take her pulse?" I asked.

"Why does that matter?"

"If it was stiff that means rigor mortis was present. Rigor sets in about four hours after death. It might help us determine when she was killed."

"When I touched her she was cold, but not stiff," Vanessa said.

Upon hearing that and after looking at the fly larvae, my guess was the body was at least six hours old. Lita probably had been killed during the night before turning off the lights to go to bed.

"Did you use the phone in the house when you called nine-one-one?"

"Yes."

"We're going to need to take a set of elimination prints and a hair and skin sample before you leave. We'll also need your shoe prints. CSI should be here momentarily and can do it."

"Okay. That works."

"You don't seem too upset," I said.

"I was born around here. I came back to this neighborhood after college. My office is at a REMAX ten blocks away. People die frequently on these blocks, Detective. I saw my first dead body when I was seven. I was roller-skating to school. He was shot, lying across the sidewalk right up from my house. That one scared the shit out of me. I've become more accustomed to the experience since then."

"Can you think of anything that could be helpful, like any enemies she had, recent disputes, or people who might want her dead?"

"I'm sorry. I don't know of anybody who would want to kill her."

I did. Half the cops in Hollenbeck. But I didn't say that. Instead, I handed Ms. Valente my card and said, "Give me a call if anything occurs to you."

She nodded and I started to leave but then turned back. "Were you also friends with the victim?"

"Lita was my client. It was hard to be friends with her. She was . . . I don't know . . . 'Driven,' I guess, is the word. She saw everything through a very unique prism."

Hitch and I returned to the house and were walking up the drive when I looked back and saw Nix Nash along with his camera crew being escorted down the street by two patrol officers. None of the TV people looked too happy.

Once we were back inside I again noted the faint odor of garlic. "You smell that?" I asked Hitch.

"Yeah, it's stronger in the kitchen. Besides garlic I also smell cooked onions with sage, or maybe it's bay leaf, like a Bolognese sauce or something."

"A Bolognese sauce? Get the fuck outta here. We're in the Mexican ghetto."

"You can eat Italian in a Mexican ghetto. I was raised in South Central and my mom made the best pasta *vongole* you ever tasted."

Among his many other talents, Hitch is a gourmet cook. When he goes on vacation, he frequently takes classes at the Cordon Bleu in Paris, something that millionaire movie people get to do. They also go to tennis camps run by ex–Wimbledon champs.

We stood for a moment, taking in the pungent garlicky odor that clung to the drapes and was mixing badly with the slight copper-sweet smell of Lita's blood and decaying brain tissue.

I saw a uniformed sergeant pull up in a department slick-back. He was holding a yellow sheet, which I knew was our search warrant.

"Better glove up," I said. Both Hitch and I pulled latex packs out of our jacket pockets and put them on.

Then a CSI van pulled up, followed by the ME's wagon. We went outside to meet them. Once they were gathered around us on the porch, Hitch,

Laguna, and I began organizing the investigation, starting by turning the house over to the videographer so he could document the crime scene. CSI and the MEs would then take over, working the body, dusting for prints, and looking for shoe impressions inside and out.

The cameraman went in alone and started doing his walk-through. After he was finished, the evidence retrieval team from CSI began the scan of the kitchen floor. We'd asked them for an electrostatic dust print lift, so one of them pulled metallic film sheets from a case and a metal ground plane to create a static charge on the lifting mat. This caused any dust prints below the mat to bond to the film surface, making a precise mirror image of the print on the film mat. They picked up half a dozen shoe sole patterns. Once they were finished securing floor prints, they waved us in.

Hitch checked the sink. It was empty, but there were a lot of pots and pans in the dishwasher. They'd already gone through the cycle, so there was no telling what she'd been cooking. The coroner would have to provide that for us with a stomach content analysis.

While CSI and the ME continued to work, Hitch and I went back outside and walked up the driveway in a cold wind that was made crisp with the promise of an incoming storm. We checked the garage and found a red '94 Chevy Caprice parked inside.

"We gotta get this towed to Cal State," I said. "Get Forensics to go through it."

Hitch made the note, then looked up. "Nix Nash is going to be all over this," he observed.

"I know."

"He's gonna make us look like douche bags on national TV."

"Yeah."

"We should pull the pin, Shane. Pitch this one back and put in our papers before this guy is leading a five-man camera crew around in our assholes."

"Probably good advice, but I'm not somebody who likes getting chased off."

I looked down and noticed a paper coffee cup in the dead bushes on the edge of the property beside the driveway. It was right where the driver's side door would be if you'd parked there. I looked closer and saw that it was a paper vending-machine cup with a delicate brown floral ring design just under the lip of the cardboard circumference. It was a fairly recent discard, because there was still some wet coffee residue in the bottom that hadn't evaporated.

One of the crime scene techs was just walking up to the porch carrying an equipment case from her vehicle.

"Excuse me." I asked her, "Could you collect this paper coffee cup for me?"

"Yes, sir."

"Then check with Patrol and make sure none of them dropped it. If it's not theirs, try and get me a DNA scan off the rim and a coffee content analysis."

"Okay," she said, and went back to the CSI truck, returning a few seconds later with a clear plastic evidence bag and forceps.

She picked up the cup carefully and deposited it into the bag, then walked down to show it to the sergeant in charge of the Hollenbeck Division, who had delivered the search warrant. He was now helping Detective Becker supervise the neighborhood canvass by his patrol officers.

My phone rang and I looked down at the caller ID but didn't recognize the number. It was a 626 area code. That's somewhere in the East Valley, I think. I picked it up.

"Is this Detective Scully?" a man's voice asked.

"Yes. Who's this?"

"Nixon Nash. I'm about a block away in your media control area. I understand you're the lead detective. I thought we should have a chat."

"How did you get my name and this number?"

"I have contacts," he said noncommittally.

"You mean you have a spy inside the police department?"

"Let's not bicker. I've got some information that might advance your case."

Then we were both silent, listening to each other breathe.

"I'm only a few blocks away. I can help you," he prodded.

"I've seen your show, Mr. Nash. My guess is nothing involving you is going to help me."

"Geez, that's kinda rough," he said as if he hadn't been trashing cops on TV for the last two years. "If you're talking about those detectives in Georgia last season, they completely botched it. I'm trying to help the police, not hurt them. How does a bad murder investigation help law enforcement?"

"I'm pretty busy right now," I hedged, not wanting to get sucked in by this guy like those cops in Atlanta.

"I discovered a witness who can help determine motive. I already know Lolita Mendez is the victim. That's gotta be a hot grounder for you guys. How 'bout you and me put our heads together and solve this thing?" I could hear a smile in his voice.

"Just a minute." I put him on hold and looked at Hitch. "It's Nash. He knows the vic is Lita Mendez. He says he has a witness who can supply motive."

"Don't swallow that hook," Hitch said.

"You stay here. There should be a patrolman on the curb with a crime scene attendance log. Get somebody out there and keep this going. I'll go see what he's got."

"What he's got is your pension and a box of matches," Hitch warned.

I gave him one of my goofy funny smiles and punched up the call again. "I'm on my way over," I said.

"Of course you are," Nash replied arrogantly.

Chapter 5

The media control area was located a block to the west of the crime scene across from the Evergreen Cemetery on Sloan Street. I found Nix Nash standing at the back of his van in the middle of a circle of ten production people. He was a slightly plump, relatively short thirty-five-year-old man about five feet, seven inches tall. He had blue eyes and a cherubic face framed by teased blond salon-highlighted hair. His clipped moustache was the standard Errol Flynn, darkened a few shades to give it presence.

When he saw me approaching, his circle of peeps and sycophants parted and he walked out majestically to greet me like a star emerging from behind a curtain. He was smiling warmly as he extended his hand.

"Gee, Detective Scully, this is really great," he gushed. "I'm Nix Nash. What a total pleasure to meet you." Napoleonic insincerity.

We shook hands and before I could reply he went on: "I can imagine what you probably already think about me, but please be assured that all I want here is to help catch this killer."

There was a warm likability about him. A charisma that I didn't trust for a minute, because most accomplished performers can affect it. He took a step back and bowed his head in a gesture of theatrical humility. When he looked up, his expression had become contrite.

"Please give me a chance to be your colleague on this," he said earnestly. "Let me show you what I can do before you judge me."

"You said you have a witness who will advance my murder investigation?" I said, sticking to my mission.

"I do. I surely do." Then he shook his head in mock amusement. "Damnedest thing, how this keeps happening to me of late. How my fans recognize me from the show or because they've read my book. They're interested in the good work I'm doing and simply want to help out. This particular fan saw me setting up, walked right over, and volunteered some amazing stuff."

There must have been more than half a dozen personal pronouns in that statement.

"People feel helpless today," he went on. "Government is too big, justice too scary; people just want a chance to get back in the game." Then his smile widened. "I'm certainly not kidding myself that you're glad I showed up here, but here's something you need to know, Shane." He paused. "Can I call you Shane?"

I shrugged.

"You need to understand that I'm a man of integrity. If you're cool, then I'm gonna be cool. I like to say any cop who does his job right has not one thing to fear from Nix Nash."

He was still overdosing on personal pronouns and had just added one third-person reference. This guy was really high on himself.

"Where's the witness?" I asked.

"In the van."

"What's he doing there?"

"Backgrounding with my producer, Laura."

"Backgrounding? What's backgrounding?"

"Fact-checking, getting corroboration on some of the things he just told us during our taped interview."

"You've already interviewed my witness?"

I was starting to get pissed, and obviously that annoyance had leaked into my tone, because he said, "There's no reason to be alarmed. For the love of Mike, I'm only trying to help move this along."

"Well, you're not helping. If he's a witness in a murder, and if you've interviewed him before the police, then you've contaminated him. You've put a statement on film that could contain falsehoods. That's going to make it much harder for me to get to the real truth, because he's

41

already locked in by what he just told you on camera. The fact that you went ahead without checking with us constitutes obstruction of justice."

I was trying to back him off with that, but it didn't work, because he quickly turned to the group of people standing behind his van and called out, "Marcia, could you help us out over here for a moment, please?"

An extremely attractive middle-aged blonde wearing a tailored pinstripe pantsuit broke away from the others and walked toward us. I immediately recognized her from her time as a prosecutor here in L.A. Her name was Marcia Breen and I'd worked one case with her in the nineties. It was before I'd met Alexa. Marcia and I had actually gone out a few times when she was in the DA's office. A few years after our short romance, Marcia had blown a high-profile murder prosecution. That loss had caused a media feeding frenzy and our politically astute DA had scapegoated Marcia, dumping her from the division to save his own ass.

After that she left town and I'd lost track but wasn't surprised to see her here, because Nix Nash liked to hire ex-cops and prosecutors like Marcia Breen who'd once been locals to give him additional tentacles into the local power structure. He liked to put these experts on the air as well, and Marcia certainly wouldn't hurt his ratings, because she was beautiful.

"Hi, Shane," Marcia said as she approached, a small bemused smile on her chiseled features.

"Is this really your new job, Marcia?" Not bothering to hide my disdain.

"The good news is I'm down to eating my pride one show at a time." She said this without a trace of rancor.

"Marcia, please confirm my opinion and tell Detective Scully that it's not obstructing justice for us to interview a volunteering witness," Nash said.

"That's right, because he sought us out," Marcia explained, still favoring me with her smile. "He's in the Evergreen gang and hates cops. There's no way he would ever have talked to you to begin with, so nobody obstructed anything. As a matter of fact, we didn't obstruct; we *instructed* him to talk with you."

"This isn't going to work like it did in Miami and Atlanta," I said to Nash. "I don't intend to stand back while you investigate my homicide behind my back. I'll file so much paper you'll think you're in a ticker tape parade."

"We've broken no laws," Nash said.

"I assume you paid him for the witness interview?" I replied. Since neither Nix nor Marcia denied it, I knew I had guessed right. "If we ever want to use this wit in court, the defense attorney will challenge his statement, calling it paid-for testimony. That violates the statute on dissuasion of evidence." I was on pretty thin ice with this argument, and from their expressions I could tell we all knew it.

"If you're talking about Criminal Statute 136.1, that only deals with dissuasion through intimidation," Marcia said. "But I'm pretty certain you already know that."

I'd lost that round. Time to move on.

"Why don't I get back to you later on the legal stuff. So where is he? Produce the witness."

Nix nodded to a man in a *V-TV* windbreaker standing a few feet away, who opened the rear door of the production van. A moment later a tough-looking gang-tattooed *vato* wearing baggy jeans and a Pendleton shirt buttoned at the throat jumped down from inside the van. It was the same guy we'd seen Nash interviewing down the street as we'd pulled up.

"Meet Edwin Chavaria," Nash said, introducing this obvious thug. "He likes to go by 'Chava.' Just to save you the trouble I had Marcia call a friend of hers downtown. We found out that Chava has a criminal record but no outstanding warrants. I'm sure you'll probably want to run him yourself, but he's trying to cooperate, so you should cut him some slack."

Now Nash was explaining my job to me. "Chava," Nash continued, "Detective Scully is going to ask you some of the same questions we just asked. It's perfectly safe to cooperate with him as we agreed." Treating me like a guest at my own party.

The banger didn't say anything but held my gaze insolently.

"Come with me," I said. "We'll talk over there." I pointed to a spot across the street.

"I ain't going over there with you. You wanta talk, *chota*, we talk here or not at all." He shot Nash a look. That little glance for approval told me they'd agreed to this provision in advance.

Just then, a slender, freckled woman with a mop of curly red hair, dressed in a work shirt, Birkenstocks, and jeans motioned at two cameramen who shifted HD cams up onto their shoulders and started flipping switches. Power lights blinked on. They were hot and rolling.

"I'm not doing my interview as a segment for your show," I said.

"Can't say I blame you." Nash smiled sympathetically. Then he turned to the freckled woman, who seemed to be in charge of the crew. "Laura, we've already done our piece with Chava. It's your call of course, but the police always prefer to conduct their business in private. Whatta ya say?"

The slender woman seemed to consider this as if it were actually her decision and not his, in spite of the fact it was actually mine. Then she motioned the cameras down.

"This is Laura Burke, my producer," Nix explained. "You'll get to know her shortly. Laura runs this traveling circus from transpo and equipment rental to music and postproduction. We all do pretty much what Laura wants around here." Nash was smiling at his no-nonsense producer, who was clocking me with brown Rottweiler eyes. "Go find a nice spot to chat," Nash suggested. "Why don't you try the other side of the white van. We'll wait here."

Chava shrugged, so I led him off. I wasn't about to go where Nash instructed, but Chava came to an abrupt halt on the far side of the production van. "This is far enough," he said. "I don't gotta do nothin' you say. If you wanna talk to me, we do it here."

Since we were out of earshot of Nash and the TV crew I decided to give in on this point and took a digital tape recorder out of my pocket, slated it verbally with the time and date, along with Chava's full name and address.

Edwin Chavaria's eyes were alive with anger. I was the hated *chota*, and he was determined to hold his ground. The big *E* on the right side of his neck and the two teardrop tattoos under his eyes marked him as an Evergreen street killer.

"Let's hear it," I said, holding the tape recorder between us.

He just glowered. I shut off the tape so I wouldn't record what came next.

46

"Listen, Chava, I'm nowhere near as good a guy as Nash told you. Actually, I'm sort of a raging shithead. My word is worth nothing. Get me angry and I'll dig up some open paper on you. I don't care if it's just an unpaid ticket, I'll find a way to slam your ass in jail."

He took a long moment just to let me know he wasn't worried.

"You should lighten up, *malandro*," he finally said, then took a breath and nodded, so I restarted the tape. After a moment, he began slowly telling his story. It sounded rehearsed.

"Last night, me and some a my boys was sittin' on lawn chairs in the front yard of my cousin's place over on Savannah Street," he began. "We was blazin' up sticks, y'know, gettin' mellow. Little later, my posse gets up and goes inside for beer and to play videos. I'm sittin' alone on my chair out there enjoyin' my *mota* when this short, really mega-fat chick rolls up inna truck and parks across the street in front a the house where that woman got capped."

"What time was that?"

"I don't wear no fuckin' watch. I use my phone and it was inside. Eight, nine, how do I know?" I nodded and he went on. "So this *chica* gets out, walks up, and bangs on the fuckin' door with her fist. Even from across the street I can see this is one very pissed-off *puta fea*. Minute later, that Lita person, she opens up. Next, these two

47

bitches start screamin' at each other. Shit gets real loud. So loud, I could even hear what they was sayin' from all the way across the street."

"Tell me."

"The fat one screams, 'I want my motherfuckin' ceiling fan back!' and the little one, Lita, she tells her to fuck off and it ain't her place no more, so it ain't her fan 'cause it was like an attached fixture or some such shit and goes with the apartment. They screamin' at each other over this stupid ceiling fan. Nobody about to give nobody no play. Then the short fat bitch grabs the little one an' they all up in each other's shit, pullin' hair and stuff. Lita knees the fat one inna pussy and before she can get upright slams the door in her face. Then the fat one screams, 'I'll get you, bitch!' and waddles back to her truck, revs the engine, and squeals out. That's it."

"What kind of truck was it?"

"I don't know—Ford, Chevy. I wasn't payin' no attention, but I got a plate." He smiled at me, showing two gold teeth.

"Would you mind giving me the tag number?"

He hesitated for a long time to show me what a *retazo macizo* he was. He finally reached into his pocket and handed me a slip of paper with the tag number 3-T-S-G-4-5-5 written on it.

Then he said, "Since I just made your whole fucking case, how 'bout you kick somethin' down, homes?"

48

"Pay you for a police statement? How long you been doing street crime, homes?" He frowned as I transferred the plate number down in my crime book. Then I shut off the tape and led him back to where the TV crew was waiting.

Nash handed me his card. "Put that in a safe spot, Detective," he advised. "There'll come a time soon when you're going to need it."

I certainly hoped not.

I walked back to my Acura, still parked in front of Lita's house, picked up my radio mike, and started by running Edwin Chavaria. He'd done five years as an accomplice to a second-degree murder in 2004, got out a year early, and was currently almost at the end of his parole. As Nash had said, there was no paper pending. Then I ran the license number Chava had just given me.

The truck was a late-model Chevy Sidewinder registered to Carla and Julio Sanchez at 1414 Lorena Street, a few miles away, also in Boyle Heights. I ran both Sanchezes and found out Carla and her husband were part of White Fence, a rival gang to Evergreen. Carla had a pile of priors—everything from drug dealing and running a prostitution ring in '03 to assault with intent to commit and illegal possession of a firearm. She'd done two short nickels in the California women's prison in Tehachapi, where she was far from a model prisoner, with a long list of write-ups for assault and other yard crimes. Her husband, Julio, had a decent yellow sheet full of assaults and drug beefs. So far he'd only done county time. Neither was currently wanted.

I walked from my car back into Lita's house, filled Hitch in on what had transpired, and then played back Chava's statement on the digital recorder. Despite the fact that this was a very good lead, like me, Hitch wasn't too impressed, because it had come from Nash. We entered the kitchen, where the ME was now working over the body with two evidence techs.

I looked up for the ceiling fan, but there was only a jagged hole overhead with stripped red and green electrical wires hanging down. It looked as if whatever fixture had once been up there had been hastily ripped out. The fan, if there ever was one, was missing.

Put with Chava's story, this offered an interesting thematic option.

It was certainly conceivable that Carla Sanchez had snuck back here later to make good on her threat to "get the bitch." Carla could have found her way inside, killed Lita Mendez, then ripped off the fan and split.

If Nix Nash hadn't supplied this lead, Hitch and I would have been high-fiving each other about now. Put another blue dot up on the homicide board. Case solved.

Carla Sanchez had motive, method, and opportunity. She had a violent prison record and a string of violent priors, along with an eyewitness to the inciting event.

A perfect slam-dunk murder case. Yet neither of us could quite get behind it.

It all just felt like a setup.

Chapter 6

The owner of the house across the street charged us four hundred dollars to rent his place for a week to use as a command post. Detective Becker was working on getting two landlines in so we could stay off our cell phones, which are too easy for the press to scavenge.

Becker also made a run for coffee and doughnuts and set them up in the new CP kitchen. The Winchells and Krispy Kremes were drawing cops and CSIs on breaks off the crime scene, keeping it less congested.

CSI was doing a grid search, marking everything with numbered tape cards. After that, they would vacuum the house, bag and tag all trace evidence, and photograph footprints in suspicious locations like outside of windows and by the side of the house.

Five minutes after I got back from my meeting with Nash, the ME rolled the body and, as I'd suspected, there were two bullet holes in the floor under her head.

The crime techs decided not to attempt fishing for the lead with forceps and possibly adding scratches to the soft lead bullets, which could confuse Ballistics. Instead, they decided to cut out the flooring with a saw and take it back to the crime lab to do the recovery there.

We had a brief discussion about both operational as well as procedural moves. We had to go interview the Sanchezes. Good investigating technique dictated we follow that lead immediately, before the suspects might decide to take off. However, the crime scene, always the temple of any homicide investigation, needed accurate supervision.

We discussed splitting up, with one of us staying here. But Carla and Julio were White Fence gangsters with records, a fact that demanded, in the interest of safety, we go after them as a team.

"How good a cop is Laguna?" I asked Hitch. "So far he set this crime scene up perfectly. Can we trust him to fill in for us?"

"When he's sober, he rocks," Hitch said. "He looks dry to me."

So my partner and I asked Rick Laguna and Pam Becker if they would supervise the evidence gathering and the canvass of the neighborhood so we could follow our one lead. They agreed.

At about ten thirty, we got in the Acura and pulled out.

"So what's he like?" Hitch asked, finally getting

around to pumping me for info on Nix Nash.

"He says 'gee' and 'for the love of Mike.' He smiles a lot and talks about himself in the third person. The words 'I' and 'me' appear frequently."

"I don't trust this," Hitch said after a moment of silence. "We're not at the crime scene ten minutes and up pops Nash with this Chava character and the supposed beef over that ceiling fan. This is exactly the same kinda shit that happened to those cops in Atlanta last year. We're being played."

"Are you saying we should just drop this lead? You can't be serious."

"Have you been watching that TV show? Did you see what he did in Atlanta? It was a train wreck. Those poor doofuses were chasing leads mostly supplied by Nash, coming up with zilch while *V-TV*'s out solving the case. Nash and his team of retired Atlanta cops turn up that schizoid bum sleeping in Piedmont Park and hand him over to those poor, confused homicide dicks on live TV. I fuckin' gagged when I saw that. The killer's actually wearing an old coat that has four of the six dead girls' DNA stains on it. The Atlanta cops looked like vacuum bag dirt."

We were a few blocks from Carla Sanchez's address when I pulled the car over to the curb and parked next to a strip mall.

"What're you doing?" Hitch said.

"You're right. I agree we're probably being screwed with. Chava's statement is probably bogus, and if we go with it and it's wrong, we look like fools. Plus, we waste important time and momentum at the front end of the investigation."

"Exactly."

"Problem is, we can't ignore this. We're in a box. If we *don't* go talk to Carla Sanchez, we look incompetent. Then that will be the next lead on his damn show."

"So, whatta you suggest? Should we just give up and put on some clown makeup?"

"We gotta cover each other. That's number one," I said. "When it got nasty on the Piedmont Murders the Atlanta cops started pointing fingers."

He nodded.

"Two. We need to stay proactive. We gotta figure this guy is gaming us. Nix Nash has issues. Ex-cop, ex-lawyer. Our department went after him, got him convicted of a felony, and stripped him of his law license. Now he's in a position to put some hurt on us. That's probably his motive here. Except—"

"Except what?"

"Does it bother you that Nix Nash and Lita Mendez were both sort of in the same business?"

Hitch nodded. "I've been wondering about that myself."

"What if they knew each other?" I said. "They almost had to, right? Both hung out in L.A. courtrooms around the same time in '05, both filing complaints against cops. I can't believe with that shared interest they didn't hook up."

"So what are you saying?"

"I don't know what I'm saying. It's just interesting that when we pull up at Lita's crime scene he's already down the street interviewing witnesses."

We sat in silence, thinking about it while ghetto cars and morning delivery trucks rattled past.

"No matter what, you gotta know I've got your back, Shane. I'll never point a finger at you. I'll go down swinging first."

"Back atcha."

We bumped fists, then I picked up my cell and dialed my wife, Alexa, who's an LAPD captain and runs the Detective Bureau, supervising three hundred detectives from the Police Administration Building downtown. She needed to know about this.

Alexa is amazing. Besides being my wife, who I'm deeply in love with, she's also the smartest cop I know. She is beautiful, with shiny black hair, high cheekbones, reef-water blue eyes, and a gorgeous figure. How she decided to be a cop instead of a model and how I ended up with her are two of life's consummate mysteries. She answered on the first ring.

"I'm in the chief's weekly COMSTAT conference," she whispered into the receiver. "Make it quick, Shane."

"Lita Mendez is dead. Murdered," I said.

There was a long pause on her end of the line.
"You hear what I just said?"

"Yeah. I'm just walking out of the meeting. Hang on a second." After a few moments she said, "Okay, I'm in the hall. How'd she die?"

"Beaten in her home in Boyle Heights, then double-tapped. According to maggot infestation, lividity, rigor mortis, and a few other things, I'm guessing it happened in the middle of last night, but the coroner will be giving us a better time-of-death estimate in a few hours."

"Look out. This is going to be a media red ball with serious anti-police overtones," she warned.

"You haven't even heard the worst of it."

"Go on."

"Nix Nash was on our crime scene when we got there. He's already turned up a neighbor who says he saw a screaming fight between Lita and someone named Carla Sanchez over a ceiling fan. I'm not sure I trust it. Hitch and I don't know what's going on yet."

"What's going on is, you're about to get your own reality show," she whispered darkly. She was silent for a second before she added, "I wonder if Nash and Lita knew each other."

That's what I meant about her being the smartest cop I knew. It took her ten seconds to make that connection.

"Listen, Alexa. Will you have somebody get me everything you can on Nixon Nash—his whole backstory? Most of what Hitch and I know is just off the stupid main title on his show, and that's probably BS. I want the real facts on this guy. If we're going head-to-head with a monster, we better know what cave he's been sleeping in."

After she hung up, Hitch and I headed on to Carla Sanchez's house. We were on either a cop's mission or a fool's errand.

Guess which.

Chapter 7

Carla Sanchez lived in a large white stucco apartment building in Boyle Heights. The structure was known on the street and at the Hollenbeck Police Station as the White House. Not because of its color but because the White Fence *Inca* leader lived in an apartment on the top floor and his entire cabinet of *veteranos* resided in apartments on the lower levels.

It was 11:00 a.m. when we pulled up in front. I hadn't recognized the address when I wrote it down, but once we arrived I realized that I'd been here before, back when I was on loan to an anti-narcotics task force for a few weeks during a citywide drug sweep.

The building was what was known as a gang module. Far from being palatial, it was an ordinary six-story stucco building. What it lacked in ornamentation it more than made up for in security. The White Fence *Inca* had mandated that shooters be on the roof 24-7 to protect the families of his shot callers, who lived under the constant threat of payback from rival sets.

After we pulled to the curb but before I could turn off the engine, people up and down the street were already standing up and walking away from porch gliders and sagging wicker chairs, heading to the safety of their homes. My car was a standard Acura, but thirty seconds after we parked we'd been made.

"We gotta start wearing better cologne," Hitch quipped.

"Okay, so this address confirms that Carla and Julio are connected to people in the top tier of White Fence."

"How do you wanta play it?" Hitch asked.

"We got two possible courses of action. One: we can back off, get a warrant, and come back with SWAT, or two: we can say the Disney prayer and go in wearing our Mickey Mouse ears."

"Never hurts to be safe," Hitch said, opting for the backup.

"Except if we come back with SWAT, we add a big testosterone factor. It's all about *ganas* with these G'sters. Besides, neither of us trust Chavaria. Since this is probably bullshit, I think we'll find out more if we low-key it."

"How you gonna low-key a police sit-down inside a gang module?" Hitch correctly wondered.

"Your call then."

"Meet ya halfway. Let's have at least one unit stand by," he suggested. "They can park up the street with their safeties off."

"Make the call."

He reached under the dash, pulled out the mike, and triggered it. "This is Delta-Fifteen requesting area backup to 1414 Lorena Street in Boyle Heights," he said. "Have the responding unit meet us on Tac Two."

"Roger that," the RTO said. "One-Adam-Fifty-Six, D-Fifteen requests backup at 1414 Lorena. Meet the detectives on Tac Two."

We heard Adam-56 affirm the call, and Hitch switched the radio to Tac Two, which was a tactical frequency for undercover ops and allows for longer, less formal communication.

"This is A-Fifty-Six. I'm George; my partner's Gately," a woman's voice said. "How can we help you guys?"

"We're two plainclothes detectives headed inside the apartment house located at 1414 Lorena Street on a one-eighty-seven investigation," Hitch said. "You know the building."

"Yeah, the White House. Gang shit hole," the lady cop's voice replied.

"We might have something and then again maybe not," Hitch continued. "If we need to make an arrest, we're gonna want you guys to show the flag. We'll keep our rover on. If we need help we'll give you two squawks."

"Roger that," the woman's voice came back. "Our ETA your location is three minutes. What's the apartment number?"

"Six-Fifty-Seven," Hitch said. "We're drawing a lot of interest out front, so we're going in now."

The cops in A-56 squelched twice in acknowledgment.

Hitch clipped a Rover hand unit to his belt; then we got out of the car and headed into the building. There were two teenaged gangbangers on lookout duty lounging on the front steps. I could tell from their alert, feral postures that they, like everyone else, had made us the minute we pulled up. Because they knew we were cops they didn't want to start anything, but that didn't stop them from insolently mad-dogging us.

"How ya doin', guys?" Hitch said pleasantly as he walked past. Neither of them replied.

The ground floor was empty. I noticed movement on the front steps behind us and saw the two lookouts walking away. Both had cell phones to their ears, spreading the word.

The elevator arrived and we got in and rode silently up to the sixth floor. So far, so good. We exited and walked down a corridor still rich with the smells of morning cooking. At Apartment 657 we stopped.

I knocked and a minute later saw the dim pin-hole of light disappear from the peephole as someone on the other side of the door put their eye to the lens. I held up my badge.

"What you want?" a man's voice called out.

"We're here to see Carla Sanchez," I said through the solid wood door.

" 'Bout what?" the man challenged.

"Is she in there? Open up! Police business."

"You got a warrant?"

"We just want to talk," I said. "There's no need to turn this into an incident."

A moment later the door opened a crack. A huge bald *veterano*, about thirty years old, with a large black *WF* tattooed on the side of his shaved head, glared out at us. Both arms were fully sleeved with elaborate gang ink. He took a menacing stance, placing his bulk in the threshold, and blocked our way.

"You can talk to me," he said.

"Who are you?"

"Carla's old man. Julio. What's the *trato*?"

"We're here to talk to Carla," I said. "We can get a warrant and come back with a SWAT team and have the talk in custody, or we can all sit down and have a friendly chat right here. Your call, Mr. Sanchez. But if we come back with SWAT, the ABGs on the roof will go nuts and this building will become the Dead House, and that's the *trato*."

He swore softly in Spanish.

"Is that a 'yes'?" Hitch asked.

"Let them in, Julio," a woman's voice said from behind him. Then she pulled the door wider and we got our first look at Carla Sanchez. She was large as Chava had said, maybe three hundred pounds, but only a little over five feet tall. She wore a lightweight long-sleeved white sweater over a tank dress that only came to her knees. She had large, corpulent arms and thick legs with ankles that looked like brown tube socks stuffed with sand. Her black hair was cut short. Because of her girth she looked uncomfortable just standing there.

"How about doing what the lady says," I suggested to Julio, who was still blocking our way.

He picked up his cell phone from the charging dock by the door and hit a number, then spoke a short sentence to somebody in Spanish. I understood enough to know Julio was getting some muscle to come over and stand in the hall. Hitch caught my eye and we traded a look as Julio finished the call.

"Suit yourself," Julio said, putting the phone back in the dock and finally stepping aside.

We walked into an overfurnished apartment. It was neatly kept, but none of the pieces coordinated. Late-morning sun was streaming through the windows.

Hitch moved to my right to check out the back

hallway, looking into each bedroom. A moment later, he returned to the living room, caught my eye, and nodded. The apartment was clear. I turned my attention back to the Sanchezes.

Then I saw it.

Sitting on the coffee table in front of the sofa was the missing ceiling fan.

Chapter 8

The fan wires had frayed and were hanging out of the fixture. They matched the ripped-out wires I'd seen hanging from Lita Mendez's ceiling. I looked at Hitch, who nodded. It was physical evidence corroborating Edwin Chavaria's story. "Can I sit down?" I asked, trying to ease the tension.

Carla nodded, anxious to get off her feet. She moved painfully on swollen ankles over to a large chair, which, I noticed, had six stout legs to support her prodigious weight. When she eased herself down, she and the chair both groaned. Julio remained vigilant, standing by the door as I settled onto the sofa across from Carla. Hitch took a spot behind me where he covered my back.

"Tell us about your relationship with Lita Mendez," I began.

"I got no relationship with that *rulacho*. Last week she rented the apartment I used to live in. I

63

hadda get outta that barrio 'cause Evergreen put a check on me."

"A check" was gang slang for a murder contract. If a rival set had put a contract out on this woman, it indicated she was a lot higher in the food chain than just some random gang *chica*. She might be what they called *la mas chingona*, one of the rare gang females who were strong enough in the set to merit the title of shot caller.

"Did you see Lita yesterday?"

"I know the bitch is dead," Carla said. "If you're over here tryin' to put me behind that murder, you're wastin' your time. I got an alibi. I was with Julio, right here, all last night."

"She was with me," Julio said predictably.

"If you were here, how do you know she's dead already? The body was only discovered a few hours ago," Hitch said.

"Don't tell me they don't got no jungle drums in your old hood," Carla said, turning to Hitch. "*Torrones* invented that shit. Ten minutes after you found her it was already old news."

This was a very hard woman. She'd been down twice. She'd survived the gangs in Tehachapi Prison. Her sheet showed she'd had her share of write-ups for violence on the inside. She held my eyes, never looking away.

"We know you were over there last night. We have a witness who saw you at her house in a loud argument at around eight or nine. He got your license plate. Stop playing us or you're gonna get arrested and we'll finish this with you in custody. I'm trying to cut you some slack here."

She looked at Julio, then back at me.

"Yesterday . . . yeah, okay, so now I remember. Yeah, I saw her yesterday. But like you said, it was early."

"Tell us. Don't leave anything out and start at the beginning."

"Bitch had my ceiling fan." She nodded at the fixture on the coffee table. "I used to live in that apartment. Like I said, it's Evergreen turf. I was only on those blocks 'cause my *tia* lived there. She rented five years ago before Evergreen took over the block. She was too sick to move. I was caring for her, but then she decided to go back to Mexico to be with her sister in Durango. As soon as she left, I knew I hadda get out."

That sounded like BS to me. If Carla was a shot caller for White Fence, living on an Evergreen block was a short step up from suicide. It seemed more likely to me that she was probably only there occasionally and the house on North Savannah was an outpost that she rented to help her White Fence drug *traficantes* encroach on Evergreen turf. When it got too dangerous, she ended up withdrawing.

"Besides, I wanted to move back here once Julio got off state paper," she continued. "Leasing agent was Vanessa Valente. She rented my aunt's

65

place to that *puta*, Lolita Mendez, but some of my belongings didn't get moved. I was supposed to get my fan, which I bought with my own money, and a primo area rug I got from Crate and Barrel and some other stuff. Bitch wouldn't give my property. Said it was hers now."

"So what happened?"

"What happened was I drove over to get my stuff back. I asked her nice and she stands there and fuckin' disrespects me. Calls me a fat *cerdo*, so we had words."

"Words."

"Yeah, I got in the bitch's face; then she knees me and slams the door."

"If she wouldn't give your fan back, then how come it's here?"

"That's 'cause a Julio," Carla said, looking fondly at her husband. "He got mellowed out in jail. Tells me to stop bangin' with the bitch and just buy the damn thing."

"You bought it?" I looked over at Hitch.

"Yeah, she bought it," Julio said from the door. "You think we're animals? That we'd kill over a stupid fan?"

That's exactly what I thought, but I didn't say it.

"Explain what happened next," Hitch said.

"I called her on the phone," Carla went on. "Was about ten, ten thirty that same night. I'm a big woman. I'm always too hot. We ain't got no air in this building, so I told her I needed my fan back. I had it installed over there with my own money, but she's saying it's attached and it goes with the apartment. I finally offered her twenty dollars. After giving me a buncha shit she says okay, if I'll pay her twenty-five. So me and Julio drove over about eleven. I went in and bought my damn fan back while he sat in the truck and covered my back."

"Can you prove any of this?" I asked.

"Julio is my witness. He was there."

"Besides Julio."

She glared at me. She was beginning to sweat despite the fact that it was February and, with the storm coming, the apartment was cold.

"Would you be willing to take a lie detector test?"

"She ain't takin' no poly," Julio said. "That shit gets rigged."

"Polygraphs are used to eliminate suspects, not include them," I explained. "You're already a suspect, so failing the test changes nothing. If you pass the poly, we start looking for Lita's killer somewhere else. Besides that, we can't use the results in court—good or bad. That's why a polygraph favors an innocent suspect."

"She ain't takin' no polygraph," Julio repeated.

Carla was still sweating and now unbuttoned her sweater and removed it. It was then that I saw multiple scratches on both of her heavily tattooed arms.

"How'd you get those scratches on your arms?" I asked her.

"We have a cat."

"You sure you didn't get them in your fight with Lita?"

"The bitch kneed me in the groin, then slammed the door. She didn't scratch me. I got this from our cat."

"Where is the cat?"

"I don't know. He's a tom. He roams a lot. All the people in the building feed him. He's like everybody's cat."

"What's his name?"

"I don't know his fucking name."

She was starting to fidget. I looked over at Hitch, who was shaking his head. She was obviously lying.

"Miss Kitty," Julio contributed from his post by the door.

"That's a pretty crappy name for a tomcat," Hitch said in amusement. Then he motioned me over. I stood and walked to where he was standing.

He leaned in and whispered, "Back bedroom. Two bags fully packed. I think these two will be in Mexico if we don't delay their trip."

"We're gonna ask you to leave now," Julio said from the door. "The interview is over."

"I'm afraid we can't do that," I said, and stepped away from Hitch to give him a better field of fire in case this got iffy.

Then my partner pulled his Glock 9 as I took my handcuffs off my belt.

"I knew this was coming," Julio sneered.

"You're under arrest. Let's all stay cool," I said.

"*Pendejos*," Julio muttered.

"We're only arresting you as material witnesses," I explained. "Be nice and maybe you're home by lunch. Turn and face the wall, Mr. Sanchez. Lace your fingers behind your head."

He turned and assumed the position while I shook him down and cuffed him. Hitch covered both of them from across the room. Then Hitch and I helped Carla to her feet and attempted to cuff her, but Hitch's cuffs wouldn't fit around her gargantuan wrists. I'd seen cuffs not fit a man before but never had that happen on a woman.

"You want to give A-Fifty-Six a piece of this?" I said to my partner.

Hitch reached into his hip pocket and squawked his radio two times.

A few minutes later the officers from A-56 were standing in the doorway. They turned out to be a Hollenbeck dog and cat patrol team. The man, Gately, was a redhead with a buzz cut. One of those standard wide-armed weight-lifting types, tough as hickory. His partner, George, was a medium-sized, compact woman with blond hair pulled back in a bun.

We led Carla and Julio out of the apartment and

locked the door for them. The four guys Julio had called as backup were standing in the hall.

"Beat it," the giant red-haired patrol officer snapped.

"You got six seconds; then you're all under arrest," his partner threatened.

After a moment, they reluctantly dispersed. We led the Sanchezes down the hall. As we passed the other apartments I could hear doors opening behind us and turned once to see half a dozen Chicanos staring daggers at our backs.

We got Carla and Julio downstairs and into the patrol car, where we Mirandized them without incident.

"Transport them to Hollenbeck Station for booking as material wits," I told the uniforms.

As the patrol car pulled away, Hitch said, "I hope that's your good side."

"What're you talking about?"

"We're being photographed." He pointed up the block at the white Econoline van with the V-TV emblem on the side, parked at the curb. Nix Nash stood near the back of the van, mike in hand, cameras rolling. He had us framed over his shoulder as he did a stand-up right in the middle of Lorena Street.

Chapter 9

A few years ago, the Hollenbeck Station was the worst rat hole in the department. Times had changed. The new station house was now located two blocks from the old one at 2111 East First Street. Our local politicians called the Hollenbeck Station, along with our new Police Administration Building downtown, shining testaments to the cutting-edge police work being practiced in Los Angeles. Hollenbeck Station was smaller than the new PAB but no less impressive. It was a steel-sculptured monument with curved mirrored sides and private balconies.

The building housed 282 police officers in four thousand state-of-the-art feet of fast track, movable walls; terrazzo floors; and vinyl-upholstered offices.

Hitch and I pulled into the high-fenced guarded parking lot and got out of the Acura. We walked inside and told the booking sergeant that we wanted the Sanchezes placed in separate holding cells in the isolation section of the jail so they couldn't pass messages to other White Fence bangers incarcerated there.

I got on the phone and talked to Ray Tsu at the coroner's office. Fey Ray was our assistant coroner, who had earned his moniker because he was a wispy character who rarely spoke above a whisper. He told me Lita Mendez's body was just coming in and that her death was big news inside the department, so she was already in the pipeline.

"Get me a stomach content analysis and as accurate a time of death as you can. Hitch will send you the room temp for larva gestation," I said. "We've got a suspect with a partial alibi, and if we come up with a solid TOD it could put this beef on her. Also, see if you can retrieve any foreign DNA off the body. Type and match the vic and check under her nails for skin traces. My suspect has scratches on her arms."

"Okay," Ray replied. Then he added, "Since it's Lita, don't bother to ask. She's already at the head of the line."

Next I checked in with Rick Laguna, who'd just arrived back from the crime scene. He said they'd collected a lot of trace evidence and sent it to the forensics lab. In the interest of time, I asked if he could help us get body warrants, so the jail technicians could take DNA samples from both Julio and Carla Sanchez. I wanted to check that against any possible DNA we retrieved from the coffee cup in the driveway or from Lita's body. Laguna said he'd run that request over to a judge he knew in the downtown courthouse and get it signed for us.

"Listen, Ricky, when you called the PAB to give

this case over to Homicide Special, did you use your car radio?"

"Yeah. Why?"

"You didn't happen to put Lita Mendez's name out on the air, did you?"

"I'm not a fuckin' ditz," he said, sounding insulted. "I also checked that out with the primary responders in Patrol the minute Nix Nash showed up. They didn't use her name either. Everybody knew her death was a giant red ball. I don't know how that dirtbag Nash found out."

I didn't pursue it, but patrol officers had cell phones as well as chalk. News of Lita's death had spread quickly through the department. Either somebody on the scene had leaked it or Nix Nash had a mole inside our system.

When Hitch and I had most of the details of the investigation in the works we went to the new station's coffee room. It was magnificent. There were fifteen different machines, all built into a vending wall like a row of slot machines at a Vegas casino. Hitch and I put in our money and punched buttons for coffee.

Our paper cups dropped down and began filling automatically. We both leaned in to study the markings. The break room used a standard vending cup. The decoration was two red lines just below the rim. There was no brown floral ring around the top like the one we'd found by Lita's driveway.

"Cops didn't kill Lita Mendez," I said defensively.

"Of course not," Hitch agreed, but we'd both checked the cups out anyway.

We sat at a table to plan the rest of the day.

"Flip you for coroner's duty," Hitch said.

Most cops don't like watching the cut, and Hitch and I were no exception. Not so much because it was a gruesome procedure, because after a while you get used to that. It was more because it was a time-consuming drag.

"Call it," I said as I pulled a quarter out and flipped it into the air.

"Tails," Hitch said as the coin hit my palm.

We both leaned in and looked at George Washington's silver profile.

"Two outta three?" Hitch suggested.

"Be sure and wear a smock so you don't get any of that nasty saw splatter on your gorgeous herringbone." I grinned.

Ricky Laguna agreed to give Hitch a ride to pick up his Porsche, which was ready, so we split up.

A few minutes later, I left the new Hollenbeck building and walked to the parking lot to get my car. I planned to head back to the PAB and start doing background research on Lita Mendez. I needed to see who was currently in her life and identify her known associates so we'd have a list of people to start questioning. It wasn't exactly a trip to the movies, but it was better than going to the chop shop to watch the opening.

Once I was outside, I saw the *V-TV* van parked at the curb across the street. Nix Nash was doing another stand-up, this time with the new Hollenbeck station behind him. He had definitely settled on our case.

His producer, Laura Burke, was watching over the shot, supervising her cameramen. When she spotted me, she leaned forward and whispered something to Nash. He stopped his rant and turned. Then he glanced at Laura and drew a finger across his throat, signaling her to stop filming. He handed his mike to an assistant and walked across the street, stopping at the chain link.

I walked the twenty yards or so to the edge of the lot to meet him. We stood two feet apart on opposite sides of the galvanized fence.

"I saw you arrested them," he said.

I didn't have anything to say to this guy, so I just stood there.

"Stuck for a response?" He grinned. "Here's one that might work. How 'bout, 'Thanks, Nix, I appreciate all the great help'?"

"You knew Lita, didn't you?" I said, and watched him carefully for a reaction.

He favored me with a small sad smile. "Of course I knew her. She was doing important work, keeping you guys honest. Back when I still practiced law in this town, she often helped out on cases I was doing." The smile died. "I'm going to miss her. But more than that, I'm going to catch her killer."

"I'd advise you not to interfere. That *is* obstructing justice. You start an unauthorized vigilante investigation, you'll think City Hall fell on you."

"So I'm supposed to leave the investigation of my friend up to the very people I think might be responsible for her death?"

"The police didn't kill Ms. Mendez," I said softly. "You're the one who gave me the Carla Sanchez lead."

"In a homicide investigation I'm sure you've discovered some things aren't quite as obvious as they appear on the surface."

I let that pass, then said, "I pull up at nine fifteen a.m., you're already up the street interviewing Edwin Chavaria. That's excellent response time, even for you. Wanta set my mind at ease about that?"

"If that's some sort of accusation that I might have something to do with this, then yes, let me put your mind at rest. I was in Florida yesterday hosting a fund-raiser at the Boca Raton Rape Clinic. You can Google it and check me out. The pictures online are great. I took an early flight and landed at eight this morning. Are three thousand miles enough of an alibi for Nix Nash, Detective?"

He was back to the third person and being damn snotty about it.

"I was supposed to take Lita to breakfast after I landed this morning. Laura and my camera crew picked me up at the airport, brought me here. After breakfast we were going to set up for an interview. Lita had agreed to be a show resource for us. She knew a lot of things about L.A. and the cops here. When we got to her house at a little before nine, patrol officers were already stringing yellow tape. Maybe my showing up was divine intervention, because I'm beginning to think maybe I'm the only one here who really gives a darn who killed her."

"You need to stop taking yourself so seriously," I said. I had nothing more, so I turned to leave. He called after me.

"Hey, Shane? Do you feel it?"

"Feel what?" I replied, turning back. He had ditched the sad, funereal expression and was now wearing an excited, hopeful look, like a teenaged boy watching his first stripper.

"I think deep down, on some level, we all know what's coming in the future," he began. "Like those stories you read about people who clean out their closets or straighten up the garage and a day later get hit by a bus. The family comes in and everything's all packed up neat and ready to go. I have a theory the reason stuff like that happens is because intuitively we can all sense the future.

It's why sometimes we're depressed for no good reason we can think of, or are unreasonably happy. What's actually causing it is a subtle knowledge of what's coming. Sometimes it's good, sometimes bad."

"And sometimes it's just too much sugar and too little sleep."

He shook his head, but he seemed happy, like he was delighted to be here, excited just to be Nix Nash.

"Maybe you're right, but I don't think it's dietary, or sleep related," he kidded. "Like right now. Tell me you don't actually feel some large sense of impending doom?"

"I don't feel anything," I told him.

"Just wait," he said, grinning. "It's coming."

Chapter 10

When I got back to the Police Administration Building, I Googled the Boca Raton Rape Clinic and sure enough, there were half a dozen pictures of Nix Nash hosting last night's fund-raiser in South Florida.

Not to be overly thorough, but I wanted to make absolutely sure he wasn't a suspect, so I checked the airlines and found that Nash had been on a flight that left Fort Lauderdale Airport at 5:00 a.m., landing at LAX at 7:43 this morning. I talked to a terminal manager who remembered Nash coming off the flight and being stopped for autographs. That meant either he'd been at Lita's house to take her to breakfast as he'd said or he'd been tipped to her death by someone inside our department. I suspected it was probably the latter and was determined to root out the spy and close that leak.

The rest of the day was spent researching Lita Mendez. Of course, I'd heard a lot about her and knew something of the trouble she'd caused for the department, but for the last few years, because I'd been investigating high-profile homicides, her crusade against the Hollenbeck Station and the Internal Affairs Group had mostly escaped my scrutiny.

As I surfed old stories about her on the Net, I was surprised by how much there was. When she died Lita was just thirty-three years old. One story revealed that she had become enamored of the court system at the age of six when she watched her mother get a restraining order against Lita's father, who had been violently assaulting them both. Her dad, an Evergreen gangster, ended his short earthly journey a year later, going tits up in an alley off First Street. Lita had been keeping herself busy since adulthood by making life impossible for the cops in and around Hollenbeck. Among her numerous activities, she'd crashed various LAPD undercover operations, taking photos of the undercovers, posting their pictures on the Internet, putting their lives in danger, and burning these cops for this kind of work forever. Most of her civilian complaints were not for police brutality but for lesser charges like rude behavior or harassment.

She had also made her share of enemies on the street. A committed Evergreen associate, she had little use for the more than forty-five competing Hispanic sets and often turned her legal skills against enemy shot callers.

An article about her titled "Talking Truth with Lita Power," by an *L.A. Times* writer named Trent Phillips, told how she was attempting to intimidate and drive rude, harassing police officers out of her neighborhood with complaints and lawsuits. Most cops thought her real motive was to compromise police activity and wrest control of Evergreen turf away from Patrol, turning the blocks back to the gangs.

She printed police corruption T-shirts with the pictures of officers she'd accused of crimes and then passed them out in community centers. It didn't matter that most of her complaints found those cops innocent. She hung sheet banners from freeway overpasses decrying Hollenbeck police officers, identifying her favorite targets by name.

On our part, the department had charged her

with two dozen misdemeanors and a few low-weight felonies, everything from driving without a license to the more serious offense of assaulting a neighbor with a gardening tool. There were eight to ten counts of verbal assaults against various cops. None of this legal vitriol had gone anywhere in court.

Last year Stephanie Madrid, a captain in charge of the Advocates Section at Internal Affairs, had used police union funds to finance a restraining order against Lita, which would require her to stay more than fifty yards away from the Hollenbeck Station. That suit had prevailed.

There was a raging legal debate being fostered within the *L.A. Times* blog community over whether Lita Mendez was a community activist exercising her First Amendment rights or a criminal menace, who was hurting her community and the quality of civilian life in Boyle Heights. By-and-large, the bloggers were throwing in with Lita, accusing the police of just about everything but double-parking.

However, even Lita's detractors admitted that she had a sophisticated understanding of how to use the court system and the complicated Federal Consent Decrees that, until recently, had governed the LAPD. She had often stated in the *L.A. Times* articles that her dream was to one day complete her GED and go to law school.

She might have made an excellent attorney,

because with no formal legal training and a closet of conservative business suits for court, Lita Mendez had managed to keep Internal Affairs and our city prosecutors embroiled in an endless legal debate. Just last week Captain Stephanie Madrid had filed a criminal lawsuit against Lita, charging her with intentionally making a false police report.

In the gang-corrupted streets, she was heralded by Evergreens as a hero. They claimed she had the courage to stand up to City Hall. Her attorney, who mostly worked her cases pro bono, claimed Lita had never been convicted of a felony, even though she did have a sealed stolen-car beef dating back to when she was a juvenile.

When I was finished, I had compiled a long list of people who hated her guts. A lot of them were cops.

Capt. Stephanie Madrid was well known to everyone in the department. She was a hard-ass who ran the Advocates Section at IA. Advocates were police officers who had the job of prosecuting accused officers. In essence, they were advocates for the department. Defense reps were the officers picked by the accused to defend them. A defense rep could be any officer on the LAPD as long as they were below the rank of captain. The chief advocate had supervisory responsibilities over both the advocates and defense reps. It was a big, important job and Captain Madrid ran a large machine that brought police officers charged with malfeasance before administrative Board of Rights hearings. Hundreds of cops had found themselves facing boards because of Lita's mostly frivolous com-plaints.

When I finished, I rubbed my eyes, which were fatigued from hours on the Internet. It was a depressing compilation of facts and angry people. I had a long list of G-sters and cops to look into, including a prickly IA captain. Stephanie Madrid was often referred to as the "Queen of the Dark," so I certainly wasn't looking forward to conduct-ing a suspect interview with her.

One thought was buzzing around me like the angry green blowflies in Lita's kitchen: this certainly was the perfect case for *V-TV.*

At five o'clock Hitch called to say he was just leaving the ME's office. I suggested we meet for a beer in a bar called the Copper Buckle across the street from the Police Administration Building. A lot of cops came in there for drinks after work, and it was usually packed.

We found a booth in the back and sat across from each other over foaming mugs. I gave Hitch a copy of my background information on Lita and he slid my copy of the ME's report over. Instead of reading the paperwork, we filled each other in verbally and would go through the paper-work later. After I gave him Lita's background info, he started recapping the coroner's report.

"The two bullet wounds to the head were made by nine-millimeter copper-jacketed Federals. They were one-hundred-twenty-nine-grain Hydra-Shok hollow points and were fired postmortem," he began.

"If she was already dead, it sounds like the doer had some personal issues with the vic," I said, thinking of my long list of angry cops.

"Lita was beaten to death first," Hitch went on. "Head trauma, body trauma, and massive brain hemorrhage on the right side of the cerebellum, which Ray says was the immediate cause of death."

"How about DNA?" I asked.

"Nothing on her body. Her nails had soap under them. Maybe she brushed her nails. Maybe the killer did. No soap where we found her, so it didn't happen while she was lying on her kitchen floor. The body was clean. No foreign hair or skin traces, no vaginal DNA. It was so clean, in fact, the coroner thinks the corpse could have been hand vacuumed, which means the unsub knew what he was doing."

Again, I thought, *cop.*

We drank our beers while I turned pages on the ME report. When I finished scanning the analysis, I looked up at him.

"We got nothing here to hold Carla or Julio Sanchez."

"I still think there's an outside chance they could be good for it," Hitch replied.

"Except we don't have enough to charge them. Even if CSI matches their prints to prints inside the house it may not matter, because Carla used to live there. How about time of death?" I asked.

"Still working on it. Her stomach content analysis came back just before I left, so it's not on that top sheet. I clipped it to the back page. Lita had a mostly digested meal of beef enchiladas and Mexican beans. Ray thinks when she died it was maybe four hours old. If she ate at eight, which is just a guess, then she might have been killed around midnight. That fits with the lights still being on and the absence of rigor mortis."

"Enchiladas? So much for the Bolognese sauce."

"Once every ten years or so, I'm wrong," he said, smiling ruefully. "That TOD estimate is also supported by lividity and maggot gestation. Ray will try and dial it in a little closer tomorrow by figuring in the ambient room temperature and adjusting for the temperature's effect on larva development."

"Carla said she was there at eleven and Julio confirms it. If you believe them, it puts Carla outside the window on this preliminary time of death," I said.

We ordered two more beers. After they arrived I said, "Just for the hell of it, I checked on Nix Nash's whereabouts, not that I think he did it, but I would have loved to get a way to stir him up a little."

"Tell me."

"He was in South Florida for some fund-raiser when she died."

"I still don't think we should cut the Sanchezes loose," Hitch said.

"They're on a seventy-two-hour hold. We could hang on to them for another day."

"I think that's what we should do. Their bags are already packed and if we guess wrong and they really are the doers, it's *hasta la vista* on those two. On a murder one, we'll never extradite them from Mexico."

I nodded my agreement. It had been a long, depressing day. Neither of us wanted this damn case.

So we packed up the paperwork, finished our beers, and went home.

Chapter 11

"So tell me about Nash," Alexa said. We were sitting in the backyard of our Venice canal house. The sun was just setting and the cloud-filled sky had turned to a mosaic of fiery colors. I can usually maximize the benefits of a beautiful sunset better than anybody can, but this evening I

86

was barely aware of the bright oranges and purples that were part of the trailing edge of the February storm that had threatened a much-needed rain but had passed on without dropping any.

After I filled her in on *V-TV*'s ubiquitous host, Alexa pumped me for case facts on Lita's death.

"Start with your suspects," Alexa said, obviously concerned about the possibility of a police doer.

"It's a very polarized list. Half my names are gang assholes from competing sets who Lita had dustups with or enemies of her brother, Homer. The other half are cops she filed complaints against. Even Captain Madrid made the list."

"Stephanie may be a bit of a hard-ass, but that lawsuit and the false-reporting case she got the DA to file were only to back Lita off from all those nuisance complaints," Alexa defended. "Captain Madrid was just doing her job."

"Easy for you to say, because she's your pit bull. I wonder what Nash's take is going to be."

We were drinking Coronas as the evening cooled. A family of ducks beat ass across the wind-rippled canal toward a thicket of reeds near the shoreline. Our cat, Franco, was hunkered in the bushes licking his chops, but the ducks were out of range.

"Nix Nash says he wants me to give him a chance to prove he's a good guy," I continued. "In one breath he calls me Shane and tells me he just loves police. Then, in the next, he tells me he can feel the future and he sees me going into a pot of boiling oil with some chopped vegetables."

"He threatened you?" Alexa said, surprised.

"You had to be there, but yeah. And he knew Lita from when he practiced law here. He told me he was going to use her on his L.A. show as a police expert. His story is he flew in from Boca Raton and landed at around eight this morning, then drove over to Lita's house to take her to breakfast and do an interview. When he pulled in, he says Patrol was already stringing crime scene tape."

"You believe that?"

"I know he was in Florida 'cause I checked. But I think he knew to go to Lita's because he's got a mole in our department. He's already spying on us from the inside."

"Be careful, Shane. I hope you remember what happened in Atlanta."

"You hope I remember? Which one of us was it who threw a shoe at the TV set over that dumb-ass Piedmont Park bust?"

"You. I threw that cute little Let's Screw pillow you gave me for our anniversary."

Alexa reached into her coat pocket and pulled out a piece of paper.

"What's that?"

"I had Danny do a full background on Nash, state and federal," she said. "There's some interesting stuff here that's not common knowledge."

I groaned loudly, then closed my eyes. "Tell me. I can't read another depressing personal history."

She glanced down at the sheet of paper before setting it on the table between us. "Nix is the third of four brothers. All of his sibs are Dade County cops. His father and uncle were also on the force down there, so it's a law enforcement family. They're all rock-hard southern conservatives. He was actually named after President Nixon. But for some reason Nix didn't qualify for the Dade County PD. I'm looking into it. I think he had a medical issue. Anyway, instead of MDPD, he ended up on the Florida Marine Patrol, which basically patrols the rivers and swamps in Dade County, including the Florida Everglades. FMP was a big deal during the drug cowboy days in the late eighties."

"I thought his TV show main title said he was a Dade County cop," I interrupted.

"Me too, but Danny checked it on Hulu. The main title says he enjoyed an early career in South Florida law enforcement, which technically includes the Florida Marine Patrol."

"Okay, go on."

"Well, he supposedly resigned, but Danny made a few calls and found out that it wasn't quite that cut-and-dried."

I sat up straighter and looked over.

"Apparently there was a killer operating in the Florida Everglades in the nineties," Alexa continued. "This whack job was killing tourists and fishermen who ventured too far back into the swamp. The unsub turned out to be an illiterate French-speaking Cajun sociopath named Lee Bob Batiste. The way this supposedly goes, Nash and his partner arrested Batiste for operating an airboat while intoxicated. When they searched him they found six driver's licenses in his wallet belonging to victims of the serial killer.

"Nash was ambitious and wanted to get off the water and into FMP Detectives. He knew a little Cajun and started interrogating Batiste about why he had these six DLs in his wallet and Batiste immediately confessed to all the murders. Problem was, Nash was so eager to make his serial murder collar, he never Mirandized Batiste.

"Lee Bob Batiste was released from custody and disappeared back into the Florida swamp, never to be seen again. Because Nix Nash had caused this miscarriage of justice, and because the victims' families were enraged, there was a lot of pressure on him to resign. Six months later, after the fuss had died down a bit, that's what he did."

"Not exactly the way it looks on his TV show," I said.

"Apparently, as a favor to all the cops in his family and because they waited the six months till it got off the front pages, the connection to his resignation was glossed over."

"Explains better why he hates cops."

"He'd say that the Marine Patrol mistake was a lesson learned and it's why he is so down on sloppy investigations."

"Right." I was getting irritated again. "What else?"

"We know most of the rest. He decided to study law and became a lawyer in the late nineties. He moved to L.A., passed the bar and made a career suing cops here, got prosecuted for embezzling, lost his license, went to prison, wrote a book, got rich, yadda yadda yadda."

I sat there thinking about all of it. The sun had dipped below the horizon and the colorful but rain-heavy sky was turning gunmetal gray. Alexa went inside, but I lingered for a few minutes thinking about my options.

The twenty-four-twenty-four-hour rule governs most homicides and states that the last twenty-four hours of the victim's life and the first twenty-four hours of the murder investigation are the two most important time frames in the case.

During my search into Lita's life, I had begun to formulate those time lines and work on setting up a victimology. Victimology is the study of the victim's life. You try to determine what she was doing when she died that might have drawn the killer to her. In addition, you are looking for personality traits, habits, or relationships that might suggest motive, method, or opportunity. That included employment, dating history, sexuality, reputation, and criminal record. I had plenty to start with.

The twenty-four-twenty-four-hour rule also postulates that something might have happened during the last twenty-four hours of the victim's life that could be the inciting event for the murder. The argument with Carla over the ceiling fan being a perfect example.

However, I was beginning to suspect that Lita's murder had nothing to do with that ceiling fan or Carla and Julio Sanchez. We would hold them a little longer to be sure, but I suspected that the real reason for Lita's death might actually lie, as Nash had suggested, in the murky depths of her tangled anti-police obsession.

Hitch and I might be hunting brother cops.

Chapter 12

I went inside and found Alexa waiting for me in the bedroom. She was lying in bed reading a crime stat report, but she was also wearing a sexy pink negligee and she looked beautiful. I needed something beautiful to end my day. I stretched out beside her and moments later we were making love.

Even though my head was spinning with this case, I could always find a way to lose myself with her. We began our lovemaking on the bed but consummated it on the floor. The way that happened was Alexa, always a playful lover, started tickling me and we ended up rolling off the side of the bed.

When we were done, I held her, feeling her warm breath against my neck.

"He's not going to get us," she whispered in my ear.

Later, when we were lying in bed and I could hear her breathing deepen and grow steady, I looked at the ceiling and tried to further sort out my feelings about Lita Mendez, Carla and Julio Sanchez, and Nixon Nash. Every fiber in my body suggested whatever was going on, it wasn't going to end well. I was beginning to buy into Nash's dire prediction for my future.

Sleep wouldn't come, so I slipped out of bed, grabbed a robe, and went to my desk in the den. I sat there, trying to categorize and systematize.

At the top of my bothersome issues list was Edwin Chavaria. Even though his tip had produced the Sanchezes, the ceiling fan, and the rest of that fire drill, there were big parts of Chavaria's story that wouldn't lie down for me.

I'm not exactly a gang squad expert, but I've worked my share of gang cases. In my experience these guys rarely, if ever, put their business in the street. They take care of their own problems in their own ways. They don't rat anybody out or bring in the cops.

Beyond that, Chava had actually gone on camera with Nix Nash, calling out Carla Sanchez, putting a murder beef on her. How was that going to look to his homies on First Street when it aired? Would a guy like Chava who had done serious prison time actually play the rat on national TV? What would that do to his street cred? I suppose it was possible, but I had my doubts. Unless, of course, somebody had put him up to it and made it fiscally worth his while. Then he could brag to his *vato* homeboys that he'd gamed the *chota*, getting them to chase false leads.

Muy rifo, homes.

Nash's MO was to get cops investigating bogus leads and then, while they ran in circles, solve the case himself. That's exactly what had happened in Atlanta, and my gut told me that's what he was trying to do here.

All things considered, I was very unhappy with our case against the Sanchezes.

I was also worried about the smells we'd noticed when we arrived in Lita's stuffy house. Both Hitch and I had smelled garlic, and the ME's report said Lita had a partially digested dinner of beef enchiladas and beans in her stomach but that there was no trace of garlic in the stomach contents.

I'd been kidding Hitch about missing the boat with his guess that it was Bolognese sauce, but Hitch really is a Class A chef. Alexa and I had been up to his house many times and he'd cooked some of the best gourmet food I've ever tasted. He knew his stuff, and he'd said he smelled garlic, onions, and bay leaf or sage.

I went on the computer and found a few recipes for enchiladas online. Most of them contained garlic. I shut off the computer and sat there thinking. I get hung up on stuff like this. Little details that fight the pattern. How could Hitch and I have both smelled garlic if she didn't have garlic in her stomach?

I opened my notebook and made a note to try to find out why. It might be nothing, but either way, I knew it would pester me until I found the answer.

Then I closed my crime book and sat back, planning tomorrow's moves. I had a lot of people to talk to, including a bunch of cops who would become pissed the minute I suggested they might be suspects.

At the top of my interview list was a name that threatened my future like the swine flu.

First thing tomorrow, Hitch and I had to go talk to the Dark Queen of Internal Affairs.

Chapter 13

The new Police Administration Building had replaced Parker Center, built in the seventies and known as the Glass House. The new PAB was a mammoth ten-story, steel and glass rectangle in downtown L.A., located right across from City Hall.

With an open atrium, a one-acre park, and an artfully designed east face to protect the offices on that side from sniper fire, it has yet to be christened with a new name, official or otherwise. I hope we've not become so politically correct that we just take to calling it the PAB or name it after the mayor. I'd prefer something more appropriately flamboyant like "The House of Mirrors" or "The Puzzle Palace." Hitch jokingly wants to call it the "Porcelain Throne" because it's where busted dirtbags get flushed into the criminal justice system.

Whatever we end up calling it, the building is a state-of-the-art police facility, six years in the making. It also houses a new computer COMSTAT center for our huge City Crime Stat Board, a 450-seat auditorium for news events, and a 200-seat first-floor café. It's been advertised as an environmentally correct green building, whatever that means.

The old Glass House was like a crumbling tenement in the projects, with broken elevators and a circulating air system designed in the dark ages.

Our new space for Homicide Special was on the sixth floor. It was well designed, with big double-desk cubicles and spacious glass windows with views of City Hall. As with all new buildings, there were stringent housekeeping considerations put in place by our über-proud city managers. No wanted posters, fliers, or taped material of any kind could be displayed on the walls. No personal paraphernalia or pictures allowed on desks, filing cabinets, or attendant work surfaces. All furniture must be kept in the areas designated for its initial use, et cetera, et cetera.

Hitch and I happened to pull into the seven-hundred-car belowground garage at exactly 8:00 a.m. He parked his Porsche Carrera just as I was locking my Acura. He looked great, as always. Purple shirt, white collar, black tie, and a charcoal gray suit with a wide pinstripe. I'm feeling more and more like the filthy Persian rug next to this guy.

We'd already talked by phone and knew that Stephanie Madrid was on the agenda for this morning. Neither of us was looking forward to that interview.

"Listen, Hitch," I said, biting the bullet as we headed to the elevator. "I think I should take the interview with Captain Madrid alone." He looked over, surprised. "One of the perks with Alexa being Chief of D's is assholes like Captain Madrid don't quite know how to deal with me."

"Good point, but I've thought it over too. I can't let you do this by yourself." He smiled at me. "You can be on point if you want and receive the preliminary pleasuring and first round of oral stimulation, but I'll be there to watch your back and cover the retreat."

"They're giving blow jobs at IAG now?" I said in mock surprise.

We rode up in the new steel elevator, got to the sixth floor, and headed to our assigned cubicle. People were still a little subdued in this building. The old Glass House was noisy, but the new shop still felt a little like church.

"You guys got a real doozie," Lincoln Fellows called softly from his desk as we passed.

"We're movie producers," Hitch said. "Our jobs here are of little import."

That begat a moderate chorus of catcalls and insults.

"Wonder if the CSI report came back," I said as we sat at our desks. I turned on my computer and found it had been e-mailed over to us at seven this morning.

"Got it," I said. Hitch came around to read over my shoulder.

The DNA on the coffee cup we'd found in

Lita's driveway did not match either of the samples we'd taken from Carla or Julio Sanchez.

"That's disappointing," Hitch said.

"We're gonna have to cut 'em loose," I told him. "We got nothing on these two."

Hitch looked skeptical. He tapped his foot impatiently. "Once we turn them loose, we're never gonna see them again. Maybe it's just with Nix Nash hovering I hate to give up such an easy slam dunk."

"Okay, we'll keep them until tonight. But then they're outta here."

I scrolled down to the coffee content analysis. The lab had managed to isolate the blend.

"It's something called Brazilian Honey Nut," I said. "Never heard of it. Sounds expensive."

"You never heard of it 'cause all you drink is Folgers. These better Brazilian blends aren't in many of the standard vending machines. What's your plan with this? Find a machine that dispenses this stuff, then arrest everybody in the closest coffee room?"

"Brilliant. One day you're gonna be a total superstar.

"Guess we can't put this off any longer," I groaned, and pulled out the department directory, looked up the extension for Capt. Stephanie Madrid, and dialed.

"Captain Madrid's office," a man whined in a very tight, humorless voice. He sounded like his tail was stuck between the cheeks of his ass.

"This is Detective Scully. I'm over at the PAB in Homicide Special. My partner and I are investigating Lolita Mendez's murder. We'd like to book an interview appointment with Captain Madrid as soon as possible."

"How 'bout ten minutes? Can you get here by then?"

"Ten minutes?" I said, looking at Hitch, who frowned. Generally, we don't get such prompt service from our division commanders.

"Captain Madrid has been expecting your call," the man continued. "She said she would make herself available anytime this morning, the sooner the better."

"On our way," I said, and hung up.

"I don't like it," Hitch said. "Something's burning."

We rode down in the elevator and took my car over to the Bradbury Building, parking in the police lot next door. We went in through the back patio, past the sculptured wall titled "Passage of Time," depicting the history of Biddy Mason, a former slave who became one of L.A.'s pioneering philanthropists. Then we headed across the marble floor toward the beautiful ornate wrought-iron elevator.

"Wait a minute," Hitch said, and turned back. He went inside the small cafeteria and walked over to the coffee machine. I followed and watched from a distance while he studied the selections.

"And?"

"No Brazilian Honey Nut." Then he put some coins into the machine and hit a random button. A cup dropped. It had a green and white design. Once it filled, he pulled it out and placed it untasted in the trash.

"You keep trying to pin this on Captain Madrid and your career really will combust," I kidded.

"Not to worry." He smiled. "Let's go kick the Bitch Queen's ass."

Chapter 14

Internal Affairs leased the top four floors of the six-story Bradbury Building. We walked past several private offices rented out to other businesses on the ground level. I saw a brass plaque on one of the doors that read:

MADRID & SLOCUM
PRIVATE INVESTIGATIONS
DISCREET INQUIRIES

I pointed at the door as we walked by. "Lester Madrid has his office here?"

"Yeah, didn't you know that?"

"No. I thought he was on Moorpark in the Valley."

"You obviously haven't been getting enough one-eighty-one complaints recently. He's been renting here for almost two years."

"That must be convenient for Stephanie," I said.

Retired LAPD sergeant Lester Madrid was an ex-gunfighter from our old SIS squad who was married to Capt. Stephanie Madrid.

Les had been involved with the Special Investigation Section back when it became famous for being an assassination squad. Ten years ago SIS had an unusual operating agenda. The unit would target predicate felons, a classification the department used for criminals we determined to be irredeemable. These were violent men who were so committed to a life of crime that no amount of incarceration or psychiatric resourcing could ever make a difference.

An SIS surveillance team would wait for these guys to come out of prison, set up on them, and follow them around. The good thing about this type of felon was, it didn't take too long for them to start piling up parole violations, often meeting up with old ex-con buddies or buying cold guns off some dirtbag street vendor.

SIS would not arrest the target for any of these transgressions. Instead, they would sit back and wait. Patience was a mighty ally in their line of work, and before long the felon and his newly formed crew of degenerate shooters would decide to take something off, a market or a bank. SIS would be waiting outside when the criminals came running out. It was then that the SIS surveillance team would attempt to initiate their arrest. These arrests tended to end in shoot-outs, and most of the time the predicate felon and his criminal buddies failed to survive the inevitable gunfight that ensued. The operative theory in the unit was a dead asshole never beat his case on a technicality.

However, the unit's violent record drew a lot of criticism, and many *L.A. Times* editorials had been written. SIS was under so much scrutiny that the chief reconstituted the unit and it now had a very stringent set of guidelines.

As a human being, I had often found myself troubled by the methodology of SIS. But as a cop, I had cheered. This unit took down violent offenders. Their brand of street justice often ended with a brass verdict. The appellate court was in heaven.

Lester Madrid had been one of the team leaders on the old SIS and had been singled out for a lot of scrutiny when the heat was on. Les was one of those tall, Clint Eastwood–looking ass-kickers with a buzz cut and a mile of jaw. He never smiled. Sergeant Madrid had managed to survive the SIS IA investigations only to accidentally discharge his weapon in the locker room a few months later, putting a 9mm slug into his lower leg and blowing apart his femur. He now walked with a cane.

After the locker-room accident, Les Madrid took medical retirement and became a private investigator. That is how this legendary LAPD gunfighter ended up doing discreet inquiries. His PI practice mostly consisted of investigating reality show contestants, to make sure "The Bachelor" didn't have an unprosecuted felony rape in his past or "The Millionaire" wasn't bouncing checks.

I occasionally still saw Madrid at police functions with his wife, who was also a non-smiler. He'd be standing in some corner, leaning on his cane, clocking the room with eyes like stones.

Hitch and I took the elevator to the fourth floor where the Advocates Section was located. The doors opened and we walked out and stood next to the large mahogany handrail that capped a beautiful black wrought-iron balustrade, which ran around the perimeter of the six-story open promenade. From all six floors you could look up to the leaded-glass ceiling above or down through the open atrium to the marble floors of the lobby below. The Bradbury Building didn't look like it belonged in Los Angeles. It looked like it should have been in the French Quarter of New Orleans.

Hitch and I took a moment outside the Advocates Section to agree on our interview technique.

"I'll take point," I said. "If you think of anything, jump in."

"Got it." He smiled ruefully at me. "First Lita Mendez, then Nix Nash, and now Stephanie Madrid. Who's next, Fenrir?"

"Who the hell is Fenrir?"

"Famous Norse monster known as the 'World-Destroying Wolf.' "

God knows where he comes up with this stuff.

"Just follow my lead," I said.

We walked inside the office, gave our names, and were informed by her terrified male adjunct that Captain Madrid kept her appointments short, with only fifteen minutes allotted to each.

Ten minutes later the adjunct led us through a door into a very small outer office with one window looking out on the Dumpsters in the alley. I certainly didn't want to be here. I would have loved any reason to escape and attend to easier police business downstairs. Where was Lord Ding Wallace when you really needed him?

From there, we were shown into the chief advocate's spacious office. Captain Madrid rose to meet us.

She was fifty-five, short and abrupt, with absolutely no overtly feminine qualities. Her ash-brown hair was cropped short in a kind of pageboy helmet. She wore almost no makeup, no jewelry, and had a stocky but muscular athletic frame. I'd seen her a few times working out on the track at the Police Academy field. She was a choppy, earnest runner. Pugnacious face, pushed out over hard-pumping arms and pistoning legs. She'd be chugging the oval, relentlessly eating up the miles on our new graphite track. I wondered if she and Lester ever did the nasty and, if they did, who got to be on top.

"Sit," she commanded.

"Thank you, Captain. I'm Detective Shane Scull—"

"I know who you are," she interrupted. "You too, Detective Hitchens. Sit."

"Yes, ma'am," he said politely, settling into the second guest chair.

"So you two got the Lita Mendez kill."

Not homicide, not murder. Kill.

"Yes, ma'am," I said.

"I understand you've made an arrest already. That's good."

"Yes, ma'am," Hitch said. We sounded like terrified Catholic schoolboys who'd just been dragged in front of the Mother Superior.

"I was expecting you to come by," she said. "It was no secret that I had my share of problems with Miss Mendez."

"Yes, ma'am. That fact has sort of bubbled to the surface," I said.

"It's what?"

"It has come to our attention," I corrected.

"Hm-m-m-m," she said, and tipped back in her swivel chair, looking at each of us in turn. "I'm curious what you've heard."

"That you recently filed a criminal case against her for filing a false police report and won a restraining order against her last June."

"That woman was eating up my advocates' budget on frivolous complaints. Almost a third of our Hollenbeck Division hearings last year were because of her. She was wasting an important department resource. IAG has legitimate police improprieties to adjudicate."

"I see," I began. "So it would be fair to say that you had a healthy personal dislike for Miss Mendez?"

"Grow up, Detective," she said, then handed me a piece of paper. "I've made up a sheet. A log, if you will, attesting to my whereabouts minute to minute for the last forty-eight hours. All of these meetings can be confirmed by the people I've listed to the right. I realize that the several loud arguments I've had in public with Miss Mendez over the years will certainly make me the subject of some interest in the press. I'm counting on you two detectives to use that sheet to deflect any such nonsense."

"Excuse me, Captain, but this isn't your interview. It's ours," I said. I'd run out of patience for this. "I intend to conduct it according to my guidelines." I saw her flinch. Hitch groaned softly under his breath.

"I beg your pardon?" She seemed astonished.

"You are not running this investigation; we are. I intend to treat this the same way I would if you didn't carry a badge. You are on my suspect sheet. I've got questions. I intend to get answers to those questions, in the way and order I want."

She sat looking at me, her face a stony visage.

"I don't appreciate your tone," she said coldly. "But go on if you must. Ask."

"When was the last time you saw Lolita Mendez?"

"Day before yesterday, in court. As you just noted, I had a felony case pending against her for making a false police report. We had the preliminary meetings in Judge Amador's chambers along with attorneys to arrange for trial dates, depositions, and the like."

"How'd that go?"

"Like all my meetings with Lita Mendez. It was contentious. She called me a bull dyke, which I'm obviously not. I called her a liar and a gangster, which she obviously is."

I looked over at Hitch. This wasn't going well at all.

"These personal insults were witnessed by a *judge?*" Hitch asked, slightly appalled.

"Listen, boys. Let's get something straight right

now. I'm an easy target, but I'm the wrong target. You made this stop to talk to me, which I guess was necessary. You've done your job, covered this base; now move the hell on. You have my time line in your hands. It clears me. I wasn't anywhere near Hollenbeck for days before the murder. If you have any further questions, consult that list."

"You willing to take a polygraph just so everybody feels all warm and fuzzy?" I asked. She was still riling me up.

"No."

"Why not?"

"Because, Detective, I don't believe police officers should be asked to take polygraph tests on less-than-solid legal grounds. If you should ever get enough actual evidence to charge me with anything, then we'll talk about it. If you want a supporting opinion on the legality of police submitting to polygraphs, talk to your own union reps. The POA has come down very strongly against law enforcement being asked to take these things and I certainly agree. Next."

"This sheet attests to your whereabouts," I said, holding it up. "You got one for Lester?"

"My husband has nothing to do with this." She leaned forward and put her muscled forearms on the desk. "You've got half a dozen better starting points. All those Hispanic gangs she dissed. There's over forty criminal sets in Hollenbeck. They're all at war over street corners.

Then, after that, you can check her brother Homer's old enemies. Some of those murderous *vatos* might want her dead, and of course there's Carla and Julio Sanchez, who you've already arrested. Concentrate on all that."

She held my gaze with hard eyes.

"Interview's over, Detectives." Captain Madrid stood, then walked to the door and opened it. Hitch and I filed out obediently, but she stopped us in the outer office.

"If you have any further questions, put them in writing and submit them to my adjunct, Joseph, here." She pointed at the terrified detective. "Good day."

We left her office with almost as little info as we had going in. We were quickly back in the hall, overlooking the magnificent atrium.

"That was fun," Hitch said. "We should vacation up here."

"Who the hell was Fenrir again?" I asked.

Chapter 15

When we got back to the PAB, we divided up Captain Madrid's time line for the prior two days. She had set it up like her appointment schedule, in fifteen-minute increments. Each day started at 7:00 a.m. and ended around ten when she went to bed. Of course, the time line was mostly useless, because our preliminary time of death was around midnight. Once she and her husband were in the sack, Lester was her alibi witness, and I had no hope that he'd contradict her version of events.

"What'd you make of that crack about Lita using up a third of her advocates' budget on frivolous complaints?" Hitch asked.

"Captain Madrid seems like she lives for her job. Maybe that rises to the level of a motive."

"Let's hope she doesn't end up on *V-TV.* She comes off like Marge Schott."

We sat at our desks in Homicide Special and I started making notes on our interview with Captain Madrid.

"You wanta go talk to Judge Amador?" I asked Hitch.

"Sure. I'll see if I can track him down. What are you gonna do?"

"I'm going to keep working on the murder book." I pointed at my computer. "According to this e-mail from Detective Becker, the neighborhood canvass turned up nothing. Not surprising considering it's a gang block, but I'm also gonna go through all the patrol officer's notes and see if I can spot anything she missed. Then, once it's dark, I'm gonna go back to Lita's house and do my Jigsaw walk."

Hitch nodded. He was already familiar with this piece of my crime scene methodology. A Jigsaw walk was something I'd learned from one of the most fabled detectives to ever work a crime beat in Los Angeles. In his over twenty years as a homicide investigator, Jigsaw John St. John had cleared a surprising two-thirds of his murder cases. Now we're lucky if we clear 25 percent. Admittedly, that was before all these senseless drive-bys where the shooters don't even know their victims, but even so, Jigsaw was an LAPD legend.

John had retired and was living in Washington near Seattle. When I first got into Homicide I'd actually made a trip up there to spend some time with him, pick his brain, and learn his tricks.

One of the things he'd told me was he used to wait until everybody had cleared the crime scene and then he would return alone, usually at night when it was quiet. He'd stand in the house, clear his mind, and try to think like the victim. He'd walk around the crime scene using the same hallways as the vic, sitting in the same chairs. He'd play CDs from the victim's music collection and do whatever he thought the vic might have done just prior to death. Basically, Jigsaw would try to become the person whose murder he was trying to solve.

Then, after he'd done that, he would go outside and try to become the killer. Jigsaw used whatever insight he'd gained from the evidence gathering and witness interviews to try to re-create what he thought the unknown subject's mind-set might be.

Jigsaw told me that nine times out of ten it was a worthless exercise, but then the tenth time he'd hit on something he'd completely missed before and that one hit made the nine misses worth the effort.

I'd been following his routine for almost ten years, and in the cases I'd had in the interim, John's methodology had actually contributed in a significant way on at least fifteen.

The day went slowly because I was calling potential wits, suspects, or uncooperative neighbors, trying to set up interviews.

At around three, Hitch went to the superior court to interview Lita's trial judge. Thomas Amador was a crusty old coot. Cops loved this judge because he threw the book at felons. The Public Defender's office called him Judge Slamador, which might give you an idea of how tough he was.

At five, I took the key to Lita's duplex from the evidence folder and drove over to Boyle Heights.

I parked up the street from the crime scene, which was still festooned with yellow tape. Then I watched the house for almost twenty minutes trying to feel the vibe of the neighborhood. It was too early for much gang activity, but because the sun sets around five thirty, the streetlights were just coming on.

A few of the living rooms up and down the

street were lighting up as residents arrived home. As with most violent hoods, I saw a number of dogs with no tags running around off-leash, scavenging.

After a while, I got out of the Acura and walked toward the house, then stood there looking at it and thinking about Lita Mendez, trying to do as Jigsaw had suggested and capture her mind-set.

How did I feel about the neighborhood where I lived? Was it too dangerous and violent? Did that bother me? Did I like it here? Did I feel safe? Was I angry? Was I sad? What was driving me? What was I looking forward to? What frightened me?

The house was in a complete state of disrepair. A house is an outer covering, just like our clothes. When we dress in colorful clothes, it can signify a bright mood. Dark clothes often signal darker moods. I first noticed this phenomenon when I went to Germany to pick up a murder suspect just after the Berlin Wall fell. It was cold and snowy, and the new Western-style economy hadn't begun kicking in yet. It was a bleak place. I noticed everybody in the street was wearing gray or dark brown.

John had taken that observation a step further. He had told me that besides clothes, the general condition of a house can sometimes hint at general personality traits of the person who owned it. This lawn was not cut. Was this because Lita had just moved in?

114

I walked up the drive and around to the backyard, where the grass was brown and dry. More of the same. The garage was padlocked shut, but I looked through a grimy window. Lita's red Chevy Caprice had already been towed to Impound, where it was being processed by forensic scientists to see if she had possibly been kidnapped somewhere else and brought back here by the killer, who, if he used the Caprice to transport her body, had perhaps left some trace or a latent print behind.

I took the back steps up to the porch, unlocked the door, and entered. Lita had been a troublesome, thoroughly organized adversary, but she was a disorganized housekeeper. The inside of the duplex looked like a fraternity house den. Our CSIs had made it worse, spreading graphite powder everywhere in their search for prints.

I stood in the kitchen where she died and looked down at the square of missing floor that we'd removed to preserve the two 9mm slugs.

I again remembered the garlic smell I'd noticed when I first hit the crime scene at 9:15 a.m. What had Lita cooked but not eaten the night of the murder that contained garlic? The thought kept pestering me, but I put it aside.

Lita had been fatally beaten, had fallen backward with her arms outstretched. Maybe she'd still been partially conscious as she fell, but probably not. The cerebral hemorrhage and the

ME's report told me Lita was most likely dead when she landed. Then the unknown subject, the killer, had stepped forward and put two head shots into her already-lifeless body. Brutal, cold-blooded, and unnecessary.

The body had been beaten badly and she was already dead when she hit the floor. So why had the unsub put the two postmortem shots into her brain? Was this classic overkill signaling rage by somebody who was emotionally involved with the victim, like a jealous lover or someone Lita had had important emotional conflicts with? Had the unsub hated Lita so much that it wasn't enough to just beat her to death? Did the killer also need to disfigure the body, blowing holes in Lita's face?

Or was it just the opposite? Were the two shots attempting to send a false message? Were they simply staging to make it *look* like uncontrollable rage while, in reality, the unsub was coldly uninvolved? I didn't know which theory was true yet. Generally staging is the less likely of the two because it suggests an organized, more sophisticated mind and most violent killers are disorganized, unstructured, and out of control.

I moved through the house. Everything was a mess. It was logical to assume the house was clean when Lita moved in a week earlier, but the closets were already in disarray. Clothes were strewn on the floor instead of on hangers. Even her expensive court clothes were thrown in a heap below the bar. Had she done this? Had the unsub?

I walked slowly through the house, sitting on Lita's furniture, sampling her extensive music CD collection, trying to find answers, making notes about my feelings and observations in a spiral notebook.

Finally, I sat on the bed and looked around Lita's darkened bedroom. She had also tacked up sheets across the windows in here. Was this because she was depressed and liked it dark or liked being in rooms without sunshine? Or were the sheets to protect her from a possible sniper's shot? When Lita died, did she already know that somebody wanted to kill her? I wondered if her life had recently been threatened and that's why she'd tacked up the sheets. I wondered if she'd confided this fear to anyone. I made a note to find out.

I stayed in the house for almost an hour. On my way out, I paused in the kitchen to stand once more where Lita had died. I could see her everyday dishes in an open cupboard. I crossed and took a cereal bowl down from the shelf. It hadn't been washed completely and still had a tiny speck of old food on the side. The glasses in the cupboard were rinsed but were a little grimy. They obviously hadn't gone through the dishwasher.

I took a few down.

I could see Lita's lipstick still on the rim of one.

Water streaks marked the sides. I smelled a glass. It had a slightly foul odor as if some of the residue of the drink it once held was still there. I checked a few more dishes and found more of the same.

I opened the dishwasher. The array of pots and pans Hitch had found were still in the racks. I picked up a saucepan, studied it. I smelled dish-washing soap. Unlike the crockery and glasses in the cupboard, the pots and pans had been run through the entire cycle.

Why were all these cooking pans run through the washer while Lita only rinsed out her regular dishware in the sink?

When you work homicides you quickly learn that people are creatures of habit. The entire house was a testimony to deferred maintenance. Lita was a sloppy housekeeper. She didn't hang up her clothes or pick up her things. She left old pizza boxes around. When she did the dishes, she only rinsed and stacked. She would have probably done the same with the pots and pans. That was her habit, the way she lived.

So why on the night she was murdered did she change this pattern and wash those pots and pans in the dishwasher? The answer to that was pretty simple. She hadn't. The night she died, somebody else had been here. Somebody else had run the pans through the washer.

Did the unsub wash the pans? If so, why?

As I was mulling this, I saw a flash of movement

through the back window. I crouched low and looked into the backyard.

A man was in the shadows of the house, sneaking toward the locked garage.

Chapter 16

I'd put the lights on in Lita's house when I first arrived and had been walking around as if I owned the place, so whoever was in the backyard had to know I was here. He probably also knew I was in here alone. However, Lita had tacked those sheets up on quite a few of her windows, so I had some cover.

I found a protected spot, knelt down, and pulled my 9mm Springfield automatic out of its custom leather holster. I tromboned the slide, kicking a fresh round into the chamber, but left the safety on. Then I kept low and moved out of the kitchen and into the bedroom.

I'd already turned the lights off in there, so I was hidden by the dark room as I carefully removed the sheet Lita had tacked up over the side window. I slid open the glass and wriggled out through the opening, falling face first onto the dirt outside, cradling my gun in one hand.

I landed in a four-foot-wide path with a rusting chain-link fence that separated Lita's house from the house next door. I gathered my feet beneath me and stood carefully, holding my gun at the ready.

I heard something clunk softly in the backyard. A muffled thump. I carefully thumbed the safety off the Springfield, then moved toward the sound. A few seconds later I approached the rear corner of the house.

Before I got there, I lay down silently on my stomach, gun out in front of me, and inched out so I could see into the backyard. I waited for my vision to adjust.

Light spilling through the kitchen window helped my eyes transition. I searched the area over by the garage where I'd last seen the figure. Then I heard some whispering off to my right and turned my head and gun silently in that direction.

"S-s-sh-h-h-h," a man whispered. "Put it over there."

"You want the three-fifty and the battery?" another man whispered.

"Yeah."

I could see them now. They were crouched low at the back of the garden. Two guys in black T-shirts and jeans, setting something up. As my eyes adjusted further, I could see the faint outline of a studded equipment box. Then I knew who it was. The two cameramen I'd already met from *V-TV*. They were setting up their digital camera and a shotgun mike in a hidden position under some bushes. One of the guys reached into the studded camera case and handed the other a long lens of some kind. He affixed it to the camera housing and then attached a battery pack.

"Okay," he whispered. "Got the infrared and battery on. Watch out for that puddle. I think a hose is leaking back here. Let's just lay down, keep quiet, and wait."

So we all waited. They were aiming their light-gathering telephoto lens at the house, trying to get a shot of me working the crime scene or planting evidence or whatever the hell it was Nash was hoping he'd be able to catch me doing. Since I wasn't inside, they weren't getting much of anything, which was beginning to drive them nuts.

"Where the fuck is he?" one whispered. "You think he left while we were setting up?"

"Damn, I just rolled in some dog shit," the other cursed.

"Sh-h-h-h-h."

Ten or fifteen minutes passed while they did a lot of low whispering I couldn't make out. Finally, the taller one stood and moved past where I was hiding and up to the house to peek into the back window of the pantry.

"He there?" the cameraman whispered a bit loudly. They were losing their stealth to a mild sense of developing panic.

"No," the tall guy said. "Can't see anybody inside. I'll check and see if his car's still out front."

The tall one moved quietly around to the far side of the house. Once he had gone down the drive, I rose to my feet and slipped out of my hiding place, hugging the shadows, and moved closer to their camera position. By the time the assistant came back, I was so close, I could actually smell the dog poop.

"His car's still out front," the tall guy whispered.

"I wonder where the fuck he is," the other responded.

"Right here," I said, and touched the barrel of the Springfield to the side of the camera operator's head.

"Shit!" he screeched in terror, and shot up to his feet. He was off-balance and I pushed him hard. He sprawled on the grass as the assistant put his hands in the air.

"Don't shoot! We give!" he shouted, spittle flying.

The cameraman scurried back to his feet, thought about running, but I stopped him by waving my gun in his direction.

"You two are trespassing on my crime scene," I said.

"Huh?"

"You got Laura's number on that thing?" I asked, pointing to a phone on the cameraman's belt.

He nodded and handed his cell over to me. "I d-d-idn't . . . I w-w-wasn't . . . We were—," he stuttered.

"Duly noted," I said, scrolling his recent calls. I found Laura Burke's name and hit her number.

It rang twice before a woman's voice said, "Talk to me, Jason."

"Are you in charge of this blanket drill?" I asked her.

"Who is this?"

"Scully. Two of your cameramen are trespassing on my crime scene. I can book them now or we can start a negotiation."

"Stay where you are," she said, and hung up. A minute later I saw her striding up the drive with another man. He was a barrel-chested gray-haired guy wearing a camel coat, jeans, and sneakers. They headed into the backyard and stopped a few feet from me.

Laura was dressed for a gunfight. She was wearing a three-quarter-length black leather coat belted tight on her pipe cleaner build. Her skintight jeans and knee-high boots made her look dangerous. With her rat's nest of curly red hair stuffed under a ball cap and her no-nonsense scowl, she had about as much sex appeal as a nine-dollar hammer.

"This kinda sucks, Jason," she snapped at her cameraman.

"Children, children, no fighting," I said. "We've got bigger problems to deal with."

"Are you gonna arrest them?" she asked.

"I don't know yet. I might. Make me an offer."

We faced off for a moment. Then she turned to her companion. "Lenny, gimme your cell. I left mine in the van."

The man handed over his cell phone and she hit a preset number. She turned away from me and had a quick, whispered conversation. I was still facing her crew, with my gun out, but it was now pointed at the ground. It didn't look like I'd have to shoot anyone, so I holstered my weapon. Finally, Laura turned back and handed Lenny's cell to me.

"Mr. Nash wants to talk to you."

I took the phone. "Yeah?"

"I'm going to do something I rarely do, Shane. But I like the way you handle yourself, the way you think, so I'm going to make a big exception."

"We've had two conversations. You haven't a clue how I think."

"I do my research. I talk to people. You rate out. That's why I want to propose something."

I wanted to give this guy enough line before I set my hook, so I said, "I'm listening."

"I want us to come to an accommodation. Enter into an arrangement. How does that sound?"

"Illegal."

"Then what would you suggest?"

"Pick another city. Go to Nevada and fuck with the Vegas cops."

"I'm not leaving L.A. I'm committed to Lita Mendez's case."

I said nothing, waited him out.

"We need to talk this out," he continued. "I don't want you as an enemy. I could use an ally on this. I think we have a shared interest. I want to find justice for Lita, who, I might add, cared desperately about justice. I think, from what I've been told, you share that trait."

Again, I remained silent.

"You still there?"

"Yeah."

"Why don't you say something?"

"I haven't heard anything yet I want to respond to."

"Okay, look. I can understand your hesitancy, but we're about to tape the first L.A. show. It will air next Tuesday, ten p.m., coast-to-coast. It kind of sets up the whole deal here. Background on Lita and her activities against the LAPD, how your department harassed her. Of course we're going to look at other L.A. situations as well, but obviously, the Mendez murder is going to be my centerpiece case. I can't leave the studio right now because we're shootin' live for tape in two hours, but I'd like to extend an invitation for you to attend the taping. How's that sound?"

"Why would I want to do that?"

"To find some common ground. This doesn't have to be Atlanta. Why don't you invest an hour and see if we can come to terms? Gee, the worst thing that happens is we go our separate ways.

But in success, maybe you and your partner don't have to become tragic secondary targets of my show."

"Where's the studio?"

"We rented a warehouse park on Pico near Century City. Follow Laura; she'll lead you here."

Chapter 17

The studio was in a new commercial park on Pico near Century City. Two concrete tilt-up warehouses faced each other across a hundred-car parking lot bordered by a nine-foot cement wall.

As we pulled through the guarded gate, I was surprised to see twenty *V-TV* vehicles parked there. Ten were TV vans, half of those rigged with satellite dishes. Parked along one wall was a fleet of white station wagons and sedans, all with *V-TV*'s fancy blue logo on the doors. I knew this was a big-budget national TV show, but somehow, in my mind, I'd been diminishing it, hoping to find some run-down rinky-dink operation with only one vehicle and half a dozen employees.

Once we were in the parking lot, I could see at least thirty crew walking back and forth between the two warehouses. One of the massive elephant doors was open and I glimpsed sets inside. Beside the door was a large sign that read:

STAGE ONE. A huge sixteen-wheel TV remote truck like the ones I'd seen at televised football games was parked next to this stage with its generator running. Rubberized cables snaked out of the side and ran into the warehouse.

Laura's van was just parking in front of me, so I pulled into a slot next to it. She was quickly out of the truck and stuck her head in my lowered passenger window. "Wait here," she said, and was gone.

I decided to get out of the Acura and stood in the fully lit parking lot, watching the preshow activity. A camera truck was being off-loaded a few feet away and lighting equipment was being pulled off the lift tailgate.

I sensed someone approaching on my right and turned to find Marcia Breen walking slowly toward me. She still had that sexy model's walk I remembered, placing one foot directly in front of the other, causing a decent amount of hip sway. She was dressed in a tailored blue suit with a skirt cut just above the knee, like the ones she used to wear during trials to distract all the drooling railbirds at the courthouse. Tonight, she also wore a sad, almost apologetic expression.

She put out a hand and said, "Hi. I was hoping to have a chance to try and explain myself to you before this got so far along."

"Some setup," I replied, shaking hands but not following her lead because I was still a little uncomfortable with our reunion and didn't need to hear an excuse for her betrayal.

"I'm sorry this case happened to land on you," she said.

"I'm a big boy."

I was wondering how much I could say to her. We'd been friends once. Lovers. Of course, now that she was on Nash's staff, I knew she had to be viewed as an enemy.

"Please don't hate me for what's coming," she said unexpectedly.

I didn't like the sound of that.

Then Laura Burke was back, full of kinetic energy. "Come on. Nix is in Makeup, but he wanted to see you before the taping." She shot a look at Marcia. "They want you in show prep."

"See you later, Shane," Marcia said, then turned and walked off.

Laura led me past the control truck and into the main warehouse. As I entered Stage One, I saw a large, ornate courtroom set off to my right. It included a raised judge's bench, jury panel, and large public seating area. We passed that and walked through another set that looked like a detective squad room, with big glass windows and a backdrop depicting the L.A. skyline. The room was full of computers and cubicles and looked a lot like our new space downtown.

I saw a retired homicide detective I knew named Frank Palgrave. He'd worked Metro but had pulled the pin two years earlier. It shocked me to see him there, sitting on the edge of a desk reading a newspaper.

"Hey, Shane," he said, putting the paper aside.

"What's going on here, Frank?"

"Life after death on the LAPD."

Then I saw a retired FBI profiler from the 11000 Wilshire building in L.A. Like a lot of Feds, he was nondescript. A blond vanilla sundae with a comb-over and blue eyes. I couldn't remember his name, but he stepped up and supplied it.

"Jimmy James Blunt. We did that Union Bank thing in Diamond Bar together."

"Right, I remember. J.J., right?"

He nodded.

"Come on, Shane; you can meet the rest of the cast later," Laura interrupted. "Nix has a preshow meeting in ten minutes. It's now or never."

I followed Laura out of the police squad room set, through a mock judge's chambers, and into the large makeup room, which was located on the far side of the warehouse.

Nix Nash was sitting in a swivel chair in front of a built-in vinyl table that ran the length of the chair-lined room under an expanse of lit mirrors. He was wearing a blue velour running suit and, as we entered, he was chewing out his bone-thin, heavily tattooed makeup man.

"Come on, Greg," Nix said sharply. "How many times do I have to go through this? You don't line it; you dot it. Otherwise the top edge fades into my skin tone. You gotta use the number nine brown pencil, not the seven. Fill in the upper lip, starting right here."

He was talking about his bullshit moustache. The makeup man leaned in with a fresh number 9 pencil and started making little brown dots along the top ridge of Nix's moustache, filling it in, creating a fuller look. Then he saw Laura and me in the mirror behind him and swung his swivel chair around, brushing the makeup guy's hand rudely away as he turned to face us.

"Hey, you made it. Gee, that's terrific," he said happily. "Just be a minute, Shane. Makeup's already on. Just gotta let Greg finish the pencil work; then we can chat."

I watched while the moustache achieved its lush TV makeover. Then Nix checked it carefully, holding up a hand mirror.

"Much better, Greg. You see what a difference it makes when you do it the right way?"

"Unbelievable," Greg replied, and then went wildly over the top as he added, "Twenty years in makeup and that's a new one on me. Great tip, Nix. It definitely goes in the book, man."

Nix got out of his chair and looked at me. "I have a dressing room right onstage here. Come on."

We exited the makeup area, leaving Laura in our wake, and walked about fifty feet to a walnut door that said: STAR on a brass plaque. Nothing too subtle about that.

Nix opened up and led me into a plush living room with wall-to-wall carpet, antique furniture, and a full mirrored bar. He went to the fridge, opened it, and poured himself a soft drink.

"I never booze before a show, but let me fix you something. Beer, wine, shooter? What'll it be?"

"I'm fine," I said, and waited to hear what he really wanted.

Nix took a moment to examine two beautiful tailored suits that were on a hanging rack near the bar. One was brown, the other blue. He pulled both off, turned, and extended them toward me, one in each hand.

"Can't make up my mind. Blue is good for our set, but the brown goes better with my coloring. Which do you like?"

"I'm not a wardrobe consultant. How 'bout we get to what it was you had in mind."

"To the point then." He smiled as he hung the suits back on the rack. "What I'm about to say is just between us. No witnesses, so don't make the mistake of thinking you can gain leverage by trying to use it against me."

"Don't worry, Nix. I know about uncorroborated statements."

"Good." He sat on the sofa, but I remained standing. "Lita's murder is a bag of snakes," he began. "But you already know that."

"Is it?"

"You know it is. You went to see Captain Madrid today. She's had it in for Lita for years. Her husband is a sociopathic killer. Les Madrid has ten notches on his gun."

"Nine," I corrected. "One of those guys didn't make it all the way onto the ark and ended up camping out in an oxygen tent."

"But you get the point. Besides him, I've got a list of half a dozen cops who had contentious arguments with Lita, some in public with witnesses present. You, my unfortunate friend, are holding an ever-expanding bag of runny doo. When it explodes you're going to wish you'd worn your rain slicker."

"Really?"

"Yep. But I can help you. We can find a way to make this, if not easy, at least livable."

"How we gonna do that?"

"I've got more evidence coming on Lita's murder. Stuff you don't even know about yet. It's substantial and it's going to make you and your partner look very stupid because you should have turned it and it points right at the killer."

"You mean at Carla Sanchez," I said, holding his gaze.

"I don't think Carla did it," he said unexpectedly.

"Except that was your lead."

"No, it was your lead. I just turned it. As cops, we know sometimes leads go nowhere."

"So where's this going, Nix?"

"I've got a proposition." He stood and set his soft drink down, then faced me. He seemed slightly taller. Then I noticed he was wearing boots with three-inch stacked Cuban heels.

"You already know a lot of my people. Marcia, Detective Palgrave, J. J. Blunt, Judge Web Russell."

"I'm surprised to hear Webster Russell is working for you. I thought he was retired and living in Tahoe."

"He's back. He's a great jurist. The point is, all my people know their stuff. Agree?"

"They're good."

"And before they retired they were all destroyed by a corrupt legal system here in L.A. and put out to pasture. I don't want to see you end up like that."

"Me neither."

"So let's you and me keep it from happening. How'd you like to be on my team? Get off the firing line and step up for a little piece of what we're doing here. Join Marcia, Frank, and the others?"

"I always try not to crap where I eat."

"Gee . . . Good one." He smiled, but I could tell I was frustrating him. "Here's the choice as I see it, Shane. You can make a deal with me right

133

now. Join my team, work this case with me, or you face the consequences like those poor cops in Atlanta. We'll talk money later, but I promise you it's gonna beat the heck out of your detective's salary."

"If I work for you, do I have to retire from the LAPD first?"

"For the time being, to be effective, our arrangement will have to be extremely confidential. You'd have to stay on the job. Later, after I leave L.A., you can pull the pin and if you've clicked with my audience, you might even be asked to join the permanent cast of *V-TV*. Become a famous talking head like Mark Fuhrman, maybe even write a few books."

"What would my job entail?"

"You'd feed me case facts. There's a five-thousand-dollar bonus for every fact you give me that I decide to run with on the air."

"Sell out my case."

"Let's not call it that. I'd rather say you're commercializing it."

"And what if I say no?"

"You won't say no."

"But if I do?"

"If you do, I will hang this stinking fish around your neck and pound you through the concrete right in front of that fancy new Police Administration Building you guys just built downtown."

"Think you're up to that?"

"Yeah." He smiled warmly at me. "Justice will be served whether you like it or not. We're not doing the devil's work here, Shane. Far from it. The perp who killed Lita was the one doing that. I'm gonna get him or her. The unsub will swing for this and if you join me we can do it together. Seems to me your choice is pretty simple. Be the agent of this killer's destruction or become the agent of your own."

"I don't think you've got what it takes to make good on that threat," I said.

"Let me give you a preview then. Why don't you watch the taping of show one in the green room or, if you want a different experience, you can look at it in the control truck. Laura's husband, Drew, is our director. Watch him work. Watch me spin it. Watch this thrashing machine come roaring down the road and see if you think you're fast enough to get out of the way."

Chapter 18

"Roll the main title! Cue the music! Camera Three, you'll be first to the conference room after the break. Stand by; we're coming out of main title tape in *five, four, three, two, one.* Slow fade on the music! Cue Camera One! Cue Nix!"

I was sitting in a three-tiered darkened control

room inside the sixteen-wheel TV truck. The main title of *V-TV* had just unfurled on a center monitor marked: PREVIEW ONLINE.

Drew Burke, the director, was thin, cranial, and kinetic, just like his skinny red-haired wife. They obviously ingested way too much coffee and not enough food. I was alone in the top-tier row of the truck. About ten other people were in the darkened control room below me, all of them busily adjusting video and volume pots or running huge consoles. A bank of smaller monitors faced the director and showed what each of the five cameras was shooting. The temperature inside the truck was held at a chilly sixty-five degrees to keep the equipment cool.

Nix Nash was standing in the center of the *V-TV* main set, which resembled a glitzy cobalt blue newsroom with scrolling tickers. About ten background actors in shirtsleeves were seated at metal desks, busy miming work in front of computer monitors. Nix had chosen the blue suit, which looked very good on his high-tech blue set. He was pumped up on adrenaline, his face round, his moustache full, bouncing happily in his hand-tooled boots as he leaned toward the camera and began to speak.

"A dangerous idea is not responsible for the people who choose to believe in it. And ordinary men become extraordinary performing remarkable feats under impossible circumstances." Now

Nix started to stroll his elaborate set. Camera One tracked him.

"Dangerous ideas can provide big opportunities, but they often get thrust on us when we can least afford it, so the call goes unanswered. We've got a whole generation now that was born in an age of extravagant semi-equality. They don't know what it was like before, so they think, 'This isn't so bad. We have our video games, our flat-screen TVs, our SUVs.' This dumbed-down generation sits lulled by excess completely unaware that all this luxury they take for granted is on the verge of being snatched away by corrupt government officials."

Drew instructed Camera One to tighten into a close-up.

"You probably think, 'Come on, Nix. Not in America.'" He stood there, his face lightly flushed, burning with this terrible concern. "Have you guys heard about this thing called the goal gradient phenomenon?" He paused and let that mouthful sink in. "It states that the farther we get away from our goals in life, the less interested we become in attaining them. When you put this in a political or a law enforcement context, the goal gradient phenomenon can become really danger-ous, because it suggests that at the midpoint in a politician's or a police officer's career, when he or she is stuck in middle management, inevitably they begin to experience boredom, malaise, and yes, even cynicism. These three emotions just happen to be the major precursors to corruption."

"Camera Two, when Nix moves go with him," Drew instructed the crew through his headset.

Nix started strolling his set again, with Camera Two tracking. They passed half a dozen extras working on computers.

"I love the concept of freedom, truth, and justice. Who doesn't?" Nix enthused. "But there's a catch. You see, in order to have a safe, free, and just society we have to first engage in a huge act of trust. We have to give some of our sacred, constitutionally guaranteed rights over to the people we have chosen to protect us."

He now stopped next to a large whiteboard, still looking directly into Camera Two.

"Ready Four; take Four," Drew Burke said just as Nix Nash turned smoothly to Camera Four, which was on a medium close-up.

"Here's something to consider. Do you know that recently in America we've been passing more and more criminal laws and using them to enforce morality? It's true. And it goes way beyond the easy ones to spot like abortion or right-to-life legislation. We now also have thousands of smaller laws dealing with everything ranging from drug or pill use, to the amount of liquor we can legally consume, right on down to whether we can smoke in our own cars."

"Camera Five, you're on a medium-wide shot.

Focus up and go," Drew said. As the shot changed, Nix turned to the whiteboard, picked a Magic Marker out of the tray, and wrote:

LEGALLY ENFORCED MORALITY

As he wrote this he said, "The very people we have chosen to protect us have now decided they also know how we should behave. And with this idea, they've begun to redefine the moral playing field, passing hundreds of these laws aimed at creating new moral standards by slowly abrogating more of our constitutional freedoms." He now wrote:

NEW MORAL STANDARDS

"I'm not here to debate the merits of these new laws; that's an argument you must take up with your duly elected officials. However, I can tell you this much. Unenforceable laws governing moral standards always promote police corruption. It happened during Prohibition, during the shoot-'em-up cocaine days of the eighties, and it's happening today. The reason is because these laws attempting to enforce morality actually provide criminal organizations and unscrupulous individuals with a huge financial interest to undermine law enforcement, and that causes . . ." He wrote:

Then he underlined it twice and set the Magic Marker back in its tray.

I sat there alone in the back of the control room watching. I had to admit Nix was smooth and good.

He stood by his whiteboard frowning. "Remember that thing we were talking about before, that goal gradient phenomenon? It also stipulates that when our police get cynical and bored, they often stray, forgetting their pledge to protect us."

He paused, cocking his head as if to think about it. "But hey, then that leaves us with nobody standing between us and these new laws and the corrupt politicians who've passed them. So what do we do now?" He gave that a moment, then said, "Well, I'll tell you exactly. We must become vigilantes."

He began walking, bouncing in his boots again, energized by this idea.

"Of course once we attempt to do this there'll be angry detractors, because plenty is at stake here. Some will call us meddlers. Others will say we're off the reservation. But come on; under these circumstances is being a vigilante really such a bad thing? I looked it up. The root word is 'vigilant.' Vigilance is an American tradition. We were vigilant at Concord when this country was born and after World War Two when our vigilance overthrew first a fascist, then a Nazi regime; then a few years later we dismantled a communist one. We were vigilant again after 9/11. Like Paul Revere in the Old North Church, we must ride forth spreading the word."

"Camera Three, go and begin racking," Drew said. A long shot hit the screen and slowly began to tighten as Nix simultaneously stopped walking. He was now standing on the far side of the set next to an American flag.

"A vigilante is further defined as a watchman, a guard, a patriotic member of a vigilance committee. So that's what we are. Vigilantes. Only here on *Vigilante TV* we're doing it one police case at a time."

"Camera One, you're on Nix and pulling back," Drew said as Nix continued.

"In each city I visit I pick one major case, one investigation that I think has gone astray due to corruption, cynicism, and malaise."

Here it comes, I thought.

"I usually try to find one with civic or legal meaning," Nix continued. "After I have chosen it, I pursue it until all of us here are satisfied that we have found the real truth. Sometimes that can be very dangerous. A few years ago, I ended up in federal prison for two years because I dared to criticize the power structure right here in L.A. But if we want a fair and just society, we've gotta take some chances."

Now Nix motioned the camera to follow him and headed toward a big threshold with open double doors. "So let's go protect the innocent and find some beauty in the truth. We'll begin in two minutes." Nix then walked through the open double doors, and when he closed them, the camera stopped on a big brass plaque affixed to one side that read:

DEPARTMENT OF VIGILANTE JUSTICE

"Stay on the placard, music up," Drew said. "Cue the bumpers. We fade to black in *five, four, three, two, one.*"

Chapter 19

The cameras all moved to a nearby set and came on one at a time, lighting the control room's video monitors. Then, after everybody was in place, Drew Burke said, "Camera Three, we open with you on Nix, then pull out."

Nix was now seated on the edge of a conference table in a large room. On one wall was a lit map of Los Angeles.

Behind him, seated in high-back leather conference room chairs, were Marcia Breen, Frank Palgrave, and J. J. Blunt, as well as three other men and two women I didn't know.

Judge Webster Russell was at the end of the table. Web hadn't changed much since I'd testified in his court a few years back. He was a big, shaggy gray-haired eminence with an honest, solemn face, wearing black judicial robes. A perfect video judge.

Nix was smiling, and as the theme music faded, he said, "Welcome, my friends, to Los Angeles, California. City of Angels. This town spans 493.3 square miles, with a population of 4 million. According to Forbes.com, Los Angeles is the eighth most powerful economic city in the world. This is a city that hosts the L.A. Lakers, a world-renowned symphony, and the Getty Center. But it also hosted one of the worst police corruptions in modern law enforcement history. The Rampart scandal saw over a hundred convictions over-turned on charges that included obtaining false confessions through torture, planting evidence, and yes, even murder. So don't say it can't happen here, because it already did.

"A lot is going on in this town. A lot of people live here, die here, and face injustice here. Tonight we're going to focus on just one."

"Ready Four; take Four," Drew said, and the shot switched to a close-up of a picture of Lita Mendez being held in Nix's hand. In the photo, she looked fragile and innocent. Her long black hair curled down on delicate shoulders.

"This woman's name is Lolita Mendez. 'Lita,'

as her friends called her, was not always a warm and fuzzy person. In fact, Lita could sometimes be a real fireball. But once you knew her, it was easy to understand why. She became a friend of mine when I practiced law in this city and, more than once, I found myself facing her moral outrage.

"Lita was mostly angry at the police because they chose to criminalize her family and friends who live in a Hispanic ghetto right here in L.A. In this eighth-wealthiest economic center on earth, there is an area called Boyle Heights, and Boyle Heights ain't doing so hot. Boyle Heights doesn't feel like it's a suburb of the eighth-wealthiest city in the world. It feels like it belongs in a third-world country."

The shot switched back to Nix still sitting casually on the edge of the conference table. "Lita is an ordinary single woman with a tenth-grade education. But more than that, she's a social activist. She has filed over two hundred civil complaints against the LAPD for violating her rights and those of her friends.

"The vitriol that came to exist between this hundred-pound Hispanic woman and the nine-thousand, nine-hundred-man Los Angeles police force became intense, personal, and often violent. So why is this lone high school dropout so important right now?"

Nix took a moment to let his audience wonder.

Then he leaned forward and said, "Two nights ago, Lita Mendez was murdered."

He paused again for effect, then continued. "It happened in the middle of the night with no witnesses or physical evidence, yet the LAPD has already arrested two suspects, a married couple named Carla and Julio Sanchez. As far as I can see, there is no reason Carla and her husband should have been arrested, because they are certainly not guilty. The police have to be well aware of that fact. So, if they're not guilty, why are Carla Sanchez and her husband, Julio, currently incarcerated in the Boyle Heights jail? The answer to that lies deep in the fabric of this particular demonstration of police corruption. Watch this."

"Music up. Roll film package one," Drew instructed.

Video of Lita Mendez came on the screen. She seemed fragile and vulnerable and was seated in her living room with the bedsheets tacked up on the windows behind her. The time-stamped date on the screen was a few weeks ago.

"My name is Lolita Mendez," she said softly. "I live in Boyle Heights, a suburb of L.A., and members of the Los Angeles Police Department are trying to kill me."

Chapter 20

What followed was a well-produced biography of Lita Mendez, starting with how she grew up on the mean streets of Boyle Heights and ending with her crusade against the LAPD. It included a filmed dispute between Lita and Capt. Stephanie Madrid shot by local TV news cameras outside the IA building. Captain Madrid was demanding that Lita and her pack of neighborhood demonstrators disperse. In the film, Lita was wearing a T-shirt with the picture of a particular police officer screen-printed on the front and a statement accusing him of shooting an unarmed gangster on the back.

The bio included an interview, obviously taken only hours ago, because it was conducted from inside Corcoran State Prison. Nash was in the visitors' center with Lita's brother, Homer Mendez. Homer was a stocky, muscular man about twenty-eight years old who had Evergreen ink all over him. He called the police murderous *chota*.

"I knew those cop bastards would eventually kill my big sis," he said sadly.

"LAPD Detective Shane Scully has been assigned to the Lita Mendez murder case and this is a very troubling choice," Nash said, narrating this piece of the film package over a stolen shot of me taken yesterday morning as I was walking toward the media control area a block from Lita's house.

The next shot showed Nix outside Lita's house, posthomicide. The police cars were gone, but there was yellow crime scene tape strung everywhere. "Why would this particular homicide detective be assigned to this particular case?" he asked with a troubled look.

A picture of Alexa now appeared on the screen. It was a publicity photo taken a few months ago when she'd made captain. She was in her dress blues but looked a little severe in the shot with her braided hat set low, shadowing her gorgeous eyes. Her hair was pulled back; captain's bars glittered on her shoulders. She was still beautiful, but off this pose you definitely wouldn't mess with her. Since this particular photo was never published, I wondered how Nash had gotten his hands on it.

"This woman is LAPD Captain Alexa Scully, and she is Detective Scully's wife," Nash intoned solemnly. Then the film package ended and the shot switched back to Nix in the conference room. "Get this," he said. "Because here's where the big questions begin. Alexa Scully is also the Chief of Detectives for the entire LAPD."

I was getting angry, but there was nothing I could do to stop this. The shot widened to show the full conference room and the other *V-TV* cast members.

"Coincidence or conspiracy?" Nix intoned. Then he turned to his panel of experts. "First, let's talk to Frank Palgrave, who used to work the homicide desk in L.A.'s Metro Division."

"Camera One, tighten on Palgrave," Drew Burke said. "Camera Two, stay with Nix. Hold sizes; we're intercutting."

"Frank, how are homicide detectives assigned to cases in Homicide Special?" Nash asked. The camera shots cut back and forth as they talked.

"They're on a standard rotation, just like at the individual divisions."

"Interesting. So Scully and his partner, Sumner Hitchens, would be given this case as part of a normal rotation."

"Yes."

"So let me get this straight," Nix said, his brow furrowed theatrically. "Along comes this red-hot grounder where a vocal police critic has been murdered, and the Hollenbeck detectives call up Homicide Special and give it over to them. Then lo and behold, who happens to just pop up as the lead investigator, but the very husband of the Chief of D's. That sound right?" Nash asked the panel.

"I think it's preposterous," Judge Web Russell said. "It's much more likely that, because of the high-profile animosity between Miss Mendez and law enforcement, the LAPD was trying to contain the situation and Detective Scully was chosen by his wife to operate as an agent of the department."

"Wow," Nix said. "Are you suggesting the cops are trying to bury this case?" He paused for effect, then said, "And then there's this."

Drew cued up a film package that showed Edwin Chavaria being introduced by Nix Nash on tape. That was followed by a shot of Chavaria exiting the *V-TV* van to come over and talk to me.

I realized that I'd been duped when Chavaria stopped at the side of the van and refused to go farther. He'd led me to a preset camera position so the encounter could be recorded by a hidden microphone and HD camera filming through a smoked-glass window from inside the production van.

The stolen interview of course included me telling Chavaria that I wasn't a very nice guy and considered myself to be a shithead. The word was bleeped, but you could read my lips. It also included me saying if Chavaria didn't cooperate, I would bust and jail him on anything I could find, including old traffic warrants. The interview between us had been edited and tightened. It included Chava's description of the argument between Lita and Carla over the ceiling fan.

After that came the arrest of Carla and Julio Sanchez. The shot featured Nash standing on the street corner as Hitch and I watched the squad car pull out with the Sanchezes in custody.

Then we were back in the conference room. The shot was close on Nix Nash. "So when you break it down, here's what the cops basically have against Carla and Julio Sanchez. No time-of-death evidence locking either of them to the murder. All the police have to support their flimsy arrest is a statement about a front-porch argument over a ceiling fan from this gangbanger, Edwin Chavaria, who my producer just found out has an extensive criminal record and was a sworn enemy of Carla's husband, Julio Sanchez. Questionable testimony at best. But that's not the worst of it. There's also this. . . ."

Drew said, "Roll film package two."

Even though the control truck was kept chilly, beads of sweat began to form on my forehead.

Now Nash was interviewing a tough-looking, middle-aged, heavily tattooed Hispanic woman whom he identified as Janice Santiago.

"I was across the street," Santiago said. "It was late. I was walking my dog and I saw a blue Sidewinder truck pull up at Lita's house and then, because Lita gets a lot of threats, I just . . . well, I shot it on my cell phone."

"This was the night of the murder?" Nash asked.

"Yes, around eleven p.m."

"Camera Four, you're up and staying wide," Drew said.

The shot took us back to the conference room.

Nash held up the iPhone. "Here's the cell that Janice Santiago shot her video on," he said. "And here's what she shot."

"Roll it," Drew said, and the cell-phone footage played on a large screen in the conference room so that all of Nix's "experts" could see it and participate.

The cell video was time-stamped 10:48 p.m. On the screen Carla Sanchez walked up to Lita's front porch and rang the bell. Lita opened the door; Carla dug out her wallet, pulled out some money, and handed it over. Then Lita handed Carla the ceiling fan, which Carla carried back to the truck. She got in the Sidewinder and Julio drove them both away.

"Camera One, move in tight on Nix," Drew said.

"So, there's your corroborating witness, including a cell video proving Carla Sanchez's story that she bought the ceiling fan just as she said she had. Yet, strangely, this innocent woman and her husband are still in jail. Why couldn't the cops find Janice Santiago? She lives just down the street in Lita's neighborhood. It only took me half an hour to locate her. What's going on here, Marcia?"

"Somebody's not doing their job," Marcia Breen said in close-up. "Or worse still, maybe somebody *wants* the Sanchezes in jail so they can charge Carla and Julio with this crime. If the Sanchezes

151

are found guilty of Lita's murder, it could cover over what's really going on, couldn't it?"

"And what do you suppose that is?" Nix asked innocently. "Let's see. . . . Hey, maybe it's this."

And we were again on the same shot of Lita Mendez inside her living room.

She was looking into the camera just as before. "My name is Lolita Mendez," she said again. "I live in Boyle Heights, a suburb of L.A., and members of the Los Angeles Police Department are trying to kill me."

The shot switched back to Nash in close-up. "We'll be right back," he said solemnly as they went to commercial.

Chapter 21

I sat in the control room fuming. I'd been outplayed and led in a big, ugly circle by this guy. I could see now how the cops in Atlanta had been made to seem like such fools. Nobody in the control room spoke to me, although a few stole looks.

After the two-minute break, Nash was on camera again.

"We're going to find out what kind of corruption is going on in Boyle Heights. This is a major *V-TV* exposé and you're not going to want to miss a moment of it."

"Camera Three, go wide and track," Drew said as Nix turned and began walking through his fake squad room set where fake detectives were working at desks, not looking up as he passed.

"Law enforcement doesn't have much time to solve a murder in metropolitan crime areas," Nix said. "They pile up fast, so if detectives don't put a case down in the first forty-eight hours, it quickly becomes something police call a cold case.

"Here on *V-TV* we like to dig into some of those old cases and see if we can supply a measure of justice and closure to the families of these tragic murder victims. In each city we visit, we select one cold case that seems to have maybe gotten more than the normal amount of short shrift and see what we can do. For our new viewers it's a segment we call: 'Cold, but Not Forgotten.' "

Nash walked into a fake captain's office to join J. J. Blunt, Frank Palgrave, Marcia Breen, and two attractive plainclothes female detectives in suits with prop badges hanging out of their breast pockets.

"You already know Frank and Marcia and ex–FBI profiler J. J. Blunt. So now meet Karen Bowman and Katie McKiernan, both retired LAPD detectives." The women smiled as Nash continued. "You guys have the case files?"

Karen Bowman handed over a stack of cold-case folders and Nash gave a brief summary of each. One or two of the cases went back as far as the seventies.

Then Nix told his audience, "I've asked every detective here to write down their vote for which case they think we should reinvestigate. So hand your slips on up."

They all passed pieces of paper forward and Nix made a big show of counting the votes before announcing: "Three out of five of you agree we should look at Hannah Trumbull's murder from four years ago." He turned right into Camera Two as Drew punched the shot up.

"Here's the dope on this murder," Nix said. "Hannah Trumbull, a beautiful twenty-eight-year-old nurse from Good Samaritan Hospital in L.A., was murdered in December of 2006." He held up her picture. She was indeed beautiful. She had shoulder-length straight blond hair and piercing blue eyes. "Hannah was shot to death in the garage of her duplex in West Hollywood. LAPD Hollywood Division Detectives Keith Monroe and John Hall got the squeal. After investigating for just two days, they determined that the murder was committed by this man."

A sketch of an African-American man in a watch cap appeared on the screen superimposed over Nix's shoulder. The suspect in the drawing looked to be in his mid-thirties.

Nix continued, "Nobody can find this dude. They say they've been looking scrupulously for four years, but I was a cop once and believe me, no cop looks for anything for four years unless it's a winning lottery ticket.

"This drawing was done by an LAPD sketch artist in 2006 working with Gina Wilson, a woman who lived across the street from Hannah Trumbull. Gina was robbed by this man one week before Hannah Trumbull's murder, and Detectives Monroe and Hall think this thief was targeting that neighborhood and committed both crimes. Working with the artist, Gina produced this drawing of the SBG, which, by the way, is unofficial cop lingo for 'Standard Black Guy.'

"So here's what these two homicide cops would have you believe. They say this home invasion specialist, this SBG, broke into Gina Wilson's house a week before Hannah's murder, tied Gina up, robbed her, and then left. He didn't beat Miss Wilson to death or shoot her in her garage. He just stole her money. So, if he didn't shoot Gina Wilson, why did the SBG shoot and kill Hannah Trumbull?"

Nix picked up the actual suspect sketch and now turned to the camera, holding it up. "I ask you, is this really a picture of Hannah's murderer or is it a picture of police disinterest and incompetence? On our next show, we're going to try and find out if this guy, who the cops have been searching to find for four years, really did the Hannah Trumbull murder. I think he may just be a convenient way for our two homicide detectives, Monroe and Hall, to dump poor Hannah's violent, hard-to-solve murder and move on.

"Next week, we're also going to see if we can run down Hannah's parents and get them in here to talk to us. We'll hear what they know about their daughter's life in the days just prior to her death. We'll ask them what they think about the service they've gotten from the LAPD so far. If you have any thoughts which might help us you can text the number at the bottom of the screen. We'll also continue to probe the troubling Lita Mendez homicide, plus a lot more. It's a pile of work, but it's God's work, and here at *V-TV* we're always invigorated. Stick around. There's more. We'll be right back."

The final segment of the show dealt with the fact that Los Angeles superior court judges were being paid cash bonuses funded by the county government. Jurists were getting up to forty-five thousand dollars extra over their base pay. So far, according to Nash, $300 million in this fiscally crippled state had been paid out to judges in Los Angeles County. Judges who, Nash informed us, were already among the highest paid in the country.

Ex-judge Web Russell weighed in. "If the county is paying bonuses, will these judges in return feel a need to favor the County of L.A. when actions are brought against it? Is this a condition where the county is in effect actually bribing these judges to get favorable results at trial?"

Nix Nash did the show close from his dressing room. He'd kicked his shoes off. His stocking feet were up on the coffee table. He was sipping a soft drink and grinning at the camera.

He set the can down and said, "So that's show one from L.A. We're in the City of Angels, but we haven't seen too many angels yet. Maybe just two." He held up Hannah's and Lita's pictures, one in each hand. "Remember this quote by the noted American humorist Donald Robert Perry Marquis: 'Procrastination is the art of keeping up with yesterday.' If that's so, then we're probably the biggest procrastinators on earth. On *V-TV*, all we do is examine what happened yesterday. We're in L.A. speaking truth to power. See you next week. God bless, and turn out the lights as you leave."

Drew Burke said, "Kill the lights."

The dressing room was plunged into darkness.

"And we're in black," Drew said. "Bring up the theme music and roll end credits."

Chapter 22

I ran into Nix just as I was exiting the control truck. He was standing in front of the open elephant doors of Stage One just outside the warehouse, dressed again in his blue velour running suit.

"What did you think?" he asked, gesturing with his soft-drink can.

"Good start," I said, "but I haven't been up to the plate yet."

"I don't think your turn at bat is going to help much," he said, a knowing smile lighting his cherubic face and twinkling in his blue eyes.

"Put a bat in a cop's hands and anything can happen. Isn't that your theme?"

He walked toward me. "Gee, don't be like this. My deal is still on the table. Come on; let's talk this over."

"What's to talk about? You shot show one. I've already been marked for evisceration."

"That's the nice thing about shooting these shows live to tape. We're still a week from air. We can always edit, change, and reshoot."

"So it's not just you against the system, speaking truth to power. You can massage troublesome corrupt facts if you want to."

"It's not corrupt to make a deal to advance a cause."

"Yes, it is," I said.

"In that case, here." He handed me a DVD. "That's a copy of Janice Santiago's cell-phone video."

"What shooting gallery did you dig her out of?"

"Not important. Her film doesn't lie," he said. "You'll need that video to clear the Sanchezes. I'm sure you'll finally want to release them now."

I took the DVD, said nothing, and started toward my car.

"I suggest you make note of this time and place," he said. " 'Cause your life just took a big turn for the worse."

I looked back. He was adrenalized and grinning, happy to be standing there in his Cuban-heeled boots and blue velour running suit. As he turned and reentered the warehouse, I promised myself before this was over I was going to flip that goofy smile of his upside down.

When I got to the Acura there was an older man and woman walking away from the car next to mine. They'd parked too close, making it hard for me to squeeze in.

"Sorry, can you make it?" the man asked.

He was one of those skinny older guys with only a few gray hairs left, but he kept them long, slicked back over his shiny pate, unwilling to surrender to total baldness. The woman was his same age and pleasant looking, if a bit plump.

"I can make it," I assured him as I squeezed between our two cars.

The man said, "We're here to see Mr. Nash. We have an appointment. Could you direct us? I'm Russ Trumbull and this is my wife, Gloria."

"Really," I said, stopping to look at him more carefully. Then I pointed at Stage One. "I think you can find him just inside that warehouse."

Trumbull and his wife hurried off.

I levered myself into the driver's seat, pulled out of the commercial park, and drove up Pico. With each block the knot in my stomach got tighter and harder. I finally called Hitch on my cell phone.

"Yo," he answered. I could hear laughter in the background.

"You in a bar?"

"Party. I'm at Joel Silver's. He's still trying to horn his way in on *Prostitutes' Ball* and keeps inviting me to these private Hollywood screenings at his house. Jamie says I should string him along. Joel's producing deal is at Warner's and we still might need their distribution. What's up?"

"We need to get together."

"You mean now?"

"Yeah."

"What's wrong? You sound different."

"I am different. Listen, Hitch, I wouldn't pull you away from your Hollywood friends unless—"

"Shit, dawg. Put a sock in it. These aren't

friends; they're business associates. Where do you want to meet?"

"How about your place?" I said. "It's closer than the office."

"See you in twenty."

"It's gonna take me about thirty. I'm all the way out in Century City."

"What're you doing there?"

"Nix Nash invited me to his studio. It's out on Pico."

"Why'd he do that?"

"He wanted me to see the taping of the first L.A. show. I just left."

"So how'd it go?"

"We're fucked," I told him.

Chapter 23

Hitch lives in a multi-million-dollar house near the top of Apollo Drive in the lush development of Mount Olympus. Most of the homes up there are big, sprawling mansions. Last year, Hitch bought a beautiful Georgian two-story with Doric pillars that span a wide front porch. When I got my first look at this place I was insanely jealous. I subsequently managed to rationalize that feeling by telling myself that Hitch just got lucky when he drew a great homicide case and was smart enough to cash it in with a big-budget movie. Maturity and good sense have since prevailed, and now when I visit I'm only mildly pissed and momentarily disgruntled. It usually dissipates in less than ten minutes.

I left my Acura in the drive. Hitch's hundred-thousand-dollar black Porsche Carrera was already parked under the porte cochere. I walked up to the front door and pushed the doorbell. *Dum-de-dum-dum,* went the chimes, sounding the theme from *Dragnet.* It struck me as being at odds with Hitch's cosmopolitan style, but I've learned that even the most sophisticated of us can fall prey to moments of cultural whimsy.

I heard the classical sounds of Dave Brubeck's jazz piano burbling away inside, once again revising my opinion. Moments later, my partner opened the door. He was wearing his Hollywood vines—leather pants and vest over a rich dark purple turtleneck. He looked like a celebrity contestant on *Dancing with the Stars*, but I guess it was a pretty good outfit for a show-biz screening at a mega-producer's house.

Hitch greeted me with a frown, saying, "You okay? You look like roadkill."

"You got one of those German lagers I can't afford?"

"Sure. Come on in. Crystal's on the back deck. I'll get three and meet you out there."

I walked through his beautifully furnished

art-adorned living room while Hitch detoured to the bar to get our beers.

Outside I greeted Crystal Blake with a hug. She's Hitch's current girlfriend and is a pastry chef at a four-star restaurant in Hollywood. The restaurant was dark tonight and she had gone to Joel Silver's party with Hitch. Crystal is talented, funny, and drop-dead gorgeous. Like Hitch, she'd been raised in South Central, but unlike Hitch, who'd used mostly charm and BS to claw his way out of the ghetto, Crystal had used a straight-A report card and a full academic scholarship to UCLA.

"What happened to you, sugar?" she said, holding both my hands and staring into my face. I must have looked worse than I thought.

"Just caught a depressing glimpse of my future," I told her.

Hitch joined us with the lagers and handed me a foaming mug. "You looked so bad, I dropped a scotch shooter in there to add a little kick," he said. "Don't swallow the glass."

I drained half of the beer and scotch as the three of us sat at a table on the edge of his deck, which commanded a spectacular view of Hollywood. The carpet of lights below his house twinkled like a jewelry store showcase.

I told them in detail about Nix Nash's first show from Los Angeles and handed Hitch the Janice Santiago cell-phone video. He brought out his laptop and watched it.

"So we got totally schmucked by Chavaria and that bullshit story about the ceiling fan," Hitch said after the video ended.

I nodded. "That whole ugly daisy chain was a setup. Worst thing is, we can't prove anything against any of them."

"Are you saying Nix Nash paid all these people to lie to you about a first-degree murder?" Crystal said, appalled.

I nodded.

"But why?"

"It's good TV. It makes Hitch and me look like cowboys so it helps Nash sell his general premise that all cops are corrupt. He'll spin it that we don't give a damn who really killed Lita Mendez as long as we can hang it on somebody quick. Carla and Julio are minorities and were handy. That's probably going to be his theme for show two."

We sat in silence for a few minutes as I finished my beer.

"You guys aren't going to take this lying down, I hope," Crystal said.

"Hitch should probably resign. That would be my advice," I said. "He should go into the movie business full-time like he wants."

"Listen, dawg, not for nothing, but I'm just horsing around with you when I say stuff like that. Every time I hint that I'm gonna bail, your ears turn red. I gotta have a few yucks on a boring shift."

"That's very sweet," I said ruefully. "I'm deeply touched."

"Besides, this guy Nash is starting to give me a bad case of blood fever, which is what the head wraps on my old block in Watts called the need to bleed."

Then I told him about the cold-case segment of the show and how Nash made a big deal out of voting by secret ballot when he selected the Hannah Trumbull murder as a second case to work.

"How's that matter?" Hitch wondered.

"I ran into Hannah's parents in the parking lot right after the show. They show up twenty minutes after Nash decided to work on their daughter's murder."

"I'm not getting it," Crystal said. "How's that change the Mendez case?"

"It doesn't," Hitch explained. "But it strikes to methodology. Nash already picked that case in advance, but he lied about it on the air."

"Exactly," I confirmed.

"I still don't see how it matters," Crystal persisted.

"It matters because it proves that almost every-thing on that show is managed content," I said. "The whole Edwin Chavaria thing, the Sanchez bust, the ceiling fan. It was all scripted, just like the vote on the Hannah Trumbull case. My guess is it's going to become a pattern with us, just like it was in Atlanta."

It was getting cold, so Crystal went inside, but Hitch and I stayed on the deck and had another German lager. This time I declined the scotch shooter. I didn't want to drive home drunk.

The drinks began to calm me, and the city view provided some needed perspective, spreading out below us, each twinkling point of light displaying another home full of dreams and fears.

After a minute Hitch looked at me and said, "What do you think we should do?"

"I don't know."

"We gotta pick our next move carefully," he cautioned.

"I don't know about you," I replied. "But when I'm on a dangerous, tricky course, I like to find someone who's seen the road up ahead."

"Like?"

"Those two cops who got smoked last year in Atlanta."

I looked at my watch. With the time difference, it was too late to call, so we decided to do it first thing in the morning.

As I was leaving, we agreed that with the arrival of the Janice Santiago video we had no case left against Carla and Julio Sanchez.

We called the jail. It was too late to get the release papers drawn up tonight, but we made arrangements to have the Sanchezes cut loose first thing in the morning.

Chapter 24

At eight thirty the next morning, Hitch and I sat across the table from Carla and Julio Sanchez and their young attorney, Alfredo Zelaya, in an I-room at the Hollenbeck Station. Zelaya should have been clocking high-dollar hours as a GUESS model. He had a swarthy complexion, wavy black hair, and two perfect rows of sparkling teeth. He was tricked out in a black suit, crisp white shirt, and maroon tie.

Carla squatted uncomfortably on a metal chair, overhanging the seat dangerously on both sides while complaining. "We didn't do nothing and still we hadda spend two days in this fuckin' shit hole."

"You and your husband were being held as material witnesses," I said. "In our opinion, you've also chosen to insert yourselves into Lita Mendez's murder investigation by making false statements. If we can prove collusion or obstruction of justice, we're gonna file it."

"Is this going to take much longer?" Zelaya said, sounding way too tired and bored for such a snazzy-looking guy. "We don't need to hear any more threats. I was told you were going to cut my clients loose, so let's sign the forms and get out of here."

Hitch slid the release forms across the table. As Zelaya was reading, Hitch turned to Carla and said, "We know you have some kind of deal with Nix Nash and *V-TV.*"

"Prove it!" Julio injected angrily.

"Was there anything else?" Zelaya had finished scanning the document. "Or can we please sign these and go?"

"You're released," I said.

All the way back to the PAB, Hitch and I were both still burning over our time-wasting runaround with the Sanchezes. We'd been set up and then stuffed like amateurs.

It was around ten thirty when we took the elevator up to Homicide Special. I dialed the Atlanta PD to get contact numbers for the two detectives who had worked the Piedmont Park murders. I'd seen half the shows and remembered one of the detectives was named Caleb Cole. I couldn't remember his partner's name.

The sergeant I spoke with in Atlanta PD's Human Resources Department gave me Cole's phone number and current address. He'd retired and was now living in Mission Viejo, near San Diego. The sergeant said that Cole's partner was named Ronald Baron, but that after he'd resigned, he dropped off the radar and Atlanta PD didn't have any current information on him. They were holding his pension checks.

Hitch and I called Caleb Cole on the speakerphone. He answered on the first ring. A bad connection full of static filled the line, sounding like bacon frying. After we identified ourselves and gave him a quick rundown on what was happening and why we wanted to talk to him and his partner, Cole told us in his slow southern drawl that he'd also lost track of Ron Baron. Apparently, after leaving Atlanta, Ron had started drinking and the last Cole had heard, he'd gone to Mississippi to work construction. Caleb Cole came west and was now aboard his cousin's lobster boat, which was at that moment a mile off the San Diego jetty, explaining the poor phone reception.

"If you're fixin' to work a case Nash is lookin' at, then my best advice for you boys is get helmets and flack vests," Cole said. "You're gonna end up looking as confused as Kmart Republicans. Me and Ronnie was running a high temperature in the press on account a two of the girls who got killed in Piedmont Park came from good Atlanta families and they kept up the political pressure. Our bosses wanted it solved fast and that's what happened. But when it was done with, I'm not at all certain we booked the right doer."

"I thought that schizophrenic bum Nash found sleeping in the park confessed," Hitch said.

"Yeah, but we're talking about a totally gassed crystal meth freak who didn't even have a regular name, just Fuzzy. Guy made Nick Nolte's mug shot look like the statue of David. He'd been scraping corrosion off of old car batteries and mixing it with crystal to amp up his fixes. When we booked him, Fuzzy was so confused he was breathing outta his ass."

"You saying he didn't do it?" Hitch asked.

"He said he did, but it's hard to put much faith in a guy with a pet spider named Louis he kept in a matchbox. This guy who prayed three times a day to a pile of rocks he'd stacked up behind the park toilet." Cole heaved a sigh. "Listen, all the captain cared about was that Fuzzy was wearing an overcoat with four of the six dead girls' DNA on it. Our department was being blasted for not getting anywhere, so when Nash finds this guy and Fuzzy cops to all six killings, everybody was so happy the case was off the board, we had him booked and cooked by sundown."

"Listen, Caleb, if you had something to tell us about Nash—a heads-up of some kind—what would it be?" I asked.

"Don't take nothing for granted, 'cause every-thing means something."

"Explain."

"Everything that happens on that damn TV show has a purpose. A reason. It's uncanny, but in the end, it will all somehow tie together. You won't think it's going to, but it will."

Then the signal started breaking up.

"I'm losing you," he said. "We're out at sea

heading south and the cell pods down here near Mexico are like nonexistent. I'm coming to L.A. next weekend. Gimme your number and we can get together if you still want."

Hitch and I traded him our cell numbers just before the line went dead.

After he was gone, I looked across the desk. My partner had one Spanish loafer propped up on his lower drawer, the pleated knee of his expensive gray slacks peeking just above the desktop. His brow was furrowed and he was blowing reflectively through steepled fingertips. His thinker's pose.

"What?" I asked. "You got something? Let's hear it."

"It's stupid, okay? A long shot."

"Lay it on me."

"Okay," he said, putting his foot down and sitting up straighter. "We know now that the argument over the fan, the Sanchez arrest, and Janice Santiago's cell video were all part of a big setup to make us look like douche bags."

"Yeah."

"And Nash choosing the Hannah Trumbull case on the air, also staged, right?"

I nodded again.

"And Caleb just said watch out because everything on that show has a purpose and it will eventually all tie together."

"Where's this going?"

"I'm just thinking, how's it possible that Hannah Trumbull's murder in '06 has anything to do with Lita's murder two nights ago? How's that ever gonna tie together?"

"I don't think it does."

"I'm thinking we're already in the blender, maybe we shouldn't be in such a hurry to get out. Suppose Caleb's right and the Hannah Trumbull case is gonna somehow affect Lita's murder. Maybe we should just go ahead and fully engage with this guy."

"You mean, put in for Hannah's cold case, get it assigned over to us?"

"That was my notion," Hitch said. "I'm not saying it's real smart; it's just an idea. You asked what I was thinking."

I thought about it for almost a minute.

"I'll give you this much," I finally said. "Nash will never see it coming."

Chapter 25

That night, Alexa had a law enforcement dinner at the Bonaventure Hotel downtown. Police chiefs and their executive commanders from all over the country were in town for a rubber-chicken banquet where Chief Filosiani was the keynote speaker.

I had to don the monkey suit and go as Alexa's arm ornament. I hate these things, but being a division commander's husband requires a few sacrifices. The banquet lasted until ten. The chief was a hit with the audience but the rest of the speeches were written by press attachés and delivered from note cards in a generally lackluster fashion.

We couldn't get out of there quick enough. Once we retrieved the car from the hotel valet, because we were already dressed up and it was still relatively early, we went to a club called the Elephant Room, which Alexa said she'd driven past a few times and had heard was spectacular.

We hit the place at eleven. The inside had a faux East India feel. The booths along the walls were only large enough for four people but were fashioned to look like big oversized baskets, like you'd sit in to ride giant Indian elephants in Nepal or Bangladesh. There was enough phony crystal hanging from the ceiling to delight a Vegas hooker. The waiters were all wearing turbans as they served their patrons while sitar music oozed out of the sound system. For my money, it was a total miss, but we were already there, so we ordered a drink and made the best of it.

While we waited for our cocktails we quickly got around to Nix Nash, *V-TV*, and his devastating first show in L.A. When I finished filling in Alexa, she sat there scowling.

"I know we're supposed to support the First Amendment and a free press," she said. "But I'm sort of losing energy for it."

"Yep," I agreed. Then I told her what Caleb Cole had said about everything being part of the whole on that show and that there were no loose ends.

"That seems a little paranoid," she said. "Maybe Detective Cole just feels that way because of the way he blew his murder case in Atlanta."

"There's probably some of that, but the whole Carla Sanchez ceiling fan runaround really got me and Hitch thinking. We talked it over. Judging from his first two seasons, the stories Nix likes to feature on the air are usually connected and part of some big overarching theme of police corruption. Those big overlapping themes are what's driven his ratings up."

"You're making it sound as if Nash could be involved in Lita's murder and maybe also in Hannah's. But wasn't he in the penitentiary in '06 when Hannah got killed?"

"I wish Nix was directly involved, because I would dearly love to book that asshole. But that isn't what's happening. His alibi is rock solid for the time of Lita's murder, plus they really were friends and you're right, he was still doing time when Hannah was killed."

I paused as our drinks were delivered by a Mexican waiter who looked like he should be a José or a Carlos but who had a name tag identifying him as Bashkir. I wasn't buying that either. Once he left, I continued.

"Nash is all about creating high-value police humiliation. He wants to set us up, then get us to make mistakes. I don't have a clue yet who killed Lita Mendez, but Hitch and I are gonna work it till it bleeds. I've got a list of potential suspects and we're not gonna let up."

"And if you find the perp, then Nash won't be able to get you," Alexa correctly surmised. "The case will be down and he'll be without his big L.A. finale."

"Yeah, but he's gonna try and keep that from happening by slowing us down and wasting our time. He's gonna feed us false leads like he did last year in Atlanta, like he already did with Carla Sanchez. He's an ex-lawyer and he knows how to pull that off so we can't see his hand and pin an obstruction case on him."

"You can't be saying he's good enough to beat you and Hitch to the solution."

"It's not so much about police science as it's about delegation of resources. Our department is spread thin. Our forensic experts are shared with a hundred and ten other detectives. Sometimes R and I, print runs, and autopsy results take weeks. There's a wait for everything these days. Nash has ten full-time cops, ex-FBI, and forensic scientists on his TV staff. Marcia Breen vets all his legal stuff so they don't get caught in a prosecutable offense. Web Russell will downfield block at the courthouse. Basically, Nash is going to float bum leads for us to chase and then try and beat us to the killer. He can probably do it, 'cause he's got us outmanned ten to one.

"Making it even worse, Hitch and I only have a limited budget while he has five or six hundred thousand dollars a week to spend on that show. He can bribe suspects and offer rewards. If he finds the unsub first, then Hitch and I get launched right up into orbit and start circling the globe with Caleb Cole and Ron Baron."

We sipped our drinks without talking for almost a minute.

Then, unexpectedly, Alexa said, "Marcia Breen is working with Nash?"

"Yeah." I didn't elaborate, but a survival alarm went off in the primal part of my brain that processes emotional danger.

"Didn't you used to go out with her?" Alexa asked.

"With Marcia?"

"Yeah, who do you think I'm talking about?"

"We dated a couple of times. It was years before I met you."

"She's very pretty."

"Next to you, it's like putting Marge Simpson next to Aphrodite." I was digging hard, trying to shovel my way out of this.

"Calm down; I trust you," Alexa said, sipping

her drink slowly, never taking her eyes off me. "You used to date her, so don't blame me for being just a little bit jealous."

I smiled and tried to get her off this subject: "Are we through with the Marcia Breen part of this conversation? Because I'd like to move on."

"What do you need, honey?"

"I'd like to get the Hannah Trumbull case assigned to Hitch and me. I checked this afternoon and it's not actually being worked right now by anyone. Hitch and I want to take it over."

"Doesn't that double your exposure?"

"Here's our theory on that: if somebody's already determined to bash your head in with a hammer, what does it matter how many additional reasons you give him to try?"

Alexa took another sip of her drink and thought it over, or at least that's what I thought she was doing. But instead, she said, "You really don't think she's prettier than I am?"

"What? Hell, no! Weren't you listening to what I just said? Marcia once had a certain earthy appeal, but she went to the dark side. My Lancelot vows won't let me anywhere near her."

Alexa finally smiled.

When we were driving home Alexa turned to me and said, "I think you guys might be right. Taking over that case is a good strategy. Keeps us on the offensive. I'll call Jeb and have Trumbull transferred over to you first thing in the morning."

Chapter 26

"That was Judge Amador. He wants to see us in the café downstairs in fifteen minutes," Hitch said as he hung up his desk phone. It was ten o'clock the next morning and we were in our cubicle, hard at work. "He's over here on another matter, but has to be back at court by eleven."

"He say why?" I asked.

"Nope, but he's probably not selling T-shirts."

"Superior court judges don't call up line detectives to have coffee," I said. "Something's up."

"He knows we're working the Mendez case, because I talked to him about it yesterday. Maybe it has something to do with that. He told me it got pretty ugly at Lita's pretrial hearing with Captain Madrid."

"Wonderful."

I groaned and looked down at Hannah Trumbull's murder book that had just been sent over from the Records and Identification Division. It was spread out all over my desk. When it was delivered an hour earlier, we'd found it in a complete mess. Report pages were missing, time lines out of order, and half the crime scene and autopsy photo pages were gone. It looked like somebody had shuffled through the papers, removed material, and subsequently not returned it. Whoever did it had left the book in shambles. I'd spent the last hour trying to reassemble it into some kind of correct order and determine what was missing.

"You get a callback yet on who checked this thing out of Records?" I asked. "When I get my hands on that gremlin I'm gonna create a fresh hospital case."

"Not yet."

"It better not connect back to Frank Palgrave," I groused.

"If *V-TV* has a mole inside this department it won't be a friend of Palgrave's. That's way too obvious for Nash." Hitch looked at his watch. "Guess we'd better go see what His Honor wants."

We put on our jackets and headed out. On the way we caught a lot of sympathetic looks from the other detectives. They knew Captain Madrid and Nix Nash were circling our case like hungry carrion, and our coworkers had already started treating us like looming pension cases.

Hitch looked sharp this morning. I checked his threads as we stepped into the elevator. He was styling a black Armani pinstripe with a gray shirt and maroon tie. His expensive maroon crocodile loafers that matched his tie must have set him back at least a grand.

"For now, because the murder book is such a

mess, I think we're gonna have to rebuild this entire Trumbull case ourselves," I told him as the elevator doors hissed closed. "I just got off the phone with the Payroll Department downstairs. Detective Hall retired in '07 and promptly went on the EOW wall." The end-of-watch wall in the lobby has the names of all deceased LAPD officers. "His current address is at Forest Lawn. Fatal car accident last year.

"Monroe got in his twenty, also pulled the pin in '07, and moved to Eugene, Oregon. I called his wife. He's on a deer-hunting trip on Mount Hood. She says he's going to be out of cell contact for at least another week. I don't want to wait a week and have Nash get that far ahead of us, so for now we gotta push on without him."

Hitch nodded and picked some nonexistent lint off his cuff. "I think I hear an oboe playing," he said sadly.

"A what?"

"The oboe is a mournful instrument that plays in movie soundtracks when something bad is about to happen."

"That's not an oboe; that's the new leather squeaking on those kick-ass maroon crocs you're wearing."

We walked into the LA Reflections Café, which is located on the ground floor of the PAB, arriving right on time. The new restaurant was a two-hundred-seat layout with cafeteria-style service on one side and traditional dining on the other. A floor-to-ceiling expanse of glass streamed morning sunshine into the café and looked out onto an enclosed patio beyond.

The lower floors of the Police Administration Building were designed with a lot of interior windows that faced out into enclosed atriums. This paranoid architecture was intended to defeat the threat of sniper fire from the buildings across the street. We went through the food line, got coffee and rolls, and then found Judge Thomas Amador reading the *L.A. Times* sports page at a table by the window.

"Judge?" Hitch asked.

He looked up and smiled. "Hey, guys, sit down."

Tom Amador was a big-boned guy with a husky build, a faded Marine tattoo on his forearm, and hair the color of roadside snow. Under his robes in court he usually wore jeans, a T-shirt, and frayed sneakers, which is exactly what he had on now. He looked more like the guy who comes over to detail your car than a superior court judge. Amador pushed aside the remains of his breakfast to make room for us as we slid our trays onto the table, straddled the small wood chairs, then both stuck perfect butt-first landings.

"I'm hearing for the first time this morning that you guys drew the black ace." He turned to Hitch. "You didn't mention that yesterday, Detective."

"If you mean Nix Nash picked the Mendez

case to fuck with, then yeah, that's us, Your Honor," Hitch replied.

"That's why I wanted to see you as soon as possible." The judge looked at his watch. "I'm running a little late. I have some motions to hear in half an hour, so let's skip the small talk and just get to it."

"Yes, sir," Hitch said

Judge Amador pushed an iPhone with a set of earbuds plugged into it across the table at us.

"You guys can share the earbuds. I don't want to play this through the phone speakers in a crowded restaurant. It's cued up. You'll see it's a little sensitive." Hitch scooted his chair closer to mine and we each inserted a bud. I positioned the iPhone between us so we could both see the screen and hit Play.

We were looking at a video being taken through the side window of a car parked in an underground garage. The shot finally settled on a department-issue blue sedan as it chirped in behind a red Chevy Caprice, blocking it just as the Caprice was reversing out of its stall. Stephanie Madrid got out of the blue sedan and slammed the door as Lita Mendez threw open the Chevy's door and angrily stormed up to confront her. From the wall markings on the garage I recognized it as the parking structure located directly behind the municipal courthouse. Both women were dressed in conservative court attire.

"I've had enough of your bullshit!" Lita screamed. It was just barely audible from the distance. Then she got right in Captain Madrid's face. "Move your fucking car!" Lita yelled.

"You little whore," Captain Madrid responded, her face purple with rage. "All that shit you pulled in there. How many lies do you think you can get away with?"

"Get out of my way," Lita said, stepping forward, moving directly into Stephanie Madrid's space. "I want to leave. You're blocking me."

Without warning, Captain Madrid pushed Lita back to create some space between them. Lita was now against the trunk of her car.

"It's not just me," Madrid snarled. "There are others. You've been warned. Continue on this path at your own peril."

Then Stephanie Madrid turned and started back to her car, but Lita stepped forward and swung her large purse, hitting Stephanie between the shoulder blades. Captain Madrid pivoted smartly and threw a wicked overhand right. It was the kind of punch every recruit was taught at the academy —straight from the shoulder. It landed in the middle of Lita's forehead. The smaller Hispanic woman went down as if her legs had been yanked out from under her. Hitch and I watched in amazement as the captain now knelt down over Lita and hissed something inaudible at her.

Then Captain Madrid stood and walked to her

department-issue sedan, her face a mask of rage. She slammed the door and pulled out. A minute later, Lita Mendez stood up, got into her Caprice, and pulled away as well.

When it was over I looked at the judge, who had been watching us carefully.

"How did we ever solve these damn things before cell phones?" he said dryly.

"Where'd you get this?" I asked.

"Court clerk. She was eating a late lunch in her car after a pretrial conference in Judge Lambert's chambers. She brought it to me this morning because she knew the Madrid-Mendez case was in my court."

Hitch and I sat looking at him, not sure of what to say.

"Of course, that video only strikes to motive and possibly to premeditation if a murder charge is ever filed," Amador said. "But as it is, I need to caution you that while provocative, this doesn't prove Captain Madrid killed Lita Mendez. Just that they argued and she hit Lita after being attacked."

"Yes," I said. "We understand."

"You need to handle this very delicately," he went on. "It certainly needs to be addressed, but if this falls into the wrong hands, careers could be destroyed."

"By 'the wrong hands,' do you mean *V-TV*?" Hitch asked.

"I mean anybody. Certainly Captain Madrid has a lot to explain. Here's a quick legal take on that video from a judge's point of view: Madrid initiated the dispute and then pushed Mendez. I'm sure Captain Madrid will argue that's because she was being crowded by an out-of-control woman and the push was an attempt to create separation. But viewed differently, it could also be called assault. Lita swinging her purse is a clear case of battery. So when Captain Madrid swung back, she can claim she was defending herself. But like most of these things, it's not clear-cut. Captain Madrid, as a sworn badge carrier, was certainly out-of-bounds. There is no excuse for what she did, but those two have an ugly, contentious history. They've been warring for years."

"Can we keep the cell phone for a few hours until we can get this video transferred?" Hitch asked.

"Go ahead, but get it back to me as soon as you can."

"This court clerk," I said. "Will she stay tight?"

"Her name is Kathy Putnam. She used to be my clerk a few years ago. She understands how sensitive this is."

"Thanks, Your Honor."

He stood, gathered up his things, said, "Good luck."

We sat there in brooding silence, neither of us speaking for a good minute.

"I think I can hear that oboe now," I finally said.

Chapter 27

"Shit," Captain Calloway said after watching the iPhone video of Lita Mendez fighting with Captain Madrid. We were in his office with the door closed. Jeb locked the iPhone inside his desk drawer as if he wanted to get the offending evidence out of his sight forever.

"Technically, that video is grounds for an administrative assault complaint against Captain Madrid," I said. "We should probably prepare a charge sheet, confront her with the video, and start a normal IAG Board of Rights proceeding immediately. But we'll be filing against our own head of Professional Standards Advocates Section and that's gonna produce a disaster. It could also lead to a criminal charge against Captain Madrid for Lita's murder."

"I get it. I don't need it explained to me!" Jeb snapped angrily.

Captain Calloway was a damn good commanding officer who we all called the Haitian Sensation. You seldom give a commander a funny nickname unless he's well liked, which Jeb was. He was born in Haiti and immigrated here as a boy, then became a naturalized citizen. The captain was only five foot eight, but he had a muscular comic book hero's build and a bullet-shaped shaved head, hence the moniker. But like most commanders, Jeb hated high-stakes situations involving internal politics.

"What should we do? We need some direction, boss," I prodded gently. "We really need to pursue this, but as you can see, it's full of complications."

"You talked to Captain Scully?" he asked, hoping Alexa had already weighed in, taking him off the hook.

"No, sir. We came to you first."

"Yeah, okay . . . okay. Good." He was fiddling with the ruler on top of his desk and finally slapped it down hard on the leather pad. Then he got to his feet and said, "You guys just took on Hannah Trumbull's cold case, right?"

"Yes, sir," I said. "It's become part of the *V-TV* show. We just thought—"

"Yeah, I know. Alexa discussed it with me. I'm not convinced you guys taking that case is smart."

"If we were smart, we'd have offices in Century City and big movie careers," Hitch said, grinning.

"Don't start up with me on that, Hitchens," Jeb warned, then heaved a big, tired sigh. "Okay, look. I need to bring a few other people in on this before we make a move on Captain Madrid —Alexa and Deputy Chief Bud Hawkins to name just two. We have to bear in mind that the cell-cam video shows inappropriate physical contact with a civilian, but it doesn't make

Captain Madrid guilty of Lita Mendez's murder."

"We know that, skipper," Hitch said. "Judge Amador already warned us."

"That video was shot by a court clerk," I said. "Even though Judge Amador told her to keep it confidential, we all know if three people are trying to keep a secret, two had better be dead. We've got to figure this is going to leak. When it does, the obvious marketplace for the information is Nash's show."

"Stop telling me shit I know," Jeb said irritably.

"I'm just saying don't take too much time before you decide, Captain. We'd hate to be running in the outside lane on this."

"Okay," Jeb said. "In the meantime, you guys get busy on the Hannah Trumbull case. I'll get back to you on the disposition of Captain Madrid by six o'clock tonight."

Chapter 28

Russ and Gloria Trumbull lived in a small, neatly cared for condo a few blocks from Universal Studios in the Valley. Hitch and I had called ahead and they were expecting us.

When we rang the front bell, it was answered immediately by Russ Trumbull, who must have been watching us approach through the front window. The Trumbulls were both dressed like breath mints. Russ in a bright turquoise golf outfit. His wife, Gloria, in a light green pantsuit with a yellow shoulder scarf held in place by an ornate butterfly pin.

After we were all seated, Hitch and I looked at them across a tchotchke-cluttered coffee table.

"I suppose you finally got interested in our daughter's murder again because of *V-TV*," Russ said, unable to hide his disdain.

He seemed on edge, as did his wife, whose face was pinched, her mouth pulled into a tight, straight line.

"I won't deny that we're here because of that show," I told them.

"At least you're honest about it," Russ said, then leaned in and studied me carefully. "Do I know you from somewhere?"

"We parked next to each other at the *V-TV* studio the other night."

"Oh, right. Right," he said, and leaned back. He fell silent but seemed puzzled. "I'm not sure I understand. Are you also working for the show?"

"No, sir, but we are reinvestigating your daughter's murder."

"Really?" he said sarcastically. "Run out of better things to do down there?"

Hitch leaned forward. "Mr. and Mrs. Trumbull, I know you're upset, and I certainly can't blame you. I know you feel that the LAPD has not given you its best work on your daughter's case, and you're probably correct. The department let it slip between the cracks. However, my partner and I have over fifteen combined years of experience working homicides. We are assigned at Homicide Special, which is the unit that deals with the most important and difficult murder cases in L.A. I can't promise you that we'll make a difference here, but I can promise you'll get the very best effort we have."

Hitch can be very charming and persuasive. I could see them loosening up slightly and Mrs. Trumbull's features softened.

"I'd like to start at the beginning," Hitch said. "Let's just go over the entire case again. Tell us the first thing you view as relevant."

"What about the other detectives?" Russ asked.

"Detectives Hall and Monroe aren't even in the department now. One was killed in a car accident a few months after he retired. The other retired about the same time and is living in Oregon. Your daughter's murder was one of the last cases they worked. Maybe that was part of the problem. They were sort of half out the door. It had been reassigned to a cold-case unit but wasn't being worked," I said. "I wish I could tell you it was otherwise, but that's the truth and I want us to start out by being frank and honest with each other."

"They didn't listen to us," Russ said. "They were so sure it was that African-American kid who robbed Gina Wilson. Aside from the fact that both crimes took place in the same neighborhood a couple of weeks apart, I didn't see much that tied the two together. But nothing we said could change their minds."

I'd seen this kind of target fixation from detectives before. Bored cops who were close to the end of their careers sometimes just went through the motions. They wanted any viable solution so they could just put out a BOLO and file the case with their bureau commander as solved.

"Did you have another theory, Mr. Trumbull?" Hitch asked.

"Well, our daughter told us she'd been threatened," he said. "I always thought that was worth looking into."

"Threatened by who?" I asked.

I looked over at Hitch. We'd found no notation of a threat against Hannah in the murder book. Of course a lot of the pages were missing.

"Hannah was a nurse," Russ Trumbull said. "She worked a night shift at Good Samaritan Hospital in the ER. She told us that a woman came in one night and threatened her life."

"When was that?" Hitch asked.

"Two days or so before she was murdered."

"Did she say who it was?" I asked.

"She wouldn't tell us," Russ continued. "I think she knew who it was, but that's just an impression, because she wouldn't actually say. It's a big hospital. All kinds of people go in there. Some of them are quite upset, because they have loved ones who are hurt or dying. She said high tension and shouted emotions came with the job."

"Did she ever tell you about any other threats she'd received at the hospital?"

"No."

"So this threat must have seemed unusual to her," I said. "Upsetting enough that she thought to mention it."

"Yes. Especially since two days later she was murdered."

"And you told Detectives Hall and Monroe about this?"

"Of course. They couldn't have been less interested. They were too busy trying to pin it on that black guy."

"You say you feel your daughter knew who the woman was? Maybe the incident was recorded in the hospital records from December of '06 and they put her name in the report."

"I actually looked into that myself," Russ said. "There was nothing." He began rubbing his forehead with the heel of his right hand. When he stopped, his brow was pink. He was obviously very distressed. "She was a great kid, you know? She loved her job. She wanted to help people." He was starting to tear up. "She chose that profession because she cared about her patients, and we've been waiting for somebody to care about her for over four years now."

"We can't change what's already happened," I told him, "but we might be able to make a difference now."

After a moment, Russ took a deep breath and nodded.

"Mr. Trumbull, you said Hannah didn't tell you about other threats or problems at the ER, but she thought this threat was noteworthy enough to mention," Hitch said. "Can we talk a little more about that?"

"That's what Russ thought too," Gloria Trumbull said. "You pressed her about it, didn't you, Russ?"

"I did," Russ agreed. "But she said she didn't want to discuss it further because it would just needlessly worry me."

"She had a lot of friends who were police officers," Gloria said. "She told us if it happened again, she'd tell one of them. She said her police friends would look after her because cops and nurses were in the same club, because they got to see the same kind of pain and death. It's why so many cops and nurses date. Since Hannah knew so many police officers, she felt she'd be all right."

"Did she mention any of these cops by name?" Hitch asked. "Did she ever say if she'd dated one of them?"

"She kept that part of her life pretty much to herself," Russ said. "I think, from time to time, she used to date a few. But we never met them or knew their names."

"Did she have any close girlfriends?" Hitch persisted. "Somebody who might have more details on her personal life?"

"Yes," Gloria said, looking at her husband. "There was that pediatric nurse she used to go to Vegas with. What was her name?"

"Linda Baxter," Russ said.

Hitch wrote it down.

We talked to the Trumbulls for another half an hour. They were rightfully angry that for four years the LAPD had been chasing after a pencil sketch and had basically been doing little else.

Russ said, "Every year we get a call from somebody down there. 'We're still working on it,' they tell us. 'Don't worry,' they say. 'We'll catch the guy.' " He looked at us and shook his head in dismay. " 'Bullshit,' is what I say. Nix Nash told us nobody down there gives a damn and he's right. You can come here and say different, but it's not hard to guess your motives. We're not stupid, you know. You guys are just afraid that Nix Nash will solve Hannah's murder and you're just over here trying to cover the department's ass."

Being perfectly honest, I had to admit that was pretty close to true.

Chapter 29

"You go first," I told Hitch. We were sitting in his Porsche parked outside the Trumbulls' condo with our crime scene interview books open in our laps. Mine was a cheap spiral notepad. Hitch had his three-hundred-dollar red leather journal embossed in gold. Captain Calloway thought Hitch used it to make notes on new screenplay ideas, but I knew it was only full of crime scene sketches and case observations made in his tight, almost illegible scrawl.

"Why do I have to go first?" Hitch countered.

"Because I went first at Lita's house."

"Okay, I think we gotta figure Hannah was probably dating cops. And that really sucks the big one."

"I agree. Fits right into Nash's overall premise that we're all dirtbag killers. He'll say Hannah and her cop boyfriend got into a fight and the cop dumped her. When Hall and Monroe found out, they were just covering for their fellow officer."

I tapped my pen on the cover of the spiral pad, then flipped it open and started to write. Hitch did the same. We were silent as we both wrote out our impressions of the Trumbull interview, getting them down while they were still fresh.

When he finished he looked up and said, "Hannah's dad was right about cops and nurses having a thing. I did that once. It's just easier. With a nurse you don't have to explain the darkness you feel, because they feel the same things."

I nodded. "Even though we're walking in a minefield here, I'm kind of glad we put in for this case. I feel bad for the Trumbulls. I don't think they got much of a murder investigation."

"Me either," Hitch said.

"I'd sure like to talk to Detective Monroe. We should stay close to his wife. If he calls in early from his hunting trip, he needs to contact us."

Hitch nodded. Just then my pager went off. A couple of seconds later, so did Hitch's. We glanced at each other as we dug for our phones. A double page meant trouble.

I hit my speed dial first and got right through to Jeb.

"Get in here fast," he said. "Bring Hitchens." He hung up abruptly.

"Don't bother," I told Hitch. "It's Jeb. Wants us both. He's in comic book mode."

"Fuck. What'd we do now?"

Fifteen minutes later we were in Calloway's small office along with Alexa and DC Bud Hawkins. Deputy Chief Hawkins was a tall, angular, dandruff-sprinkled guy who had short gray hair that grew in about four different directions on his head and was also sprouting out of his ears and nose.

Alexa wasted no time: "We're going to suspend Captain Madrid on administrative charges pending a Board of Rights hearing," she said.

"For hitting Lita?"

"For that and for mishandling that whole damn situation. She got so involved in that dispute she completely forgot to open her chute. Deputy Chief Hawkins and I are going to appoint Lieutenant Jasmine Nishikido as temporary chief advocate and get her to take over immediately."

"Given this video, we need to question Captain Madrid again on Lita's murder," I said. "That assault could constitute provocation."

Alexa nodded. "But let's take this a step at a time. We don't have any direct evidence tying her to Lita's murder, so there's no criminal case yet. I'll call the DA's office and put them aboard, but they'll just tell us to get more evidence before we bring them in or try to book it. That means all we've got so far is this administrative complaint.

"We've already filled out the IA charge sheet. Captain Madrid's two blocks away at the Bradbury, but I don't like picking up armed police officers. We did that once a few years back and it turned ugly and got dangerous. We're having a sergeant at the jail call her and tell her that one of his detainees has volunteered important information on an IAG case she has going in her division. The sergeant will say that the informant will only discuss it with her."

"Okay," I said.

The reason this was a good idea was because all police officers have to surrender their weapons before entering the jail. Once Captain Madrid was disarmed they would be able to safely detain her without incident for an interview. Not that anybody really thought that she'd go for her gat and start blasting, but you never know.

Since Hitch and I were the lead detectives on the Mendez case, we would be the ones to interview her. It was a path fraught with career danger. If we swung and missed, we'd have a lifelong enemy with a grudge who was still a ranking IA commander.

Alexa was ahead of me on this. "I'm going to handle the suspect interview," she said. "Shane, you and Detective Hitchens will be there, but only to observe."

Captain Madrid was called and given the message. She hurried to the Central Jail to hear whatever dirt the fictitious incarcerated detainee had to contribute.

She left a Glock 9 in the police lockbox at the jail reception desk. As soon as she was inside an I-room, Alexa entered and handed her the charge sheet. Hitch and I stood behind Alexa and watched as the shock slowly registered on

Captain Madrid's pugnacious features.

"Even though you know all this, I'm required to inform you that the two-week clock on this complaint starts at this time and date," Alexa told her. "You retain all of your administrative rights and privileges, including your right to a Skelly hearing, which will take place anytime before the end of the two-week period. At your Skelly, you'll be allowed to bring a defense rep and a POA rep, and will be able to respond to these charges in detail. Until then you are suspended."

Alexa read Stephanie Madrid her Miranda rights and the captain sat on the bench in the jail I-room glaring as if Alexa had just crawled up through some trapdoor from hell.

"If that charge sheet is trying to suggest that because of some shouting match in the court parking garage last week I had anything to do with Lita Mendez's murder, you really are insane," she said. "I don't know who told you about that, but there are two sides to everything. That sheet hardly captures the incident. What happened is completely open to interpretation."

"Maybe you should take a look at this," Alexa said.

She turned on a small monitor we'd brought into the room and played the video the court clerk had taken in the garage. When the video ended, Stephanie Madrid sat there stiffly.

"Comments?" Alexa said.

"I want to see my union rep," the captain replied.

"You don't want to make a statement to me and just clear this up for us?" Alexa asked.

"Clear what up? You saw what happened. I pulled up to discuss the case and Mendez verbally assaulted me. I gently pushed her out of my space, and then she attacked me. I didn't like her, but I sure didn't kill her. As far as I'm concerned, we're through talking until I get some professional advice."

"Okay," Alexa said. "That's it, then."

"Are you planning on holding me here?" Captain Madrid asked. "Because as I see this, all you have is a potential administrative offense. You can't connect me to the death of Lita Mendez. I have an alibi and I've already given Detectives Scully and Hitchens my verifiable time line."

"Are we finally at that point where you would be willing to submit to a lie detector test?" I asked, trying to keep from sounding pissy.

"What do you think, Detective?" Captain Madrid snapped.

"My intention is to OR you, Captain." Alexa was referring to a release on Madrid's Own Recognizance. "However, I'd like you to remain here until you talk to your union rep in case he advises you to cooperate more fully."

Twenty-five minutes later, Stephanie Madrid met with her rep from the Police Officers Association. Her POA rep was a retired lieutenant named Beau Butler. After they spoke, she refused to give further statements, on his advice. She agreed to a set of restrictions, including the promise that she remain in Los Angeles unless notifying us first. Since she would be tried at IA, Alexa agreed that Captain Madrid could retain the use of her office in the Bradbury Building and the use of her adjutant in the preparation of her defense. Then, escorted by her POA rep, Captain Madrid left the Police Administration Building.

Hitch and I stood in the lobby and watched as she crossed the quad with Lieutenant Butler. They made their way across a wide setback, which separated the PAB from the street barricades designed to prevent a car bomb from taking out the mirrored front walls of our new monument to twenty-first-century policing.

Captain Madrid got into her POA rep's Lincoln Town Car, leaving her sedan in the parking garage. We watched as they drove up First Street until the car disappeared.

Chapter 30

Hitch really is a gourmet cook. For the past several years he has used his two-week vacation time to study at the Cordon Bleu in Paris. His multi-millionaire status has also given him a lot of celebrity friends and he travels in a high social orbit.

At five o'clock he told me that he was invited to a private cooking demonstration being given by Wolfgang Puck at Hollywood mega-producer Neal Moritz's Beverly Hills home. Very exclusive. Hitch wanted to duck out a little early to catch it.

As he started gathering up his things I said, "I'd like to get some of Captain Madrid's DNA so we could see if it matches the DNA on that coffee cup we found in Lita's driveway. She said she hadn't been near that house for days before the murder, so if it's a match, it turns that time line she gave us into a work of fiction. Got any ideas how to do it?"

"She's never going to agree to give us DNA swabs," Hitch said. "You saw how she was about the poly. Since we don't have enough evidence yet to get a judge to write a body warrant, we can pretty much forget that."

"See ya tomorrow," I said.

After he left I went back to work piecing together Hannah Trumbull's murder book. I also made an attempt to locate her friend Linda Baxter through Good Samaritan Hospital. They said they would see if they could find her and have her call me back. I left my number.

After about an hour I needed a break from Hannah Trumbull, so I switched cases. There were still a lot of loose ends on Lita's preliminary evidence pull and street canvass, so I turned back to the list of patrol officer interview notes taken after talking to Lita's neighbors. Despite the fact that Nash said he'd found her in less than an hour and that she lived right down the street from Lita, nowhere could I find a mention of Janice Santiago being interviewed.

I also checked with the courthouse, got a number for Edwin Chavaria's parole agent, and called him up. He told me Chava had gone off state paper a few days ago and changed addresses immediately. It looked like Chava had scooped up his TV money and split. Probably wouldn't be seeing that *calabazo* again.

My next call was to a friend of mine named Sue Shepherd, who was currently working as an investigating officer at Internal Affairs. After a minute of small talk I asked her, "Listen, do you ever eat in that cafeteria downstairs at the Bradbury?"

"All the time. It's convenient and the food's pretty good," she said. "On nice days people like to eat outside in the patio by the Biddy Mason wall."

"Do Lester Madrid or his wife ever eat there?"

"Sure do. He and Captain Madrid are fixtures there at least three times a week. What is this?"

"Listen, Sue. I could use a heads-up the next time you see them eating down there. I can't tell you exactly what's up, but I can promise you I won't burn you. How 'bout it?"

She agreed to help me, so I left her my cell number and hung up. About an hour later, my desk phone rang.

"Is this Detective Scully?" a woman asked.

"Yes."

"It's Linda Baxter. I understand you were trying to reach me."

"Yes, Ms. Baxter, I was. I've recently been given the Hannah Trumbull cold case to reinvestigate. I was wondering if we could meet."

"I'm on duty now," she said. "I could meet you at eight, when I get off."

"That would be great."

We agreed to meet in a restaurant called the Short Stop Grill, located just across the street from the Good Samaritan Hospital.

By seven thirty it was time to get going.

I closed up shop and took the elevator down to the garage, got in my Acura and pulled out onto First Street, turned left on Lucas Avenue on my way to the meeting.

I hadn't driven five blocks when I noticed a white *V-TV* station wagon tailing me about three cars back. These guys weren't anything if not persistent. I had no intention of leading them to my witness, so I picked up the dashboard mike and called the Communications Division.

"This is Delta-Fifteen. I need a traffic stop on a

new white Ford station wagon heading south on Lucas Avenue at West Third. I don't have a plate, but the vehicle has a V-TV Productions logo on the side door."

"Roger, Delta-Fifteen. What is the nature of the problem?"

"It's a press vehicle and I'm being followed. My case is extremely confidential. Have any available unit pull the wagon over for a vehicle check so I can ditch them."

"Roger," the RTO said. "One-Adam-Forty-Five, Delta-Fifteen requests a traffic stop on Lucas near West Third. Vehicle is a late-model white Ford station wagon with a *V-TV* logo on the door. No available plate number. Detain briefly for vehicle check, then release."

"One-Adam-Forty-Five roger. ETA that location three minutes."

I watched my rearview mirror and a few blocks farther on saw a squad car pull in behind the white wagon and light it up. As soon as the *V-TV* mobile unit pulled over, I turned right and quickly found my way to Wilshire Boulevard.

The Short Stop Grill was right across the street from the Good Samaritan Hospital but didn't have a baseball theme, which I'd been expecting. Once inside, I realized the name referred to the length of time it took to get served. A lot of doctors who were on short breaks and were tired of hospital food ate there.

Linda Baxter had told me she would be in her uniform, carrying a large red leather bag. I spotted her sitting in a booth at the back of the crowded bar.

"Ms. Baxter?" I asked.

She looked up and smiled. She was a pretty brunette in her early thirties with a full-bodied, vivacious quality. She'd probably had to chase off half a dozen requests to buy her drinks before I arrived.

"Detective Scully?" she asked.

"Yes." We shook hands as I slid into the booth.

"Glad you got here. It's been a hard day and I could really use a drink, but I don't drink alone."

We waved over a waiter. Linda ordered a Manhattan. I had a Corona with lime.

"You're still investigating Hannah's murder? I thought they had that solved. They even have a picture of the guy."

"I'm starting from scratch, going over the whole case again."

"God . . . poor Hannah. That was so awful," Linda said with a shudder as the drinks were delivered. "When it happened, I was numb for a week."

"I just got assigned the case," I said. "I think you spoke to Detectives Monroe and Hall a few years back."

"I only talked to Hall. Monroe seemed to always be in court."

"They're no longer on the case. Detective Hall was killed in a car accident and Detective Monroe retired."

I worked my way into it slowly, talking about her friendship with Hannah and their trips to Las Vegas.

"It was fun traveling with her. We both loved to play blackjack, so we'd hit Vegas about three times a year. She was one of those people who didn't judge you. She saw things for what they were, if you know what I mean. No bullshit."

"I understand she worked in the ER."

"She liked it there. She had nerves of steel, that one. Didn't rattle. Hannah was very passionate about her work. A special girl in all ways."

We talked for a few more minutes about Hannah and her work at the hospital and then I segued into the threat against her life that occurred two days before the murder.

"She mentioned that, but she never really told me who had screamed at her," Baxter answered. "A woman. That's all she'd say. It bothered her, but there's so much going on in the ER, she didn't have a whole lot of time to remain focused on it."

"Was she also dating a police officer?" I asked.

The minute I said that, Linda recoiled as if I'd just touched her with a live wire.

"Who told you that?" she demanded sharply.

"Her parents. Were they wrong?"

She was looking around the bar as if someone might overhear us.

"Are you okay?"

"Yeah, sure. I guess."

"Listen, Linda. You were her friend. Somebody killed her. I don't think it was the black guy who robbed that house across the street. I think that theory just let Hall and Monroe file the case. I want to find out who really killed her. To do that, I need your help."

"We're not all as brave as Hannah," she said softly.

"What are you afraid of?"

She fidgeted but didn't speak.

"Okay, look . . . you tell me and I promise I won't reveal where I got the information. Fair enough?"

"If you catch the killer, once it's in court, won't they make me testify?"

"We're a long way from court. Please, help me help Hannah. She can't speak for herself any longer. It's up to us to do that for her."

Linda sat for a long time, trying to come to grips with it.

"You promise?" she finally said.

"Promise."

A moment later, she began, haltingly at first, but then she picked up speed. "Okay, you're right. Hannah *was* dating a cop. . . . He was more than just a regular cop. One of those officers who keep getting in gun battles and killing people. He was huge—almost six-five—and scary looking. I told her what I thought of him. I told her she should give that guy a wide berth. But, as I just said, Hannah was strong willed. She told me he wasn't anything like I thought. She said she cared for him and underneath he was very sweet."

"Do you remember his name?" I asked, but I already knew who it was.

"His name was Lester Madrid."

Chapter 31

"What on earth are you wearing?" Jeb asked sharply as Hitch slipped into the captain's office, where four of us were already waiting. He was dressed in a white chef's smock with a Spago logo on the breast pocket.

"Sorry, skipper. I was at a cooking class and Dina Lohan accidentally spilled some red wine on my shirt. This was all I could borrow." He smiled an apology and dropped into a chair next to the door.

Alexa and DC Bud Hawkins were already seated. Jeb was standing near his desk and I was on the sofa across the room.

"Okay, now that we've all *finally* arrived, let's hear what you've got," Deputy Chief Hawkins demanded, pinning me with a cold look. He'd delayed dinner plans to be here and was making no attempt to hide his displeasure. Hawkins was Chief of Operations and Alexa's immediate supervisor.

I ran them through my interview with Linda Baxter. When I got to the part where Baxter told me that Hannah Trumbull had been dating Sgt. Lester Madrid in 2006, I felt most of the air go out of the room.

"You can't be serious," Hawkins said, appalled.

"While I was waiting for this meeting, I went on the computer and found out Lester and Stephanie got married in 1998," I said. "So if he was dating Hannah Trumbull in '06, that means Sergeant Madrid was having an extramarital affair with Hannah just before she was murdered."

Everyone just sat there trying to process that.

Bud Hawkins finally asked, "How does Nix Nash keep getting so fucking lucky? This is worse than Atlanta. Captain Madrid is on the short list of suspects for Lita Mendez's murder and now we find out Nash is also featuring the Hannah Trumbull murder from '06. A case that happens to involve Captain Madrid's husband, Lester."

"What are the odds that these two completely unrelated murders could both involve the Madrids?" Alexa said.

"Astronomical," Jeb replied. "And how the hell can they both just happen to randomly pop up on that damn TV show? What's going on with that?"

Morale in the room was plummeting.

"Well, it might not be so far-fetched if you look at the situation back to front instead of front to back," Hitch said quietly from his seat by the door.

"What the hell are you babbling about?" Hawkins snapped. He had very little patience to begin with and was not displaying what little he had.

"This may seem a little off the point, but when you plot a movie you often work from the resolution backward to the inciting event," Hitch said. "That way you're able to keep the story tight. If Nix Nash just happened to pick these two cases randomly, then yeah, the odds *are* astronomical that they'd both involve the Madrids. But let's say that's not how it happened. Suppose Nash knew before he started that Lester and Stephanie touched both situations and he picked those two cases precisely for that reason."

"I see what Hitch is getting at," I said. "Nash doesn't take chances. He knew he was moving to Los Angeles, so working backward, like Hitch says, this isn't quite so far-fetched. Let's say Nash researched the whole LAPD in advance of his arriving here. He has his team of researchers digging into the thousands of open homicides. Then after Lita was murdered, he throws all that info on the table and starts looking for a connection. He has his staff investigate Lita's life. It wouldn't take him long to come up with Captain Stephanie Madrid and the long-running battle she'd had with Lita. There's no direct evidence against the captain, but Nash would certainly know she'd make our suspect list because of their numerous public disputes."

"So how does that get us to Hannah Trumbull?" Hawkins asked.

"It's like the six degrees of separation. He starts digging around in Captain Madrid's life and up pops her husband, Lester, who's a real gold mine. The guy is ex-SIS, just the kind of rogue cop Nash loves to feature on that show. Nash researches him, talks to some sources inside our department, and finds out there's a rumor that Lester had been cheating on his wife with Hannah, who also just happens to be an open murder case from '06. It's just what he's looking for. Lester doesn't have to be guilty. He just has to look guilty. After all, this isn't about justice; it's about Nielsen ratings."

They all sat there looking doubtful.

"I'm not buying this," Deputy Chief Hawkins said. "It's too far out there."

"Out of the thousands of uncleared murders all he had to do was tie one of them loosely to the Madrids," I said. "I think Hitch may be right. This guy is plotting his shows in advance by working backward, not forward."

"It does make some kind of crazy sense," Alexa said thoughtfully, although I think she was just trying to save us from Deputy Chief Hawkins, who looked like he was about to start giving birth to a chair.

"All we need to do is clear the Trumbull murder fast," Hitch said. "If Lester is innocent of that murder, it destroys Nash's conspiracy theory."

"And what if Lester was cheating on his wife and Stephanie found out?" Hawkins said. "What if Stephanie Madrid is the woman who threatened Hannah Trumbull in the hospital ER and then, two nights later, killed her for sleeping with her husband?"

"We better pray that's not what happened," Jeb said.

When the meeting broke up, nobody was happy. We were standing in the squad room outside Jeb's office and he took a parting shot at Hitch just because he was handy.

"Stop going to cooking classes while you're on duty, Hitchens."

"I was off duty, Skipper."

"I don't care. You look like . . . like . . . like a fucking cook."

"Yes, sir," Hitch said softly. "Sometimes I am. But I'll take that under advisement."

As we walked to our cubicle, Alexa caught my eye and pointed toward the elevators, then went up to her office, leaving me with Hitch.

When we were alone, Hitch said, "While we were rolling that out, it sounded pretty damn weak even to me. It's very dangerous to pursue an offbeat idea like that if we can't prove it."

"A dangerous idea isn't responsible for the people who believe in it," I said.

"I really hate this," Hitch said. "Our theory sucks."

"There are no coincidences in police work," I said, trying to reassure him. "I agree that there is something more than we know about going on here. We're obviously missing a big piece. However he's doing it, Nash has a great source that's giving him an edge. We just have to keep working it until it all makes sense."

It was almost midnight now and the administration floor was deserted. Alexa was waiting for me in her new tenth-floor office. It was larger than her old digs at the Glass House, where she had no view. This new office had wide double windows that faced City Hall. As soon as I entered, she shut the door.

"Do you really believe any of that?" she said. "Working backward hardly explains this coincidence."

"Caleb Cole told us everything would tie in and look what just happened."

"And you think it's not random, the way he picks the cases?"

"I think the guy is writing a script like Hitch said. Then he's shooting it. None of this is coincidence."

"It still doesn't explain how he's doing it," she persisted.

"I know, and if we don't find out fast, we're all going to be looking for new professions."

Chapter 32

That night at home, as I lay in bed with Alexa asleep beside me, I kept wrestling with the same gloomy feeling I'd had in the *V-TV* control room. It was a growing certainty that this case wasn't going to end well for any of us. I felt like I was being led by the nose through a maze that had no back door.

I finally got up and, without waking Alexa, went out to sit in the den. I thought about Lester and Stephanie Madrid and, despite the theory Hitch and I had advanced in Jeb's office, how improbable it was that the murders of Lita Mendez and Hannah Trumbull each touched one of the Madrids.

I kept looking at the problem and turning it over like a Rubik's Cube, examining all sides, twisting facets. No matter how I tried to get all the same colors to line up, I couldn't make it come out right.

A random thought struck me. We'd all assumed that Nix Nash picked Los Angeles as the city he wanted to feature in the show's third season because this was where he had lost his law license. We'd assumed he hated the LAPD for putting the fraud case on him, which sent him to prison and got him disbarred. It made such perfect sense that he was here seeking revenge against us that we'd never looked at any alternate theories.

What if that wasn't the reason he chose L.A.? What if the reason was because he'd lived here for years? He'd associated with cops and criminals. He had contacts. He had to already know about the Madrids because Stephanie was chief advocate even back then and she was fielding a lot of his lawsuits against cops. Taking it a step further, it would have been impossible for Nix to miss Lester with all the press coverage he got in the *Times* for dumping assholes in the street back when he was in SIS.

Maybe it was usable information, and not revenge, that had brought Nix back here for his third TV season.

I would discuss it with Hitch in the morning and see if he could think of a way to twist my cube further and make the colors line up closer.

I was just getting up to head back to bed when a text message signal sounded from my cell phone in the charging dock across the room. I walked over and read it.

YOU ARE INVITED TO JOIN NIX NASH
AND THE CAST OF V-TV ABOARD

THE HMS BOUNTY FOR BRUNCH AND A
CRUISE CELEBRATING THE PREMIERE
OF OUR THIRD SEASON. WE'RE LEAVING
FROM FISHERMAN'S VILLAGE, MARINA
DEL REY, AT 10:00 A.M. TOMORROW.
GROG AND HORS D'OEUVRES.
DRESS CASUAL.

I stood in my den holding the cell phone, looking down at the improbable invitation. What the hell did this guy take me for?

Even though it was late, I dialed Hitch.

"What up, dawg?" he said as he came on the line, still fully awake.

"Listen to this," I said, and read him the text message.

When I finished, he said, "I'd view it as an incredible opportunity. We decided to engage. Full contact, remember?"

"So you'd go."

"Bet your ass."

"I'd like it better if we were betting yours."

"Listen, dawg. If it makes you feel better I could go as your date. We could wear matching sailor suits. But you'll get more if you go alone; it will keep his guard down. This guy is arrogant. Arrogance is his weakness."

We were both silent for a long minute.

"I'm tempted," I said. "But my gut tells me it's a trap."

"Unless he pushes you overboard, which I doubt, you'll get back safely, and then you and I will debrief. We can use whatever intel you get to find a way to net this tuna. While you're on that cruise, you can also try and pump those other sellouts—Marcia Breen, Frank Palgrave, and J. J. Blunt. See what they have to contribute."

"Okay," I finally said. "I guess I'll do it."

Chapter 33

Alexa left before I did the next morning. I hadn't slept well. When I awoke at eight, my head felt so fuzzy I was mainlining coffee trying to develop some focus and a heartbeat.

By nine o'clock I was struggling with what the hell you're supposed to wear on an ocean cruise. Should I take my fancy nickel-plated 9mm Kimber automatic with the white bone handle or go unpacked? What should my nautical look be, or should I even try for one? I finally opted for a beige Brioni sport shirt, khaki slacks, and a pair of canvas deck shoes. For bling I added my small ten-ounce Airlight .38 in an ankle holster.

I got in the Acura and was backing out of the driveway when I noticed a gray Navigator with smoked windows parked at the curb at the end of the alley. I figured it was another *V-TV* mobile unit.

Then the door to the SUV opened and a gaunt six-foot-five giant with a silver-headed cane got out.

Lester Madrid.

He leaned against his front fender and crooked his index finger in my direction, beckoning me over like I was some crack whore on Main Street. I could see no way past him, so I opened the door and reluctantly walked over.

Lester had aged some in the last five years. He still looked nasty enough to eat your children and still didn't carry an ounce of fat, but now his hair had begun to thin and go gray.

As I got closer, I said, "I don't want to get into a dustup with you, Lester."

"I came to deliver a message," he growled in the ruptured, gravelly whisper that served as his normal speaking voice. "Stop trying to put your fucking Mendez homicide on my wife. If you don't pay attention to this warning, you'll be dealing with some critical issues."

I was assuming he didn't know yet that his name had become a part of the investigation in the Hannah Trumbull case. But with *V-TV* covering it, that probably wasn't going to last long. I was trying to decide whether to lay it on him now to gain some tactical advantage or let it just come out naturally.

As I was pondering this, he said, "When did

you turn into such a pussy? The Shane Scully I remember didn't try and fuck up brother cops. He used to go to the asshole."

"Go to the asshole" was an old department reference to cops who were so committed to catching criminals they would risk their own lives in the breakneck pursuit of any bad guy. Lester Madrid always went to the asshole. Trouble was, he killed most of them when he got there.

"Lester, this is a mistake," I told him. "You don't want to threaten me."

"I'm not above a mistake," he rasped. "How you recover is all that matters."

"I'm sure Captain Madrid told you about the cell-phone video with her and Lita fighting."

"Lita Mendez was a bleeding hemorrhoid. Somebody finally put that bitch at room temperature, which is exactly what needed to happen. We oughta throw the doer a parade. But either way, my wife isn't the one who dropped her. You and your bullshit movie-producer partner are gonna get played by Nash like the douche bags you are. I'm here to tell you that will be the mistake you can't recover from. My wife didn't kill that *chola*."

"Racial slurs?"

"I'm not a cop anymore. I don't have the faggot PC police telling me what I can and can't say. I call people exactly what they are now."

I tried to evaluate this. Lester Madrid was six

feet, five inches of gristle and bone, leaning on a cane, glaring, eyes cold and sharp as a box of tacks. He was no less dangerous today than he was ten years ago. This was a cop who had chilled almost a dozen bad guys and then gone home and slept without conscience. Had killing people just become too damn easy? Was that now Lester's preferred way of solving his problems?

It was certainly conceivable that he or his wife could have been involved in Hannah's death. I could easily see a chain of events where Stephanie confronted Nurse Trumbull in that hospital ER, threatening her over the affair with her husband, and then, when they didn't break it off, killing her.

It was also possible that an argument had developed between Nurse Trumbull and Lester over his refusal to leave his wife. He could have been the one who killed Hannah. Both scenarios tracked. I decided this was probably the right moment to confront him after all. I took my shot.

"You used to date an open homicide named Hannah Trumbull back in 2006," I said. "You and Stephanie were married when Hannah was murdered. That puts you on a very short list of suspects, along with your wife. Nash knows about it. He's going to be using this stuff on his show. My suggestion is you should tell me what went down with Hannah. You'll get a better hearing with me than with him."

Lester didn't even flinch.

"Just remember who you're fucking with," he said in that menacing whispery growl. Then he turned, got back inside the Navigator, started the engine, and sped away.

The morning was getting off to a bad start.

Chapter 34

The HMS *Bounty* was moored beside the big dock in front of Fisherman's Village in Marina del Rey. Its 215-foot masts towered above the marina. I'd read up on it before driving over. It was an exact copy of the original HMS *Bounty*, launched in London in 1787. Since then several replicas had been commissioned. This particular ship was built in Nova Scotia in 1960 for the Marlon Brando MGM movie *Mutiny on the Bounty*.

Green and brown paint glistened brightly on her hull and reflected the morning sunshine bouncing off the water, lapping against her wide beam. The massive vessel was pulling against half a dozen two-inch-thick mooring lines in the brisk breeze, causing the ropes to creak loudly.

I stopped my Acura in front of a red velvet rope cordoning off the gangplank and gave my car to the valet.

Nix Nash was greeting guests, standing in front of a banner that said:

He was decked out in British yacht attire—white pants and a blue blazer that had an ornate pocket crest of some kind. Under the jacket he wore a crisp white shirt with a three-inch-tall Tony Curtis collar. As I walked up, a warm smile broke wide on Nash's cherubic face.

"Didn't figure you'd come," he said, happily clasping my hand in both of his.

"How could I pass up a swell invite like this?" I replied, matching his phony delight.

Out of the corner of my eye I saw my Acura being pulled off by a valet in a red coat, and I wondered how many bugs would be installed while I was out at sea. I would have to make an appointment at the Scientific Investigations Division to have the car electronically swept when I got back.

"We're casting off in about ten minutes," Nash was saying. "Go aboard and get yourself a drink."

"This is some boat," I said, admiring the vessel.

"Not a boat, it's a ship. Actually, as you'll come to see, the HMS *Bounty* is sort of a metaphor for my life's work." A statement that made no sense to me at all. "I went to a good deal of trouble to get it up here for this party. It usually berths in San Diego. See you aboard."

He turned to greet other arriving guests as I climbed the gangplank and stepped onto the crowded wooden deck. There was a man standing amidships wearing a period British naval officer's uniform and giving out information about the *Bounty* to a crowd of partiers.

I hovered in the back of the group and listened for a minute as he said, "She's a hundred-twenty-feet long at the waterline and one-eighty at the rail, so you can see there's a nice overhang, both fore and aft. This vessel has four hundred thousand board feet of lumber and ten miles of rigging on two masts. She weighs slightly more than five hundred displaced tons. There are four carriage cannons, two on each side. Each cannon has been decommissioned, but they once fired four-pound lead balls."

He went on, but I wasn't here for a lesson on old sailing ships of the Crown and stepped away to wander the deck and check out my fellow guests. It was a well-dressed, affluent crowd with a definite Hollywood tilt. I recognized the usual smattering of B-list celebrities and reality-show stars. Most of the women were young and dressed to distress. A four-piece string quartet was playing period chamber music on the fantail. Two bars set up on the main deck were doing a brisk business. A sign on a nearby easel announced their specialty was the *Bounty* mai tai, made with actual grog. Most everybody was trying one. So far, I estimated at least a hundred people were onboard.

I stepped up to the bar and ordered a bottled

water. I intended to keep my wits about me for this cruise.

"You'd be in the category of last person on earth I'd expect to see here," a man's voice said.

I turned to see Frank Palgrave standing behind me, holding a mai tai, wearing white slacks and an aqua-colored Palm Springs–type shirt. A red sweater was tied jauntily around his neck. Back when I knew him, this kind of screwy Troy Donahue look would have never been a choice. In the intervening years Palgrave obviously had experienced a big emotional refit of some kind. In this glitzy setting, in my beige-on-beige getup I was beginning to feel like a smudge of dirt on polished glass.

"Nash invited me. Some bash. He sure knows a lot of rich, flashy people," I said, indicating the crowd.

"He practiced here for six years. Hard not to get connected when you have a big, exciting personality like his."

"And these swells don't mind that he went to prison for embezzlement," I said.

"Only makes his star shine brighter," Palgrave said, smiling. "Fantasies of shower rape—it's a secret Hollywood turn-on."

We stood for a moment, neither quite sure how to continue.

"So Frank, what's really going on here?" I finally said, trying to get something going.

"In what context?"

"Pick the context. You were a good cop once. Let's start with what you're doing working for this police saboteur?"

He hesitated, looked around, then pulled me away from the group at the bar and led me over to a vacant spot by the rail. He turned his back to the water so he could keep an eye on the crowd over my shoulder as he spoke.

"I work for him 'cause I got this troublesome little problem I haven't been able to solve," he began.

"What's that?"

"I gotta eat to say alive."

"You have a pension."

"My ex-wife has my pension. After the divorce, all I ended up with is a shack so far out in the West Valley even meth cookers won't go there."

"So you sold out to this cop hater?"

He took a moment and then leaned in closer. "Listen, once you get past all the obvious bullshit, Nix isn't such a bad guy."

I started to speak, but Palgrave held up his hand.

"I know; I know. It looks bad on TV, but honestly, Shane, that Atlanta case was being screwed up. Nix actually performed a service there. Those APD cops were working it like a couple of Alzheimer's patients. You wouldn't believe the stuff they missed. That schizoid bum Nix found was crazy as a shit-house rat. He had a yellow sheet full of violent priors and he'd been wandering around in Piedmont Park for six months threatening people. Twice he attacked Atlanta PD patrol officers when they were called to get him to stop sleeping in the public toilet. Cole and Baron walked right past him and he was standing in plain view the whole time."

"I talked to Cole. He says he's not sure Fuzzy was the doer."

"Right. Fuzzy. Those two imbeciles couldn't even put a real name on him. Nash had to do that too. Before we aired, we did a deep background, found out the guy was named Joffa Hill." Palgrave smiled. "Just another example of the slipshod fast-food way those two were working the case. God knows how many girls' lives were saved because of Nix, and all Cole and Baron could do was bitch about it."

"So, Nix Nash is straight and you're happy to be working for him."

"I'd rather be playing golf, but since I shank every other shot, my game won't support me. As far as private gigs go, this one ain't half-bad. Give him a chance. You might be surprised."

Half an hour later, the mooring lines were thrown from the dock up to the deck crew, all of whom wore British navy uniforms, circa 1800. Then with two 375-horsepower John Deere diesel engines chugging stoutly beneath us, the magnificent vessel motored out of Marina del

Rey at a stately four knots. We turned south, passing the Coast Guard station, then the UCLA Marine Aquatic Center, before finally clearing the breakwater and heading into open water.

I watched as the crew scaled rope ladders and unfurled the topsails on both masts. With 20 percent of the canvas up, you could feel the wind begin to take the boat, heeling it over slightly as we continued out.

I was here to collect intel, so I went looking for former FBI agent J. J. Blunt, Judge Web Russell, or Marcia Breen.

I found Marcia in the middle of a group of people. She spotted me and winked. A few minutes later she found a way to break free and joined me by the rail.

"You look really great," she said. "It's nice to see a little beige cotton mixed in with all these sequins."

"My sparkle comes from inside." I smiled and said, "You look pretty great yourself."

She nodded demurely to accept my compliment. "So how's the marriage going?" Holding my gaze longer than was necessary. "That working out like you wanted?"

"It's great. We're very happy."

"As an old friend, I guess I should be glad," she answered. "Unfortunately, I'm not."

"We had our shot, Marcia. It didn't gel. We've both moved on. Besides, when I was at the studio, I saw the way Nix looked at you."

"The things some of us are willing to do for what's left of our careers." She smiled ruefully, then turned her gaze toward Nash, who was mingling with guests about twenty feet away on the far side of the deck.

"We won't be able to talk for long because Nix doesn't quite trust me with you," she said. "He knows we used to date. He's afraid I might get all giggly and accidentally let a few show secrets slip. You, on the other hand, know what a hard-ass I can be, so that's never gonna happen." She toyed with the plastic swizzle stick in her drink.

"Frank thinks Nash is a good guy," I prodded.

She was silent for a few seconds. "I guess we all see what we want to." Then she leaned slightly closer and lowered her voice: "Be very careful, Shane."

"You want to give me something a little more definitive?"

"I can't."

"Why not?"

"Just can't. If you knew why, you'd understand. All I can tell you is watch your back, 'cause what's coming will probably hit you hard."

"There you are," Nix Nash enthused as he moved up.

Now that we were at sea, he had added a white captain's hat with gold braid on the visor. The snazzy lid was taking his already over-the-top costume to the edge of comedy. I would have said it made him look ridiculous, but I've learned any committed adversary, even one wearing a tutu, should command your complete undivided attention.

He looked at Marcia and said, "Would you excuse us, honey?"

"Of course," she said brightly. "I was just on my way to talk to Brad and Larry about the script for next week's show." She smiled at me again and left.

"You have scripts?" I asked, in mock surprise.

Nash was shorter now because he was wearing boat shoes, not risking the three-inch Cuban heels on this rolling deck. He laughed good-naturedly and said, "I'm going to view your being here as a hopeful sign, Shane. Come on; I want to introduce you to a new, potentially exciting concept."

I walked with him across the deck, then followed him down a narrow ladder to the crew quarters below.

I had no idea where we were going or what would happen next.

Chapter 35

Nash led me aft through a dim, lamp-lit corridor to the stern area and stopped in front of a large mahogany door. The gentle roll of the ship was pleasant as we crossed the mostly calm bay outside the jetty. I could hear the faint sounds of laughter along with the string quartet on the fantail directly above us. Nix took out a key to the captain's quarters.

"I've kept this cabin off-limits," he said as he worked a key into the lock. "Because of who I've become, I've found of late I need to have my chances to get away, create some distance between myself and the fawning public."

Nothing too humble there.

We stepped inside; then he closed the door and turned the latch. The cabin was richly appointed in red leather with plenty of teak and oak. Across the entire stern was a row of mutton-bar windows, which provided light while affording a view of the frothy white wake stretching out behind us as we rolled along.

"Drink?" Nash asked, smiling congenially.

By way of an answer, I held up my bottle of water.

"Not taking any chances, are you?"

"You go ahead," I told him. "I'll use any advantage I can get."

He poured himself a drink from a bar setup on the port side of the room while I checked out the rest of the magnificent cabin. The area ran the entire width of the ship and included a large table and seating, which I guess was designed to duplicate the captain's mess where William Bligh entertained fellow officers while at sea.

Nash turned, drink now in hand, and studied me carefully. "You're making a huge mistake not joining up with us," he said. "We've got a good team."

"I'm sort of a loner."

"I don't mind loners. I'm sort of one myself. There're all kinds of ways to fight this fight, Shane. For instance, I'm no longer a cop or a lawyer, but right now I'm making an even bigger contribution to the legal system than ever before. If you join me you can also be more effective. We have right on our side and we have a powerful electronic megaphone, so people actually hear what we say. It's important work. I won't keep asking. This is sort of it. Last call."

The ship lurched in a trough. I was braced, but Nix grabbed for the edge of the captain's table. He regained his balance as the ship steadied its roll.

"Was this last-call concept the exciting idea you wanted to expose me to?" I asked.

"No," he said. He took a moment to study me. "I

wanted to expose you to a negative civic phenomenon, which you've been participating in. I'm going to try to get you to stop. It's something called the broken-window theory. Ever heard of it?"

"Never."

"Pretty simple, really. All it says is, in troubled neighborhoods when a window gets broken you must fix it immediately, because when people see broken windows they tend to lose hope and that loss of hope causes anger and anger causes more broken windows. I know you see me as some sort of anti-police spokesperson, but all I'm doing is going around fixing broken windows."

"So am I."

"Not so. You're actually the guy breaking them. Arresting the Sanchezes was a broken window. Hannah Trumbull's blown murder investigation, another."

"Look, Nix, in the interest of not spoiling your premiere party, I don't want to get into that whole Edwin Chavaria snipe hunt. Let's just leave that and move on." He held my gaze, looked speculative for a moment, and said nothing.

"I spent some time reading about you on the Internet," I continued. "Made some calls to departments in Atlanta and Florida. I'm trying to understand why you have such a hard-on for cops. That's the primary reason I accepted this invitation."

"And what did you learn?" he said, his slightly superior smile in place, never taking his eyes off me.

"Getting thrown off the Florida Marine Patrol over losing that serial killer might explain some of it. At least that's what the Marine Patrol cops in Dade County think. However, my bet is there's a lot more than just that going on."

"Lee Bob Batiste was a mistake," he said. "I don't make many, but that was a big one. Borrowing money from my law firm and not correctly accounting for it was another. I paid my debt to society on the so-called embezzlement charge and I count Lee Bob as an important lesson learned."

"That swamp rat kills nine people in the Everglades, he's still walking free because you blew up the case, and you think it's an important lesson learned? You're going kind of easy on yourself there, don't you think?"

He frowned, then took a minute to gather his thoughts. "Since you seem so interested in that chapter of my life you might as well hear the real facts." He sounded frustrated now, even annoyed.

"Bobby Batiste was illiterate and semi-educated. He barely spoke English. He was Cajun, raised in the Louisiana swamp, but he moved to Florida in the eighties. The guy was so loony he lived up in a giant cypress tree on the west side of the 'Glades. He ended up killing campers who crossed the imaginary boundaries of an imaginary empire he thought he ruled. He drew lines of death for miles around his tree house. Anybody who wandered in there got killed. He was a scavenger who'd steal food out of his victims' backpacks and turn it into Cajun dishes over their own campfires. He had this strange dream of creating a kingdom in the swamp where he would bring kidnapped women to help him repopulate. He had actually already started building his capital city using money and credit cards he took off the dead bodies."

Nash set his drink down before he said, "I wanted that collar. I wanted the killings to stop. I arrested him and had him in cuffs. He had some of the victims' DLs in his wallet; I got a little anxious and started asking questions. I never thought Bobby would just flat out confess to nine murders right when I grabbed him, but that's what he did. He thought he was a demonic angel, immune from human prosecution. I'd never seen that kind of deep psychotic illness before, so yeah, I learned a big lesson there. Before I end my time on earth, I intend to fully atone for that mistake."

"Good shit," I said dryly.

"You don't like me much, do you?" he said softly.

I let that hang there.

He took another moment before he smiled and said, "It's okay; a lot of people feel that way. It

235

sort of comes with this gig. Because of what I do, it can get sorta pronounced, but there's a deeper reason than just fame or jealousy. Wanna hear?"

"Sure."

"If you make people *think* they're thinking, they will love you. But if you really make them think, they'll hate you. Since I really make people think, I have picked up a fairly long list of enemies. The good news there is, a nonthinking enemy is usually very easy to deal with."

The boat lurched again. Nash was ready this time, but I almost went down. My bottle of water flew from my hand and rolled across the room. I started after it, but Nash waved me off.

"Leave it," he said, and took a step closer, forcing me to turn back and focus on him.

"Do you know where we are right now?" he said.

"The point of no return?"

"I was thinking more about where we're standing. Our location on this ship. Ever since I was a boy, the mysteries and social crimes perpetuated in this cabin have fascinated me."

Oh, brother.

"HMS *Bounty* was rebuilt by King George of England and sent all the way to Tahiti to get breadfruit plants to take to the West Indies for cultivation. Do you know why?"

"Haven't a clue."

"It was a cheap food source, which could be

236

used to feed American plantation slaves. So at its heart, the mission the *Bounty* was rechristened to perform was a gross social corruption. But in the end fate had other plans."

He moved closer to me. His eyes were wide and shining. There seemed to be a glazed insanity hiding behind that cherubic face and Cary Grant costume.

"Commander Bligh was just thirty-three and something of an innocent," Nash continued. "He's been portrayed in books and film as a terrible tyrant. But if you read the ship's logs as I have, actually Fletcher Christian was the real malcontent. Christian had once been Bligh's protégé. Christian organized a mutiny with eighteen out of forty-two crew members. After it was over and he'd taken the ship, only these original mutineers wanted to remain on the *Bounty*, while all but four of the loyalists boarded a leaking, unsafe lifeboat and went with William Bligh. They preferred to set off across thousands of miles of open ocean with their courageous captain rather than remain behind with the treacherous Mr. Christian."

I had no idea what we were actually talking about. I was pretty sure it had nothing to do with Fletcher Christian or the mutiny on the *Bounty*.

Nash paused, then asked, "Why do you suppose Fletcher Christian took the ship? What caused him to put his saber to William Bligh's throat and force him into a lifeboat with only a sextant and a watch to navigate with? Can you discern the reason?"

"The goal gradient phenomenon?" I answered.

"You're a lot smarter than you look," Nash said. "Exactly right. William Bligh, if you read his logs, was a great commander. A great sailor and leader. Fletcher Christian was a young officer stuck in middle management, bored, unhappy, and filled with malaise. This is what spawned his moment of corruption. It's the same situation I battle every day."

Nash crossed the cabin and picked up my water bottle, then dropped it into the trash. When he turned back, he was smiling again.

"Our municipal police and politicians are the Fletcher Christians of modern society. They want control, but not responsibility. They're staging a mutiny against the laws of democratic justice. Like Bligh, I'm backed up at the rail with a saber at my throat, offering you a chance to get in my leaking lifeboat. To sail a courageous voyage to help me free society from these lawless tyrants."

"So you're cast as our misunderstood commander, sent to prison by a bunch of ungrateful pricks because of a rigid management style?"

He stood there, his brow furrowed, angrily flexing the muscles in his jaw.

"The way I see this, it's all part of the same fabric," I continued. "We can talk about corruption and the broken-window theory, or the goal gradient phenomenon, but that's just camouflage. What this is really about is revolution against social order and the real joke is you're getting filthy rich while you're doing it."

He was standing opposite me, his eyes shadowed in the dark cabin, staring malevolently.

"A man can't take everything and be everything at the same time. It creates isolation and that causes failure," I said.

He pinned me with a withering gaze, then said, "If you'll excuse me, I have other guests to entertain." He turned abruptly and walked out.

Chapter 36

While I was at sea learning about broken windows and social corruption, Hitch had spent the day doing scut work on our two cases, trying to set up interviews with Lita Mendez's balky neighbors and putting together a victimology profile on Hannah Trumbull. It had left him in a prickly mood.

One of the most important parts of a homicide investigation is establishing victimology. Neighbors and friends often know things about a victim that can be surprisingly helpful. I once worked a case where a neighbor told me the vic couldn't wear cotton because it gave her a skin rash. The dead woman's body was found in a motel lying on cotton sheets. But the neighbor had explained that when the victim traveled she always took silk sheets in her luggage to remake hotel beds. That information led us to realize the killer had obviously not known the woman well and was unaware of her allergy. He was trying to make it look like a suicide and had purchased new sheets to get rid of his semen stains. We were able to trace the sheets to a nearby Walmart, and a credit card led us to the killer. You never know where a case-breaking lead might come from.

The problem with Hannah's victimology was the murder was more than four years old and over time memories for detail fade.

The problem with Lita's death was nobody on her block wanted to talk to us. Hitch was visibly frustrated by the time I dropped into my chair at Homicide Special a little past 2:00 p.m. and propped my feet up on a wastebasket.

"That was an interesting day," I said.

"Can't have been as much fun as having forty neighbors bitch you out."

"Palgrave thinks Nash is good people. Marcia told me to watch my back and Nix threatened me."

"Just another rollicking good day with the animals," Hitch replied.

"There was a moment there down belowdecks in the captain's cabin when Nix started acting like a fifty-one-fifty," I said, referring to the police code for a head case.

Hitch looked surprised. "You think he's nuts?"

"I'm not sure." I recounted Nix's rant on William Bligh and how he saw the HMS *Bounty* as a metaphor for his career.

"At the end we had a real Jack Nicholson moment," I concluded.

Hitch sat back and pondered it. Then he said, "So that's all you took away? That a guy who we already know is an egomaniac also has delusions of grandeur?"

"Yeah, kinda."

"Already knew that," Hitch said, and picked up the phone sheet he was working his way through.

"Well, maybe there's one other thing," I said.

He glanced back up.

"It's more of an impression than anything else. I was trying to goad him with the Lee Bob Batiste bust and he said something that came off strange."

"Yeah?"

"He said Bobby was illiterate and semi-educated."

"He probably was."

"He didn't say 'Lee Bob'; he said 'Bobby,' like he was friends with him."

"Now you are grasping. You can't believe Nash intentionally blew that bust."

"I didn't say that. It just hit me funny."

241

My phone rang and I picked it up. "Detective Scully," I said.

"Shane, it's Sue Shepherd. I'm sitting in the patio behind the Bradbury Building. You wanted to know when Captain Madrid or her husband was eating here. Well, they're on the patio right now, having a late lunch."

I checked my watch. Two thirty-five.

"Thanks, Sue."

I disconnected and got to my feet. "Grab your coat. Let's go."

"What is it?"

"Fill you in on the way."

We made it to the underground garage in two minutes and took Hitch's car because I wasn't sure the Acura hadn't been bugged. On the six-block drive to the Bradbury Building I filled Hitch in.

"Since we can't get a body warrant, I asked an investigating officer I know at the Bradbury to keep an eye on the cafeteria. She just called. Lester and Stephanie are on the patio having a late lunch."

"Wanta do a Dumpster dive?"

"Got a better plan?"

"As long as you do it, I think the idea smokes."

We pulled in behind the building and moved carefully toward the patio dining area.

"Listen, I guess I should mention that Lester showed up outside my house this morning and tried to warn me off his wife's investigation."

"All we need now is Internet posts of us with strippers," Hitch said.

"I think we should treat Lester with extreme care. If we blunder in there and start clocking these two, it could get nasty."

"I'm testifying on that Quadry Barnes case anyway, so I've got a reason to be here. I'll go get a sandwich and sit out there, keep an eye on 'em. You wait in the Porsche. I'll call you on your cell and keep you posted."

So that's what we did. Hitch went through the food line and took a seat at a small patio table. I went back to the car. He called once to tell me Stephanie and Lester were still seated at a table by the Biddy Mason wall, talking in low voices.

Ten minutes later Hitch called me again.

"You'll never guess what I just noticed," he said.

"What?"

"They're both drinking from paper coffee cups with that same brown flower decoration like the one we found near Lita's driveway."

"Where'd those cups come from? We checked the cafeteria."

"I don't know, but I'd hate to end up filling out one-eighty-seven complaints on these two."

"Just hang in there. Watch those cups. Don't let them out of your sight."

"Duh . . . ," he said, and hung up.

Five minutes later my phone rang again.

"They're bussing their table now. Haven't made me yet. Oops . . . spoke too soon."

I heard Stephanie Madrid's voice coming over my cell speaker. "Have you started following me around now, Detective?"

"No, ma'am," Hitch said. "Just here doing my third depo on that damn Quadry Barnes deal."

Then a minute later I heard his cell phone being picked up and he was back.

"They've left," he said. "Come on. There's a crime kit in my trunk. Take what we need. I'll go protect the evidence."

I took two pairs of latex gloves and some evidence bags out of his crime kit and made it to the patio area in about ten seconds. Hitch had already located the cups in a trash can and was keeping other people from dumping their lunch clutter on top. I put on one set of gloves and handed a second pair to Hitch. Then I stuck my hand in the barrel, pulled the cups out one at a time, and passed them to Hitch. Both were identical to the one we found at Lita's house.

"We need evidence bags," Hitch said.

"Got 'em." I pulled them out of my coat pocket and he dropped the cups inside. "Let's go talk to Food Services."

We found the Hispanic guy who supplied the cafeteria and the coffee rooms on all six floors of the Bradbury and showed him the cups inside our clear plastic evidence bags.

"These aren't in the main cafeteria," Hitch said. "You know where they came from?"

"The exotic blends machine up on four," he said.

"Exotic blends?" I asked.

"Yeah, we've got a machine up there for the senior staff in the Advocates Section—captains, commanders, and lieutenants. It's got all kinds of blends, Brazilian, Caramel Mocha. You know, expensive stuff."

We thanked him and hurried back to the car.

"This ain't gonna end up good," Hitch said.

"I know." Then, because we were heading to the forensic lab at Cal State where our electronics surveillance unit was located, I had Hitch drop me at the PAB so I could pick up my car and follow him there.

Chapter 37

The LAPD has had a major face-lift in the past few years. Besides the PAB downtown and the Hollenbeck Station, the Hertzberg-Davis Forensic Science Center at Cal State Los Angeles is fully operational. It's a five-story brick and terrazzo building with inward-leaning sides, which makes it look like a long, rectangular pyramid with the top third cut off. The LAPD shares the

209,000-square-foot space with the Los Angeles County Sheriff's Department, a fact that causes a little elbowing in waiting lines but on balance is a big improvement over our old space.

The Forensic Science Center has specially equipped areas for ballistics and firearms identification as well as forensic biology. The old DNA facility had space for about eight people, but with the ever-increasing demand for biological evidence, by the time we moved, there were almost forty CSIs camping out in the hallways. It was an overcrowded hive of squashed-together scientists, all buzzing angrily, about to sting. Over here everyone had wide smiles and they served you coffee.

Hitch and I handed over the two cups and gave instructions to run them for a match against the cup we found in Lita's driveway. We asked for our results ASAP.

I went to the ERT area to check on our footprints. I found a young guy named Adam Rush who pulled the results up on his computer.

"Lotta Blackhawk! Warrior, light assault, lace-ups," he told me. "They're real popular in Patrol, so we're starting by checking those against the cops who were on the scene." He clicked to another shot.

"And here's Waldo," he said, pulling up another footprint. "This guy doesn't fit the others. Sole pattern is from a rubber Baffin outdoor boot.

Size thirteen. It doesn't lace up, so no cop would be wearing it. You can see it's got a triangle-shaped nick in the left heel and some pronounced tread scuffs. Also, the dust we recovered on the footprint has traces of ammonium polyphosphate, which is a chemical used to put out fires. Not sure what that means yet." He printed me out a copy of the boot print and I left, feeling like it was progress. A tiny bit of physical evidence.

I called Alexa and gave her a heads-up on what was going on, ending our conversation by asking her to call Forensic Biology and put a little command staff oomph behind our request.

Hitch was still filling out the paperwork for our DNA, so I used the time to visit the Electronic Surveillance Department. I got one of the lab techs to go out in the parking lot with me and wand the Acura for bugs. I was pretty sure I'd picked up something at the marina, and I had. There was a little satellite voice transmitter with a GPS function buried inside the Acura's rearview mirror. I had to make a decision as to whether to leave it there or to have the bug removed. If I took it out, it would alert Nash that I had found it and that might change his behavior. In the game of chess I was playing, knowledge was power, so I left it where it was.

When Hitch came downstairs I showed him the Baffin boot print and told him about the bug in the Acura. He was buoyed by the size 13 rubber boot and agreed it was a good idea to leave the bug where it was. If we rode in the Acura, we'd have to keep our discussions off the case.

"This is our unsub," Hitch said, still looking at the boot print in his hand. "He went to Lita's house to kill her. He knew it was going to get messy, so the guy wore rubber boots."

I agreed. We caravanned back to the PAB and closed out the day making phone calls.

I drove home at six and went out to the backyard to watch the moonlight on the water. Alexa wasn't home yet and I was feeling lonely and a little afraid for my future.

I hadn't spoken to Chooch in at least a week, so I dialed his cell. He was in midterms at USC and didn't sound like he had much time to talk, but he did let one gem slip.

"Listen, Dad, next semester I'm thinking about taking Introduction to Police Science," he said unexpectedly.

"You're a finance major. What's a finance major need with police science?"

"You and Mom are cops. I just want to understand what you do. How can that hurt?"

"It just seems like it's not something you'll need, is all."

"Todd McNear, my left-side tackle on the scout team, took it last semester and he says it's really interesting and kind of easy. Never hurts to pile up a few easy credits to pump up the GPA."

My alarms were ringing. Chooch has a 3.5 average while playing Division I football at USC. DI ball's a huge time commitment, and even so, he'd been an academic All-American for three years straight. His GPA was fine. I wasn't keen on the idea of him taking police science. I didn't know where it might lead.

"Listen, Dad, I gotta get back to this review sheet. Call me on Sunday."

"Right. Love you."

"Love you too."

After he hung up I sat there watching the moon on the water and tried to keep my mind off the possibility of my son being wooed into a law enforcement career. I guess you naturally set higher goals for your children than yourself. I had visions of him using his finance degree to run a large multi-national corporation or something. I chose police work because of who I was and a need for an identity back when I didn't have one. It was a perfect choice for me, but I had larger ambitions for Chooch.

I finally pushed that thought away and also tried not to think about the two cases Hitch and I were working on. I've discovered that a little separation can be helpful. If I create some distance, the next time I open the folder I might see things I'd completely missed before.

But my thoughts kept pulling me back into that strange meeting with Nash aboard the *Bounty*. I wondered about his insistence on equating a British naval mutiny that took place over two hundred years ago to current law enforcement practices in Los Angeles. The more I thought about it, the more it had me wondering about his mental state. Or maybe I just wanted him to be crazy because crazy people are easier to catch.

So far, Nix Nash had not made any obvious goofs that I could spot. It wasn't hard to figure out why he kept inviting me to go to work for him in rooms he controlled. I was pretty sure Bligh's cabin and Nash's studio dressing room were both outfitted with hidden cameras or mikes, just like the one in my car. My new paranoid theory was Nash wanted me to agree to sell out the department on some hidden camera so he could unpack me in front of his national TV audience.

The front door opened and I heard Alexa drop her briefcase on the table.

"I'm home," she called out.

"Bring me a beer," I called back.

A moment later she appeared on the patio and handed me a Corona. Then she sat down beside me.

"I've been worried about those two coffee cups ever since you called me," she said. "If the science lab puts Stephanie or Lester Madrid in Lita's driveway the night of her murder, then we're going to have to bust one of them, and that's going to set our inner city on fire."

"Let's hope that doesn't happen," I said.

But of course the next morning that's exactly what happened.

Chapter 38

The call came in at 8:00 a.m., just as Alexa and I were about to leave. I picked it up in the den.

"Detective Scully?" a woman's voice asked.

"Yeah."

"This is Erica Hobbs with Forensic Biology. We got back the overnight on that DNA scan you requested."

"Whatta you got?" My heart rate started climbing.

"We have a solid match to the cup you found in Lita Mendez's driveway. One in fifty billion probability."

"Which one is it, Lester or Stephanie?" I asked, hoping it was Lester, because at least he was not an active police officer anymore.

"I'm afraid it's Captain Madrid's DNA," Erica said.

"Shit," I muttered softly. "Listen, we really need to keep this on the DL. How many people know about it yet?"

"Just me and my lab partner."

"Okay, look. You know what's at stake here. We're going to have to move fast. Just guard that info."

"It's guarded," she said.

I hung up and found Alexa in the bedroom, loading rounds into her light Spanish Astra, which she jokingly called the lady's home companion.

"That was CSI. The DNA matched on Stephanie Madrid."

Alexa paused mid-motion, then turned slowly to face me.

"Na-a-aw-w-w," she said softly.

"I gotta call Hitch. We better pull this together fast. We're going to need an arrest warrant. If it leaks before we can release a statement to the press, we're fucked. We've gotta control the message. I'd like to pick Captain Madrid up before ten." I looked at my watch. "That's in a couple of hours."

The next hour was a flurry of activity. I called Hitch, told him the bad news, and agreed to meet him downtown in forty minutes. I rode in with Alexa in her BMW, leaving my bugged Acura in the garage. All the way to the office, Alexa was on the Bluetooth in her car, setting things up, giving instructions.

"Notify DC Hawkins and Chief Filosiani," she said to her adjunct. "And get Captain Myer from Media Relations over to my office right away. We're going to need a prepared statement and I want somebody full-time on media tamp downs. Also, get a warrant delivery team on standby and send a UC out to Captain Madrid's house to keep her under surveillance until we can pick her up. I think she lives in Valley Village or Sherman Oaks. Get the address from Records. I want to make sure we know where she and her husband are at all times."

We arrived in the PAB at eight forty-five and convened a meeting in Alexa's office on the command floor. In the room were Jeb, Hitch, Bud Hawkins, and Sgt. Britt Mills from the warrant delivery team. Mills was another one of those expressionless, hard-eyed gunfighters who always seem to end up in our high-risk shooting units.

Chief Filosiani stuck his face into the room but said he couldn't stay. The superchief was a short, lunch box–shaped guy with a shiny bald head and Santa Claus cheeks. He didn't look as much like a police chief as he did a market manager, but this morning he was a grocer with an attitude.

"Two things," he said sharply, standing in Alexa's doorway. "This has to be a no-incident takedown. That means you screen Lester Madrid off first. Second, everything, and I mean every little scintilla of info headed to sources outside this immediate venue, gets processed through my chief adjunct, Rodello Morales. I want RoMo to have strict control of all facts and be the sole distributor of information."

Capt. Bert Myer from Media Relations showed up and waited in the corridor behind the chief until he finished. Dubbed Myer the Liar by the troops, he had a thankless job. Myer ran the LAPD Media Relations office and he was going to have to manage the press fallout, which would be huge. How often does the head of Internal Affairs get arrested for killing the city's leading police critic?

After the chief left, we got down to it. The undercover was already out at Stephanie Madrid's house and had notified us by phone that both Lester's and Stephanie's cars were still in the driveway.

"Let's do this," Alexa said after we ran through our arrest plan.

Forty minutes later, we were parked half a block down the street from the Madrids' well-cared-for faux Italian two-story house in a middle-class Valley neighborhood. The gray Navigator with the tinted windows was still in the driveway. Parked in front of it was Captain Madrid's deluxe dark blue department sedan. When we got there and relieved the UC, it was just a little before ten.

At ten thirty, Lester Madrid exited the house, got into the gray SUV, and pulled out. Once he was gone, the warrant delivery team moved. While Hitch, Alexa, and I covered the outside, SWAT Sergeant Mills knocked on the front door.

Stephanie Madrid answered, dressed in jeans and a T-shirt. We watched from positions of advantage as the three cops on the front porch spoke to her for a few seconds, then took her into custody, cuffed her, and drove her to the Police Administration Building.

The arrest was quick and easy, but booking Captain Madrid for suspicion of Lita's murder was a little more complex. What happened now was going to be part of the public record and would be on the evening news. Nix Nash would have a field day.

As soon as she was Mirandized, Captain Madrid demanded her attorney. It turned out that, as a precaution, she had already hired Clarence Moneymaker. He was L.A.'s new Johnnie Cochran —an elegant, spindly African-American who fit his name remarkably well. He oozed confidence and diamond accessories. His client list spanned everyone from A-list celebrities to unrepentant gang killers. However, he was shrewdly effective when he got to the defendant's table.

Of course, he immediately pointed out that a coffee cup outside a crime scene wasn't enough to charge his client with Lita's murder, suggesting it could easily be planted. Captain Madrid had an alibi, supplied by her husband. Alexa called the DA and after a heated ten-minute discussion it was determined that we should hold off a day or so before booking Madrid. She was labeled a person of interest and we were instructed to let her go. The DA had cold feet and pointed out to us that we'd collected similar cups by Dumpster diving, agreeing with Moneymaker that somebody could have planted it. Of course Clarence Moneymaker forbade all future LAPD or DA contact with his client. After that, all that was left for us to do was start writing search warrants for Stephanie's house and car. I would have loved to find a box of 9mm Hydra-Shok Federals like the ones we pulled out of Lita's kitchen floor somewhere in Captain Madrid's possession, but I didn't think she, or Lester if he was involved, would be that careless.

One really unsettling thing happened as Hitch and I were heading out to get a taco for lunch. Lester Madrid was sitting on the bench in the atrium, across from the elevator, silver-headed cane leaned between his legs, waiting for us. As we stepped into the lobby, he stood.

"I don't think you two ass wipes see what's really going on here," he said in his whispery growl.

Since I didn't want to guess what he thought was *really* going on, Hitch and I waited him out.

"Steph isn't going down behind this horse-shit murder beef. She's being set up. If I have to rip out a few yards of somebody's colon to prove it, then that's what I intend to do."

"Stop threatening us," I said.

"I'm not threatening, Scully. I'm promising. In SIS they said we were assassinating criminal dirtbags. But that wasn't what we were doing at all. We were just eliminating problems. Cleaning up the city. You two idiots have been parked in a cul-de-sac, jerkin' off while this fucking case went down the road without you. That means I'm gonna have to get involved and fix the problem. When I get involved there are conse-quences."

He turned and left us, walking out of the interior atrium into the midday sunshine. Hitch and I just stood there.

"Isn't that a crime, threatening a police officer?" Hitch asked.

"Yeah, Section Seventy-One of the Penal Code. I had one filed against me once in the Valley when I threatened to knock my training officer's teeth out."

"Then let's hit that guy with a seventy-one and give him a ride in a squad car," Hitch said. "I don't want him hunkered down in my bushes tonight with a SWAT rifle."

"It's borderline. All we got is his promise to eliminate a problem and a warning of conse-quences. Let him cool off and we'll take his temperature again tomorrow."

Two hours later, we'd finished with the IA paper-work for Stephanie Madrid's charge sheet. We filed it and took off early, both emotionally wasted.

When I got on the freeway, I thought I saw a

gray Navigator a few cars behind, tracking me from two lanes over. I couldn't be certain. I kept changing lanes, trying to spot it again, but it never reappeared.

I finally decided it was just my imagination.

Chapter 39

Ten minutes after I got to Venice, Alexa called to tell me she wouldn't be home until later that evening. Deputy Chief Hawkins had put the Stephanie Madrid case under Alexa's direct supervision, and she was stuck in the office working on a media plan with Bert Myer. The press had already scooped up the arrest report, which was now public information. An hour after that, Nix Nash had a mobile unit parked in front of the Police Administration Building and was doing shotgun interviews with anyone who he thought might conceivably touch the case.

I hung up with Alexa and, to take my mind off this disaster, was trying to decide what to do for dinner or if I was still even hungry. Just then the phone rang again. This time it was Hitch.

"Dawg, get your skinny ass up to my place, *inmediatamente!*"

"I was just gonna go down the street to get something to eat," I told him.

"Got that covered," he said, sounding excited. "Stop arguing and get up here."

"All the way to Mount Olympus? Man, can't we at least meet halfway?"

"No. Gotta be here. You'll thank me. Just get moving!" He hung up.

I don't much like being commanded, so in a self-involved show of indifference I wandered slowly into the kitchen, poured some orange juice, swallowed it down, taking my time about it. Then I ambled out to the Acura, took the keys off the visor, got in, and inched back slowly onto the street. I know, I know, pretty juvenile.

All the way up to Hitch's place in Hollywood, I kept checking behind me for gray Navigators. Every time I looked in the rearview mirror, I remembered Nash's bug sequestered in there. I've had these devices planted on my vehicle once or twice in the past. They can often be turned into a very effective source of disinformation. I was circling a few ideas as I drove.

Thirty minutes later, I parked in the drive of Hitch's magnificent house and rang the bell. The familiar *Dum-da-dum-dum* chimes sounded, followed by Hitch's voice over the intercom.

"Come on in!" he yelled. "It's open!"

I entered, leaving the *Dragnet* theme behind, and was greeted by the classical sounds of some turn-of-the-century European composer like Strauss or Rachmaninoff. The music was coming from Hitch's thirty-thousand-dollar wraparound sound system. Then the aroma of something delicious engulfed me. Hitch was cooking.

"In the kitchen," he called out.

I went into his beautiful living room–sized, professionally outfitted kitchen and found him perched on a wood stool beside the stove. He had a drink in one hand and a cooking spoon in the other.

"You gotta fix that doorbell," I said. "I go from *Dragnet* to Rachmaninoff. It's giving me whiplash."

"Not Rachmaninoff, it's Bach. Sonata Number Five in C Major." Hitch set down the drink, then looked at me expectantly and said, "Well?"

"Well, what?"

"The smell. You recognize it?"

I took another sniff. "Kind of, but I'm not sure from where."

"Lita's house, man. This was what was in the curtains. It's been driving me nuts. I've been combing through cookbooks ever since we found her. I finally came up with it."

I realized he was right. This was the same smell that we'd experienced when we first walked into Lita Mendez's living room.

"You're right. It's more pungent of course, because it's still being cooked. But you're right. It's the same."

"You know what it is?"

"Uh-uh."

"It's fucking gumbo, dude."

"It is?"

"Yep. Look."

He showed me the cookbook. The page was open to a recipe for gumbo.

"Besides the chicken, your main ingredients are garlic, onions, tomatoes, cayenne, okra, and ta-da-a . . . andouille."

"What's andouille?"

"A spicy country pork sausage. It's what gives it that pungent odor. They use it in a lot of Cajun dishes."

As I read the recipe, he removed the lid from the pot and waved some of the steam in my direction.

"I thought it was the bay leaf and garlic," he said, grinning. "But I tried that and it didn't do it. Then I found that recipe. It was the andouille."

"Damn," I said, smiling at him. "Lita couldn't have had all these ingredients. You think the killer brought his own groceries?"

"Don't know. Let's eat this stuff before it gets cold. I've got the rice all steamed."

"Isn't that like eating evidence?"

"Right. Grab a plate, dummkopf."

We each dished up a large helping on rice, then grabbed some lagers from the fridge and went out onto the deck.

The view tonight was partially eclipsed by a

low blanket of fog hanging over Hollywood, but the air wasn't too cold and we sat at the table and tasted the gumbo. Masterful.

"So who do we know in this big, ugly, bullshit case who could be cooking Cajun?" Hitch asked.

"Lee Bob Batiste," I said.

"Correcto mundo." He beamed. "Our Creole-French chucklehead from Louisiana."

"Okay, okay. Hold on. Let's not get carried away. This is a big jump. Let's take it slow."

"Fine," he agreed. "But remember what you said about Nash calling Lee Bob Bobby? I think you were actually on to something there."

"Now you think Lee Bob and Nix Nash knew each other when he was a cop?" I asked. "I thought you said I was grasping at straws."

"Maybe the bust in the Everglades was for real and Nash fucked up on the square, or maybe he knew the guy and arranged to get him kicked loose. Either way, it's the same result. What's important is, I think he knows him now."

I thought it over for a minute before I said, "So you're saying Nash cut a deal with Lee Bob Batiste to commit these murders at times when Nash is out of town and alibied up. Then Nash solves the case on his TV show, looking like a genius, making huge ratings and multi-million-dollar grosses."

"Exactly," Hitch said. "Going back to Atlanta, what if Lee Bob Batiste, not Fuzzy, was wearing that overcoat when he killed those girls in Piedmont Park? During the murders, Batiste gets their DNA on the coat. Then Nash finds Fuzzy sleeping in the public toilet there. He's brain-dead from all the meth and doesn't know if he's upside down or inside out. They give Fuzzy the coat. It's December and he's glad to have it. Then, a day or so later, Nash just happens to find poor old Fuzzy in the evidence-stained overcoat, and the Atlanta PD busts him while Nash is rolling cameras, taking all the credit. How hard would it be to get a schizophrenic to cop to the six kills? Fuzzy had a pet spider named Louis, for chrissake."

"It also helps connect the two murders here in L.A.," I said, warming to Hitch's idea. "Obviously, Nix had nothing to do with Hannah Trumbull's death in '06, because he was still in prison, but this could explain how he was able to link Lita and Hannah to Stephanie and Lester Madrid. He worked backward, like you said before. But the second death, Lita's, wasn't random like we thought. He selected her because of the fights she'd had with Stephanie and then he had Lee Bob kill her."

"Bingo," Hitch said. "He starts with the cold-case Trumbull murder from '06. Nash, or some L.A. contact, finds out Hannah was dating a cop and that turns out to be Lester Madrid. He probably turned that up just like we did, by asking around. Then he starts looking at Lester's life and up pops Stephanie, who runs IA and has a history of public dustups with his old compadre from the Anti-Police League, Lita Mendez. She's an acquaintance of Nash's, but she's also a perfect murder victim who will be a high ratings getter for *V-TV*, so she goes into the chipper."

This take wiped out the impossible coincidence of both those seemingly unrelated cases touching the Madrids. "Nash sets up his alibi in advance," I said, ironing out a few more wrinkles. "He accepts an invite to be at that fund-raiser in Boca Raton while Lee Bob, or Bobby as he calls him, sneaks over to Lita's house. Batiste beats her to death and then double-taps her with the nine-millimeter Federals."

"A perfect murder," Hitch said, nodding.

Then I remembered another detail from the meeting in Captain Bligh's cabin. "Nash told me that in the Everglades, Batiste was stealing food out of his victims' backpacks and cooking it over their own campfires. Could that be some kind of MO? The Gumbo Killer? He whacks Lita, cooks a Cajun meal in her kitchen just like he cooked food from the backpacks of the campers he killed in the Everglades."

We both thought about it. The gumbo feast over Lita's body seemed a little far-fetched. He would have had to bring all the ingredients. But in ten years of solving homicides I've seen some very strange behavior.

"Sociopaths and psychopaths have strange realities," Hitch said, picking up my unspoken thought. "Remember that gay unsub in Santa Monica who killed boys on their twenty-first birthdays? He brought them home, sat them up at his dinner table, and served the corpses birthday cake."

"Okay, let's put a pin in that for a minute. We don't know why he actually cooked a Cajun dinner, but let's assume he did. Then he washed the pots and pans, vacuumed the body. This guy used very strict crime scene protocol. The kind an ex-cop or an ex-lawyer like Nix Nash would be able to give him."

I pulled out the photo of his boot print. "Let's go on the Internet and see if we can get a picture of this Baffin rubber boot," I suggested.

We went into Hitch's office, logged onto his Mac, and found it on the Baffin Web site. That particular boot came in black rubber and neoprene and was calf high.

"Lookit this," Hitch said. "They're called Marsh boots. Good choice for a guy working the Florida swamps."

We went back to the porch feeling like supercops and kicked back on the deck chairs.

Finally, Hitch broke the silence. "What do we do now, Batman?"

"Let's start by finishing this great gumbo you cooked. Then we need to go down to the PAB and get this theory blessed by a rabbi."

"Thank god you're married to yours," Hitch said somberly.

Chapter 40

It was nine thirty that same night and we were gathered in the public affairs conference room, just down the hall from the new four-hundred-seat auditorium, which would soon be getting a lot of use with this media-intense murder.

Deputy Chief Hawkins was seated at the head of the conference table, flanked by Jeb and Alexa. Hitch and I remained standing as we presented our theory. When we were finished, silence prevailed.

"You're saying that this famous, internationally known TV personality is committing serial murders and then solving them to make his show more entertaining?" DC Hawkins finally asked skeptically.

"He's not doing the actual murders himself," I said. "Lee Bob Batiste is. And let's not forget the ratings this is producing. *Variety* just reported Nash signed a new two-year deal with his syndicator for forty million dollars up front, plus fifteen percent of the back end. That's huge. Don't tell me money can't be a motive for murder. Guys in this town can get washed out over a ten-dollar spoon of heroin."

More silence.

I could feel sweat beginning to form under my ass. This was a very cold house. Only Alexa seemed neutral, but to be fair, she trusted my instincts on cases and had seen me be right too many times. Our captain, Jeb, sat Buddha-esque, impossible to read.

"It certainly straightens out that bizarre coincidence that has Lita Mendez's murder and Hannah Trumbull's both involving the Madrids," Alexa said. "All Nash needed was one open murder, Hannah's. It touched Lester. Then he kills the second victim, Lita, and plants Stephanie's coffee cup with her DNA evidence in Lita's driveway just like he did with that overcoat in Atlanta."

"Detective Cole told us that everything would tie together," I said. "And this is how he's doing it."

At that point, Deputy Chief Hawkins stood and walked to the door. I thought we'd lost him, but he stopped abruptly and turned to face us again.

"Okay," he said, surprising me. "Let's say I go for it. You still don't have enough to write either a search or arrest warrant on Nash. That Baffin boot print certainly isn't enough unless you can prove it belongs to Batiste, which you

267

can't. So how do you propose to do this?"

"We need to find Lee Bob Batiste and bust him first," I said. "If we can get him to flip, we'll have Nix Nash. I've got no proof that Lee Bob's still in L.A., but my bet is he is. This isn't a guy you're gonna fly around on United Airlines. Nash probably hired somebody to drive him out here and parked him some place out of the way. If that's the case, he's probably still here. We need to find him and pick him up."

"And how are you going to do that?" Hawkins challenged.

"I'm gonna try and scare the shit out of Nash. He thinks he's way ahead of us. He's not used to getting pushed. If he knows we're on to him, he might do something stupid. If Nash contacts Batiste to warn him, then we try and get to Batiste before he splits."

"You walk in there and tell Nash about all of this and he's gonna throw you out. Then he'll send his lawyers after you. You don't have a shred of proof."

"I have something else in mind," I said. "But before we do it, we need to get a citywide phone trace set up. Then we need units parked strategically around the basin. If Nash calls to warn Batiste, we need to be ready to pounce."

Then I explained the rest of what I had in mind.

Chapter 41

When he first moved to L.A., Shaq O'Neal bought a huge, modern house for his mother on the east end of town, in the hills above La Cañada Flintridge. It sat on a point that overlooked the Rose Bowl to the south and the 210 Freeway and Mount Wilson on the north. The front of the triangular house was three stories of rounded green glass that jutted out on a promontory point and looked like the prow of an ocean liner. When Shaq left the Lakers to play for the Miami Heat, his mother soon followed and the house was sold. With the real estate downturn, it was on the market again. When Hitch and I did our background investigation on Nix Nash, we found out that Nash had worked out a short-term lease deal for the property. He had moved into the mansion two months ago for his six-month stay here.

Even during off-hours in L.A. traffic, La Cañada was at least a forty-minute drive from the *V-TV* studios in Century City. At peak rush hour I figured it could take as much as two hours. The estate was located well outside of the glitzy Hollywood limelight Nash seemed to covet. While it was a magnificent property, it seemed like a strange residential choice, and that got me wondering.

At eight thirty the next morning, Hitch and I were standing beside my bugged Acura in the parking lot of La Cañada High School. Three hours earlier, ESD had begun to organize electronic surveillance teams and position them in various strategic spots around the L.A. Basin. The teams were now setting up receiving equipment so they could initiate a trap and trace on any cell calls transferred from Nash's rental house to one of the hundreds of cell towers in the greater metro area.

We needed a warrant to do a regular hard line phone tap and we couldn't get one, so Alexa and Deputy Chief Hawkins talked the phone company into temporarily shutting off service to Nash's house, which would force him to use his cell if he wanted to place a call. We would not be listening in on his conversation but merely tracking it, so there were no evidentiary or procedural hurdles requiring a judge's permission. No one knew where Lee Bob Batiste was hiding. It could be anywhere in the 490 square miles of Los Angeles. We were hoping the trap and trace would narrow our search to a single cell tower.

"You really think we should be way out here on the east end of town?" Hitch asked as he sipped from a cup of Starbucks coffee we'd picked up on the way out here.

"If you had a guy like Lee Bob Batiste under

wraps, what would you do with him?" I asked.

"I'd have him chained up in the basement with a pound of raw meat."

"But if you couldn't do that, where would you put him?"

"Close enough to know what he's up to."

"That's why I convinced Jeb to give us this sector. There've been dozens of fires in the Angeles National Forest and that dust we got off his boot print had traces of fire retardant."

"So your theory is, Nix Nash leased this house way out here because it was a good out-of-the-way spot up in the hills where he could park Batiste?"

"Yeah."

Hitch cocked a skeptical eye at me but said nothing.

By nine thirty, I got a text message from Jeb informing me that the ten ESD geeks were set up and ready to go. The operation was code-named Black Swan. I don't know who picks these corny op names. When I asked, I was told that Nash was a dirtbag celebrity, a black swan. Some genius on the command floor had come up with it.

We had learned that Nix never left for the *V-TV* studio until after ten in order to miss the rush-hour traffic. At exactly nine thirty, Hitch and I got back into the parked Acura and I called Hitch's cell from mine. As soon as he answered, I hung up.

"What up, Captain?" Hitch said to nobody,

miming the conversation. "You got a latent print from where?" He was playing to the surveillance bug buried in my rearview mirror. "Okay. Gimme it." He paused, then said, "Thanks," and disconnected.

"You won't believe this, Shane." His voice was full of excitement. Like most cops who had risked their lives undercover, he was a remarkably good actor. "The science division got a palm and three fingers off the wall above the toilet in Lita Mendez's bathroom. The print hit came back to somebody named Lee Bob Batiste."

"That's the serial killer Nix Nash busted in the Everglades back in the nineties," I said, giving it my best gee-whiz reading. "Why would he be out here in L.A.?"

"Maybe he and Nash are somehow in this together," Hitch suggested.

"Son of a *bitch*," I said.

By now, both of us were staring at the rearview mirror, hoping our little-theater production was being transmitted to Nash. We got out of the car again so we could talk freely.

"I wonder how much time this will take?" Hitch asked as we sat on a metal bench at the edge of the high school parking lot.

"If somebody is monitoring this bug twenty-four-seven, we should get something immediately. If they're only picking up tapes and checking them later, who knows?"

As it was, it took almost two hours. The sun was high overhead and we were still sitting on the metal bench when Hitch's cell phone rang. It was Jeb.

"You guys must be clairvoyant. He just made a single call. It was received by a cell pod tower in La Cañada off Inverness, up in the foothills near where you are."

"We're on it, Skipper," Hitch said. "Send us some backup from the sheriff's substation in Flintridge. Tell them it's a Code Two run and that we need them nearby but to hold back. Once we get a location we'll radio the sheriff exact directions."

We got in the Acura and hauled ass from our parking place at the high school with Hitch on the GPS giving me directions on how to get to Inverness Drive. We took Berkshire under the 210 Freeway up into La Cañada, climbing into the hills above Nash's rented mansion. When we got to Inverness we started driving west along the winding street, checking out the forest on the right side of the road.

"Look for an old burn," I said as we both scanned the hills for either blackened trees or a patch of new growth.

It made sense that an outdoorsman like Lee Bob would be camping out in the wilderness. From what Nash had told me I sure couldn't see Lee Bob kicking back in a suite at the

Four Seasons cooking roast pig in the bathtub.

We continued to look for old fire areas as we passed Corona Drive and headed up to Haverson, where we merged right. There were more small dirt offshoots up here than I expected. Finally, we found a twisting one-lane road that looked promising and which led us farther up into the hills where a new growth of brush marked a recent fire. The growth only looked to be a few months old. About half a mile up the road we spotted an old rusted-out Airstream trailer sitting on a burned-out, junk-strewn clearing. Off to the right was a crude fire pit.

I dialed up the sheriff's substation and relayed the location; then Hitch and I got out of the Acura.

"You wanna wait for our backup?" Hitch asked.

"Do you?"

"Kinda not our style," he said. "Besides, he's only one guy, and if he's in there, he had to already see us pulling up."

"Okay then, let's clear it," I said.

We both pulled our guns and approached the dwelling slowly, staying away from the front window to defeat a possible line of fire.

Just then a shot rang out from the hillside on our left. Hitch spun around and went down, blood blossoming from his right leg.

"Shit!" he screamed.

I fell on top of him to protect him from additional fire. I couldn't tell exactly where the shot had come from. I had my gun trained on the hillside but couldn't see anyone. When I looked back down at Hitch I saw that he was bleeding badly from his thigh.

"Up there," Hitch grunted, pointing to a scorched stand of trees on the right edge of the old burn.

I could hear someone crashing through the dried foliage up in the tree line. I rolled off Hitch and checked his leg. The shot hadn't hit an artery, but he was losing a lot of blood from a huge exit wound. I pulled off his belt and fixed a tourniquet around his right thigh, a few inches above the wound.

"Hold this in your teeth and keep it pulled tight," I said, handing him one end of the belt, which he clamped between his molars, keeping the pressure on by pulling his head back while still aiming his Beretta in the direction the shot had come from.

I ran back to the car and grabbed the dash mike, switched to the county sheriff's frequency, and made my broadcast. "This is LAPD D-Fifteen. In the hills above Flintridge. We have an active shooter with shots fired and one officer down. I'm at a mountain trailer site in an old burn area half a mile up a dirt road east of Haverson. Cross street Corona. Send backup and EMTs."

I jumped in the car as that call got retransmitted and rogered. I pulled the Acura up to the spot where Hitch was lying and put the car between him and the hillside to shield him from any additional fire. The shooter might have a scoped rifle and could be dialing up a kill shot.

"Go get me some payback, dawg," Hitch hissed through teeth still clamped tightly around the belt tourniquet. "I'm good. I'll cover your run."

"Paramedics are coming. You sure?"

"Go."

I left him and started across the open clearing. I made it with no additional shots fired. Clutching my weapon, I clamored up the mountain grade toward the stand of burned trees. It was a charred hillside, the leafless, misshapen, burned-out trees giving the landscape the blackened look of a war zone.

I searched for broken branches, scuffs in the dirt, or anything that looked like a recent track of any kind. I will admit right now that I'm not much of an outdoorsman, but it didn't take me long to realize the shooter was gone and I was actually sort of lost.

I turned and headed back down, finding my way by stopping occasionally to listen for traffic noise from the 210 Freeway, which I knew was to the north.

After about fifteen minutes I made it down to the clearing where a half a dozen sheriff's cars and an EMT fire unit were now parked near the Acura.

Hitch was lying in the back of an ambulance

with his leg in a compression bandage. The bleeding had stopped, but he had refused to be transported to Huntington Hospital in Pasadena, insisting instead that he remain in charge of our crime scene until I got back. He had also refused to let the uniformed deputies search the trailer without my being there.

"This is a secondary crime scene in a current LAPD homicide investigation," I explained to the lead sheriff.

Before going inside the trailer I told the ambulance driver to get going. The EMTs rolled out using red lights and siren, taking Hitch to the hospital. Then, with two sheriff's deputies flanking me, I approached the trailer. There was a Vespa motor scooter chained to the trailer hitch, which I assumed was Lee Bob's only transportation. That meant he was probably on foot until he could steal something. I kicked open the Airstream's door and stepped across the threshold.

The trailer reeked inside. The smell was a pungent mixture of chemicals. I was familiar with this odor from taking down meth labs in the past. It's produced by cooking a mixture of ephedrine, anhydrous ammonia, red phosphorus, paint thinner, Freon, and battery acid. The reek told me that at one time in the not-too-distant past this Airstream had manufactured crystal meth. Biker gangs had these things parked in remote wilderness areas all around L.A. In the middle of the night with the windows closed to keep the telltale odors from escaping, stringy-haired crystal cookers would fire up their stoves and brew bubbling batches of crank. They picked remote spots like these because of the hard-to-disguise stink these chemicals produced when heated. Most meth cookers ended up inhaling copious quantities of their brew, which killed millions of brain cells and turned them into mumbling idiots. Meth labs also tended to explode more frequently than suicide bombers, and from the look of the Airstream that's exactly what had happened. The original stove had been ripped out, but there were extensive burn marks where it had once stood. A boarded-up window told me that one of these brain-dead assholes had thrown his flaming pot of crystal out the window, where it had promptly ignited the brush and burned down the adjoining hillside. With the trailer ruined, Lee Bob had moved in.

I checked over the rest of the room. A stained sofa was pushed against the wall opposite a new small one-burner butane stove, which looked to me like a recent addition. There was a paint-chipped, cigarette burn–scarred dresser. No mirror, no shower. In the back of the trailer, a toilet sat behind a dirty brown curtain.

I knew I was in the right spot because on the dresser I saw a half-empty box of 129-grain Hydra-Shok Federals.

Chapter 42

A quick survey of the Airstream trailer revealed a potential treasure trove of evidence. A pair of rubber boots were in the back of the small but cluttered closet along with some wadded-up camouflage clothing. As soon as I had done a quick no-touch search, I backed out of the trailer with the two uniformed sheriffs, secured the site, then got on the phone to the crime scene techs and got them rolling.

While I waited for CSI to arrive, I talked with the sheriffs about trying to track Batiste up into the hills by utilizing their mountain rescue team and a fire department chopper. They said they'd get on it. As soon as the techies arrived I turned the crime scene over to them and took off for Huntington Hospital.

As I drove, I began to fit a few more pieces of the puzzle together. The original stove from the burned-out Airstream had been removed and replaced with a small camp stove, a less elaborate cooking device. I wondered if that was Lee Bob's purchase. It was the kind of unit you could pick up in any outdoor supply store. The stove had only one butane burner and no oven and would barely heat a pot of coffee or can of beans. It would never accommodate a complicated gumbo recipe. Maybe Lee Bob had grown tired of eating warmed-over supermarket pork and beans. Maybe that was why he brought the groceries to Lita's the night he planned to kill her. Admittedly strange behavior, but my gut told me that might have been what had happened.

Alexa and Jeb were in the waiting room when I arrived at Huntington Hospital. Hitch was already in surgery, so we went down to the cafeteria to get some coffee. On the way they explained to me that the admitting docs in ER had told them the wound was through the meaty part of Hitch's thigh and, barring infection, wouldn't cause any lasting damage.

"This whole deal is pretty much blown," Alexa said as we returned to the surgery wing and settled on the waiting room couch with cups of cafeteria coffee. "We still don't have any direct evidence against Nash, and if Batiste gets away, all we've got is just an interesting theory."

"There's gonna be plenty of direct evidence in that Airstream," I told her. "There's a pair of rubber boots in the closet that look like Baffins, and I'm betting there will be a triangular scar on the left sole which will match our crime scene print. He also left a box of nine-millimeter Federals on the dresser. If we can match up the lead content in that box to the slugs in Lita's floor, that could put Lee Bob in her kitchen with the murder weapon. It's more than enough to bust him. Like you said, it doesn't directly tie Nash to her murder, but it's a start. All we have to do is get our hands on Batiste and flip him."

She heaved a deep sigh. "If we don't catch Batiste, it's just a semi-weak circumstantial case."

"The good news is this probably takes Stephanie Madrid off the hook," Jeb said.

An hour later my partner was out of surgery. At Hitch's insistence they'd only used a local anesthetic to clean and close the wound, and when they wheeled him back he was still awake. I went in to see him, along with Jeb and Alexa. They left after twenty minutes when it was obvious Hitch was going to be okay.

Once they'd gone, Hitch grinned up at me.

"What was all that Audie Murphy BS?" he asked. "Throwing yourself on top of me. Next time you pull shit like that, I'm gonna need a kiss first."

We reached out and bumped fists.

The docs wanted to keep him overnight as a precaution against infection, so after another hour I headed home. It was around four when I left the hospital. I called Alexa as I drove. She was still at the PAB in a meeting with Clarence Moneymaker and the DA, bringing them up-to-date. They were discontinuing the investigation against Stephanie Madrid. Alexa told me she wouldn't make it home for a few more hours because she had to work on the press release.

I didn't have much hope that Batiste would be apprehended, because a swamp rat like Lee Bob could go to ground indefinitely in the vast 650,000-acre Angeles National Forest.

I was pretty sure an egomaniac like Nash wouldn't leave this hanging and would feel compelled to prove his superiority. I was also pretty sure he'd make the next move. When he did, I resolved to be ready.

The problem was, I never expected what he did next.

Chapter 43

Once home, my body began to crash. I'd been pumping too much adrenaline for too long and was coming down fast. I needed an emotional boost and some sugar, so I went to the fridge and got one of the expensive blond lagers Hitch drinks and grabbed a few Oreos. I walked outside with this feast and came to a stop next to my low white picket fence a foot from the edge of Venice's Grand Canal. I hadn't seen our cat, Franco, in a few days, but it was cat season and he was out hunting up a love connection. I stared down into the murky depths, all two feet of it, and started munching down cookies. The canal is fed by the ocean, and a school of saltwater minnows was swimming in the shallows near where I stood. I watched as a few of them nibbled the mossy rocks at the edge of the bank. The beer was light gold and ice cold. As I chugged half of it down, it made my throat ache.

You can sense when a case is coming to an end. It seems to have a heartbeat. As pieces begin to fall into place the vibe always changes like a big momentum shift in a football game. I could feel the road we were on narrowing and getting slick. I wanted to make sure I didn't finish this one upside down in a ditch.

It was hard for me to wrap my head around the insanity of Nash creating these murders solely for the purpose of driving up his TV ratings. Could there be something else going on with him that I still didn't understand? As I stood watching the little inch-long silver fish nibbling at the moss by my feet, I tried to find a rationale that would explain it. I tried to get inside Nash's head, predict his game.

Going back over what I already knew, he was from a family of cops. When he was on the Florida Marine Patrol, he had humiliated the family name by screwing up a high-profile, media-intense serial killer bust in the Everglades. Lee Bob Batiste had slipped off the law enforcement hook and disappeared like a deadly water moccasin back into that teeming swamp. As a result, Nix had been forced to resign from the

Marine Patrol. His father and brothers were all Dade County cops and they had defended him, argued to keep him on the FMP until the heat died down so his departure wouldn't feel like cause and effect. Then half a year later Nix had quietly resigned. But for a law enforcement family that must have been humiliating. I wondered what Christmas dinner was like at the Nash house that year. Had Nix felt ostracized? Had that chapter in his life changed him, or was Nix a damaged personality from birth?

I walked back inside to my den and pulled down a revised fourth edition of the *Diagnostic and Statistical Manual of Mental Disorders*. I've found in the past reading the *DSM-IV* could be helpful in understanding warped criminal psyches.

I had little doubt by now that Nix was some kind of deviant psychopathic personality. Psychopaths are the most dangerous criminals you can encounter because they share several alarming traits. They're without conscience and are extremely manipulative and, without exception, very smart. This combination makes them extremely dangerous and difficult to catch. Unlike sociopaths, who are rough impulsives who will break social norms with impunity, the psychopath plots, schemes, and executes his plans with cold-blooded precision.

I found the designation in a large section on severe psychotic disorders. I skipped down past delusional paranoid psychosis and sexual sadism and began to read. The further I went, the more certain I was that Nixon Nash fit the category of a pure psychopath almost perfectly. He was cunning and manipulative, narcissistic and a user.

The *DSM-IV* said that pure psychopaths are completely lacking in remorse or empathy. This was certainly the quality that would have allowed Nix to so easily order Lee Bob Batiste to kill Lita Mendez, a person Nix claimed to have an abiding friendship with.

The *DSM-IV* went on to say that the symptoms of psychopathic personality disorder can set in as early as age three or four but are rarely diagnosed until fourteen or fifteen. I made another note to call Miami and check into the reason Nix had not been allowed to join the Metro-Dade Police Department, where the rest of his family served. I began to wonder if the medical issues that had barred him from the department were mental instead of physical. Had the more in-depth psychological testing required by the Dade County police turned up his deviant personality? Was that why he had joined the FMP instead?

The chapter continued listing elements of psychotic personality disorder. Psychopaths tended to have white-collar jobs and generally didn't resort to committing crimes in order to survive, choosing that course only when a huge reward justified the risk. They were frequently articulate, charming, and charismatic. All classifications that pretty much fit Nix Nash. According to the *DSM*, the thing that most motivates a psychopath appears to be a love of control and power. They are masters at reading and exploiting other people's vulnerabilities. Psychopaths' primary weakness tends to be egotism.

Nix had scrupulously planned the killing along with his alibi and, being an extreme egoist, believed he could get away with almost anything. This prevailing weakness was leading him closer and closer to the edge.

As I sat back to think it over, I realized it was almost six o'clock. I'd been at this for over an hour.

Then the phone rang. I reached over and picked it up.

"Yeah?"

"Shane, I need your help," a woman's tense voice whispered. She sounded terrified.

"Marcia?"

"Yes. Listen. He—Nix—he, he's out here," she sputtered breathlessly. "I can't go home. I—"

"Calm down, Marcia. Where are you?"

"He's gonna kill me."

"Where are you?" I demanded again, sharply.

"I'm parked up the block from my apartment. I'm afraid to go in there. He knows I found out what he's doing. I think he could be—" She stopped, then said, "I don't know where he is, but when he gets like this he—"

"Marcia, I need an address."

"Two-Three-Five-Eight Ocean Way in the hills above Malibu. It's just off the Coast Highway. I'm in my car parked up the street. He's crazy, Shane."

"What kind of car are you driving?"

"It's a white Cadillac convertible with the top up. I'll tell you exactly how he keeps doing this, how he solves these cases, but you've got to come now. Only you, nobody else! I can't trust anybody. You've got to promise you'll protect me!"

"I'm on my way. It's gonna take me twenty minutes. Can you stay safe until then?"

"I think so. I'll try."

I hung up, and as I ran through the pantry grabbed a hammer out of a drawer before I continued out back to my car. I got inside and used the tool to knock the rearview mirror off the Acura. I threw the mirror out of the window and into a box next to the driveway. I started the car and pulled out.

I'd be lucky if I could make it in twenty minutes. It would all depend on traffic. I tromped on the accelerator and peeled out, speeding down the alley. As soon as I hung a left on Abbot Kinney Boulevard I could see that the street was hopelessly clogged with 6:00 p.m. traffic.

You aren't supposed to go Code Three without

getting permission from the Communications Division first.

Fuck it, I thought, and flipped on my red lights and siren.

Chapter 44

As soon as I got on the Pacific Coast Highway, I shut down my emergency package but hauled ass, using my horn to get around slower traffic. I wrestled with a tactical dilemma as I drove. Despite Marcia's demand that I come alone, it definitely presented a risk. I didn't know if I could trust her or whether she was setting up a trap. Correct police procedure demanded that I call in and get backup and I was about to do that, but my instincts told me it might not be the right move.

Jurisdictionally, the address in Malibu was in the county, which meant calling in the sheriff.

Marcia Breen sounded panicked. Supposing for the moment she was on the level and Nix was lurking around out by her apartment trying to get his hands on her, then bringing in a bunch of Malibu uniforms in black and whites could spook Nash before I got a chance to scope it out. If Marcia really had solid information that could prove Nash's guilt and could make a statement tying him to Lita's murder, then my case was made. But that still didn't put him in custody. The last thing I wanted was to bust the piñata and not get any candy. In addition, if I showed up with a bunch of cops how would that affect Marcia, who had insisted I come alone?

Part of this thinking, I will admit, is produced by my natural tendency toward lone-wolfing. I've been in situations before where I've specifically asked a sister agency for covert backup only to get surprised by ten fully lit black and whites boiling in looking like a presidential motorcade. I decided the better option was to wait till I got to Ocean Way and then check out the neighborhood, looking for Marcia's white Cad. I'd get her into protective custody, debrief her, and then decide what the next step should be.

It took me over half an hour to get to Ocean Way, which turned out to be a tree-lined canyon street up in the Malibu hills above the PCH. I found her apartment building at 2358 and slow-rolled the address. The development was a beautiful tile-roofed, Spanish-style structure built into the canyon hills. The units looked large and each had a balcony that faced down the canyon toward the ocean.

I drove the narrow street, looking for Marcia's car. I finally saw her white Cadillac Eldorado with the top up parked a block up from her apartment complex on the right. I drove slowly past but could see nobody in the car. Maybe she had ducked down when she saw my head-lights.

I hung a U and came up behind the Cad, parking in a slot two down from her. I pulled out my Springfield XD(M), took the safety off, and chambered up a round. Then I held it surreptitiously down by my right leg as I got out of the Acura, stood beside my car, and made a careful visual sweep of the street. Nobody seemed to be around. It was still early, only a quarter to seven. There was occasional drive-by traffic, residents heading home after work. I walked up to the Cadillac and looked inside.

Empty.

I tried the door and found it unlocked, leaned in, and popped the trunk. Then I walked back to check inside.

Spare tire and jack.

I took another careful look up and down the street, checking behind me. I didn't want to get surprised, but the whole area seemed quiet. Nobody on any of the balconies or between the houses across the street.

I was just getting set to close the trunk when I heard a strange sound. It started as a faint whir but scant seconds later intensified like the buzzing of a large flying beetle. Then it hit the right side of my chest. Sudden intense pain followed.

I looked down and, to my horror, saw that a

large red dart was sticking out of my shirt, just above the right nipple.

"Fuck," I muttered, and snatched at it. But in the one or two seconds since it hit me I was already losing coordination. Sudden numbness spread through my upper body. I missed pulling the dart out on my first try. Whatever drug was in there, it was extremely fast acting, because in the next few seconds I was not even able to lift my right arm for a second attempt. I stood behind the open trunk of Marcia's car, teetering like a drunk, as all the muscles in my body began to spasm and shut down.

I sensed someone walking toward me from my right. Paralysis had already hit and I couldn't even turn my head to see who was approaching. The footsteps came closer.

A tall strange-looking man in camouflage clothes stepped into my field of vision. He was narrow shouldered and almost six and a half feet tall. He had a grotesque face that was a sharp collection of bony planes. Above it rode an unruly shock of red-orange hair. His long, stringy goatee was set off by snow-white skin and freckles. He had a lean body, ropy, as if fashioned out of twisted twine. But his worst feature was his eyes. Gray, predatory, and lifeless. I'd only seen eyes like those on the tiger sharks that sometimes cruise the reefs north of Rincón.

"*Ils demandent dat chu shoot homme,*" he

said in a thick Cajun accent. Then he pulled the dart out of my chest and pushed me roughly into Marcia's open trunk.

I landed next to the spare tire. Then the lid slammed closed and I lay paralyzed in the dark, unable to move a muscle.

Chapter 45

When I woke up, I didn't know where I was. It appeared to be some kind of windowless concrete room. I heard a radio playing bluegrass. A rendition of "Foggy Mountain Breakdown" with guitar and banjo. I was in a straight-back wooden chair. I had regained some mobility and tried to move my arms and legs but couldn't budge. I could only move my head a little. I didn't seem to be tied to the chair but for some reason couldn't move. I turned my head slightly to the right. The room was a large, garage-sized bunker made entirely of gray unpainted concrete. A lone light hung from an electrical cord overhead, but it only lit the center of the room. The periphery fell away into darkness. I could hear the distant hum of a generator outside supplying power. I turned my head farther right. The fin of Marcia's white Cadillac was at the edge of my peripheral vision.

I saw the tall, stringy-orange-haired man sitting at a workbench to my left, his back to me, hunched over working on a project of some kind. The bluegrass music was coming from a CD player at his elbow.

Off to his left, I could see a portable camp stove like the one I'd found in the Airstream trailer. Next to that was a big ice chest. Sitting on top of the chest, a crossbow and a leather shoulder quiver full of red darts.

"Aughhh . . . ," I said, trying to get his attention. I was groggy, but as I continued to regain consciousness, I could feel some of my strength coming back. Whatever he had shot me with seemed to burn off quickly. He turned from what he was working on and looked directly at me.

"Where am I?" I said weakly.

He studied me for a moment with those cold gray eyes but said nothing. Then he turned and went back to his project. I tried to move my arms and legs again but still couldn't. I looked down a second time and now my vision had cleared slightly and I realized I was lashed to the arms and legs of the chair with heavy fishing line. It was looped around my wrist at least ten times, hard to see and impossible to break.

"Lee Bob?" I asked, forming the words carefully around my thickened tongue.

"*Bouche ta gueule*," he said, in Cajun French, his voice strangely reedy and high-pitched.

"You in my *cachot. Ecoute-moi, no gris gris.*"

Not a clue what that meant. He turned back to his workbench and refused to look at me or say anything more.

Half an hour later I heard a metal door slide open and footsteps moved into the concrete room. Nix Nash was suddenly standing in front of me, wearing a tailored tuxedo with a bow tie and cummerbund. He had a festive red carnation pinned to his lapel, a black overcoat draped across his left arm.

"Guess you should've joined my team after all," he said dryly.

"Where's Marcia? What did you do to her?"

"She's waiting in the shed outside."

"What . . . what did he shoot me with?"

"Lee Bob hunts gators with a crossbow in the 'Glades. It's his thing. Loads those darts he makes with succinylcholine. It's a fast-acting skeletal relaxant. A neuromuscular blocker. It can fully paralyze a bull gator in fifteen seconds. It's an animal tranquilizer, so no coroner ever puts it on a blood tox screen. Won't show up at your autopsy, if you even get one."

"You actually think you can get away with killing me?" I asked.

"Yeah. After Lee Bob does his thing, he's gonna get lost for a while, go home. Things will cool off."

Classic psychopathic egotism. Nix was studying me carefully. I saw flashes of adrenalized excitement in his eyes.

"I sorta knew it would come down to this after we had our talk on the *Bounty*," he said. "I tried to warn you. I offered you a fortune and a chance to work this with me. If you'd listened, none of this would have happened."

"You can't kill us," I said slowly. "I'm a police officer. Marcia's an ex–L.A. prosecutor. We both have important friends in Los Angeles. You'll never get away with it."

"You obviously haven't been paying very close attention," he said softly. "I would think by now you'd know I don't leave much to chance." He grabbed a nearby wooden chair, pulled it over, and straddled it, sitting backward. Then he put his chin on his crossed arms and leaned forward, studying me lazily.

"The final confrontation," he said, smiling. "One winner, one loser. It's like great sex without the complaining."

"You haven't won, and you won't. People in my department know what's going on. We found Lee Bob's Airstream. It's loaded with evidence. We're already working on getting a warrant for your arrest."

"Not in any law school I attended," he said. "I admit, you surprised me by finding his hideout so fast, but the fact is, I saw that possibility coming over two days ago. I've been covering my bets ever since we took that sail. None of that stuff you found up there in that Airstream is gonna tie up to anything. I had Bobby throw it all away, buy new. His clothes, tread wear on the boots, all the ammo. It will match nothing at Lita's crime scene."

"Then why are you here? Just come to gloat?"

"I want you to tell me anything that I might not already know."

"Why would I do that?"

"So you and Marcia won't have a horrible last hour with Lee Bob before you both die. He's got a black heart. You don't want that Cajun miscreant experimenting on you with one of his cane knives."

"You knew him in Florida, didn't you? You blew that bust intentionally so he could get away."

Nash paused for a moment pondering that before he said, "I wish it could have been that easy. Unfortunately, I blew that case on the square. It was a mistake, but I was young and impulsive. It was one of the few times I didn't think things all the way through. It cost me dearly, but it also allowed for me to move on, to grow, to explore my psyche. There were dark parts of me I needed to understand. Then, fifteen years later, after I was out of prison and had sold my show in Miami, I knew I needed some kind of an edge for it to be huge. I knew what Lee Bob was. I understood what drove him, even back when I first busted him in the nineties. He couldn't speak proper English, which made him impossible for anybody to talk to. That made him a perfect, watertight partner."

A small, arrogant smile crossed Nash's face as he continued. "I learned Cajun. I'd been working airboats, so I already knew that swamp. After I sold *V-TV* to that local TV station I went back into the 'Glades. It took me a week, but I found him. He'd become even more dangerous than before. He caught and almost murdered me, but using Cajun, I was able to talk him out of it. One day, after things calmed down, he took me to a mud clearing in the middle of the swamp. Nothing but gators, water moccasins, and mosquitoes big as flying beagles. He told me he was building a beautiful city there. 'Le Gran Batiste,' he called it. Dreams are powerful things, Shane. They can define or destroy you. There was nothing there but a bunch of stolen lumber and plastic sheeting, but Lee Bob could see a beautiful sun-washed city. I pay him a monthly salary. He's living to build Le Gran Batiste. It's all he cares about. Since I sold *V-TV*, he's been paid a fortune for the services he's provided. There's enough lumber and plumbing stacked on that sandbar now to open up a Home Depot."

"And you think you can control him? He's a serial killer."

"You're wrong. He's only delusional and territorial. Like the first Cajun settlers, he kills to protect his land. He's not crazy. He's motivated by his dream."

Nash took a moment to think this over before he said, "I have, however, seen Lee Bob at his tortures. You don't want to experience that. Marcia's already come clean. Now you need to tell me what you've learned and I'll see he ends this civilly."

"Not interested."

Nash heaved a disappointed sigh and stood. "Sorry you feel that way, but I can promise you this much: the ending will be great TV."

He looked over at Lee Bob, who had never turned away from whatever he was working on at the bench. "*Sors de la chambre à onze, cher,*" Nash said, then turned back to face me. "Gotta go. The Children's Cancer Auction awaits."

Then he walked out, leaving me there.

Lee Bob finally stood up from his workbench and walked toward me. He was holding a damp white washcloth.

"*Avancez,*" he said, and grabbed my neck, pulling my head roughly forward. Then he clamped the cloth over my nose and mouth. I held off breathing for as long as I could but finally had to inhale. My nose was suddenly filled with a sweet, pungent odor that clogged my senses.

Chapter 46

When I opened my eyes, it was dark outside.

I was in the backseat of Marcia's Cad convertible, my hands firmly tied behind me, my feet still lashed together with fishing line. I tried to speak but quickly realized a gag was jammed deep down my throat. I had to be careful breathing to keep from aspirating.

I looked over and saw that Marcia was also tied up and gagged beside me. Her eyes were bulging with terror.

Lee Bob Batiste was in the front seat behind the wheel, paying no attention to us, tapping his bony fingers on the dash. We were parked off a main road in a dirt lot. To my right, half a block down, I could just make out a road sign that said:

BUENA VISTA

Buena Vista was in Burbank. Out the other window I could see the exit ramp off the 5 Freeway at San Fernando Boulevard a block and a half away. Something about this location began tugging at my memory, but I couldn't pull it together because my head was still freewheeling.

Marcia started to gag from the cloth down her

throat. Lee Bob stopped drumming his fingers and turned sharply around in his seat.

"*Tranquille, cher*," he said. "*Da loup-garou ça s'advance.*"

I didn't know what most of that meant, but I'd taken a trip to Mardi Gras when I first got out of the service and thought I remembered that a loup-garou was some kind of fictitious Louisiana wolfman-monster that wanders around in the night and eats the dead.

Lee Bob checked his watch, turned back, and continued to look out the front windshield. He seemed to be waiting for something. I looked again at Marcia, whose eyes were now darting back and forth in panic; the cords in her neck were rigid.

I was so damn mad at myself for having let this happen. One of these days, if I live, maybe I'll just follow the fucking manual.

I tried to gather my wits. After a few more minutes, I pinned down what was familiar about this particular location. It had a bloody ten-year history.

The railroad intersection with San Fernando and Buena Vista Street in Burbank had produced a number of fatal collisions with the Metrolink. The cops called it the Death Crossing. In the past few years, there'd been twelve train hits on cars at this spot. The intersection was formed like a Y, which made it hard to see up the tracks when you merge from the left. The crossing was equipped with the normal array of warning lights and crossing guards, but the lights face south and are not easily seen by cars crossing the tracks from San Fernando Boulevard on the east. According to half a dozen lawsuits filed against the City of Burbank and the Metrolink, it's possible to make a turn onto the tracks before the metallic crossing guard drops and you can see the flashing lights that warn you a train is coming. Because of this flaw, cars have become trapped on the tracks, unable to get off. Several deaths have resulted from train hits at this spot in the last three years. Because the crossing meets all of the NTSB technical and safety requirements, to date the Metrolink and the city have won each lawsuit. As a result, the intersection has yet to be redesigned.

It didn't take much deduction for me to realize that Marcia and I were about to become the next fatalities.

There would be no prolonged investigation into our deaths. Probably no autopsy, as Nix had suggested. It would be assumed that we were just the next two unfortunate motorists to die here.

We would be victims of a tragic mistake in engineering. It would be covered by the news but dispatched with quickly.

Chapter 47

Lee Bob looked at his watch, then got out of the car, opened the back door, and lifted Marcia out. He put her in the passenger seat, then came around to get me. He lifted me up with almost no effort and carried me to the driver's side of the Cad, shoving me behind the wheel beside Marcia.

It's hard on a man's self-image to be lifted, then carried around and dumped like so much garbage.

"*Da gran rêve pesant, cher*," he said, looking at Marcia. "*Da loup-garot, ça arrive.*"

Then Lee Bob pulled out a vial of clear fluid and poured it on a rag.

He grabbed me by the neck and pulled me toward him, covering my nose and mouth with the cloth for the second time. He held it there until I began to lose consciousness, then pulled the rag quickly back. I was still awake but totally paralyzed. He reached across me and did the same to Marcia.

We were still parked in the dirt lot on a slight rise when I saw the headlight from the approaching Metro train. It rounded into view a mile away, coming toward us at over sixty miles an hour.

Lee Bob shoved me over, then crowded behind the wheel and started the car. I could see the train barreling down the tracks toward us. At sixty miles an hour, that would put it at the intersection in about a minute. Lee Bob had the car moving and was heading toward the track. It wasn't even going to be close. He was going to beat the train by at least twenty seconds.

He pulled the Cad around the corner on San Fernando and drove it up onto the tracks just as the signal lights started flashing and the guard arm dropped both in front and behind us. Then he scrambled out of the front seat, pulled a thin curved knife from a scabbard on his belt, and slashed the fishing line holding my hands and feet. He did the same with Marcia.

"Bonne chance," he said, then slammed the door and sprinted off the track. I could feel the car shuddering with the vibrations of the approaching train. The red lights across the street from us were clanging, the bar arm lights flashing. I was unable to move.

Marcia was staring dumbly up the tracks at the approaching train. We were both trying to claw at the door handles to get out but had no strength to accomplish it.

Then the headlights swept around the last bend in the track and the train was bearing down on us from less than a block away. The engineer saw us and started leaning on the horn. He was going way too fast. The train whistle kept blaring as the white headlamp on the lead car wigwagged back and forth, strobing the car as the train thundered toward us.

We sat there, staring helplessly, watching the end of our lives approach at breakneck speed.

Chapter 48

I've heard that at the moment of death your life will sometimes pass before your eyes as a series of living tableaus. As I stared in terror at the approaching train, I had no retrospective vision— no precious insights. I was just sitting there, unable to move, locked in full panic. The only thing that kept running through my brain was, *This can't be happening.*

The train whistle blared relentlessly now less than a hundred yards away as a hundred and fifty tons of metal and glass bore down on us. The brakes were shrieking as they locked up on the track, throwing out sparks on both sides. Metal squealed against metal. We were seconds from impact.

First I heard the crossing guard arm behind us shatter. Then our car was hit from behind. As Marcia and I were thrown forward the airbags deployed. Next we were being pushed violently across the intersection and off the tracks. The nose of the Cad hit the crossing arm on the opposite side of the intersection, broke through it, and kept going.

Once the Cadillac broke through the guard arm, the tires cramped and it brodied right, spinning sideways. For a second I could see out the driver's side window. A gray Navigator with smoked windows was behind us, powering us off the tracks. As we skidded sideways, the big SUV turned sharply with us and both vehicles barely cleared the rails. Seconds later the Metrolink flashed past.

The door to the Navigator opened and Lester Madrid climbed out. Leaving his cane behind, he limped quickly over to us and opened the car door. He pulled me from the front seat and laid me on the ground. Next he limped around to the passenger side to free Marcia. As he pulled her out, the train was still screeching by, trying to stop, but it was going so fast it would keep going for almost two more blocks. All I could see was the taillight as it finally came to a halt almost a quarter mile away.

I struggled to sit up. My head was spinning. Lester came back around the car and looked at me with disgust.

"I can't believe I'm down to rescuing ass-wipe pussies like you," he growled.

"Help me up," I said.

He pulled me to my feet, and as soon as he did I started teetering. I felt a mile tall and six inches wide. I swayed and finally leaned against the Cad, trying to keep from falling down.

Marcia was lying on the grass on the far side of the road. She was beginning to regain some coordination and was struggling to get to her feet. She couldn't make it but managed to prop herself up in a sitting position with her arms out behind her.

"Who parked you up there?" Lester asked. I couldn't answer, so he went on. "I've been following you for two fucking days, Scully. How did you miss me? You should work on getting your head out of your ass."

"Lee Bob Batiste. We need to get him, Les. He killed Lita."

"Come on," he said. "I saw where he went."

Lester helped me into the front seat of the Navigator and then pulled Marcia to her feet and helped her into the seat behind.

I heard some train crewmen running toward us, their footsteps crunching the gravel beside the tracks as they approached. Lester got behind the wheel, slammed the door, and swung a U.

"Hey!" somebody yelled. "Come back! Where you going?!"

But Lester already had the Navigator in a smoking turn and squealed it back up and across the tracks.

"Where'd Lee Bob go?" I asked.

"Took off running up that side street back there," Lester said. "Looks like designer houses and a cul-de-sac. Ends up by the foothills."

He had the pedal down and the engine roared as the big SUV screamed across San Fernando Boulevard and made a right. We headed toward the foothills about a mile and a half away.

"Oh, shit," Marcia muttered, ducked her head down, and threw up in the backseat.

Lester glanced back angrily at her. "You gonna puke, lady, do you mind doing it in your fucking purse?"

We flew up a residential street toward the hills beyond.

"There's a backup piece in the glove box," he said.

I fumbled with the latch, but I couldn't get it open. My coordination was still shot.

Lester reached over and opened the glove box, then pulled out a .38 and dropped it on my lap.

"Try not to shoot me with it," he growled.

We reached the cul-de-sac at the end of the road and Lester smoked the Navigator to a stop. I looked past the new designer houses and caught a glimpse of what looked like a man running in the moonlight through the brush up into the hills beyond.

Lester got out, then turned to Marcia. "Can you drive?"

"I think so," she said. Her hair was in tangles.

She had vomit stains on the front of her once-stylish gray designer pantsuit.

"Take this car back down the hill. On the way, call nine-one-one and give them this location. There's a police station a mile away on San Fernando. Get help up here."

Then, as Marcia pulled out, Lester led the way up toward the hillside. I stumbled along behind him clutching his .38 in my still-numb hand.

Chapter 49

Lester was limping without his cane but making damn good time. I was struggling to keep pace.

We made our way between two houses and exited a back gate to a wilderness area behind the designer development. I saw Lee Bob loping across a large field of dry, brown grass cover. He was almost a quarter mile away, heading toward a three-hundred-foot rock cliff. If he got over the top, he could disappear into the mountains. He was barely lit by moonlight as he got to the rocks and began climbing the craggy surface, using his ropy build to pull himself effortlessly up.

Lester Madrid knelt in the dirt at the edge of the brown grassy meadow and watched Lee Bob scale the cliff.

"Fucking little spider monkey, ain't he?" Lester said.

"I don't think I can make that climb," I said, as I dropped in beside him. "I don't know what drug that nut-job gave me, but my coordination is shot."

"With this leg I sure as shit ain't gonna climb no rock wall," Lester said. "Come on."

We moved out into the field, breaking through tinder-dry brush, and hurried to close the distance to the cliff face.

Lee Bob was now almost halfway up, moving faster all the time as the degree of ascent lessened near the top. He must have heard us crashing through the brush below, because he paused and then turned to look down. He studied us for a minute, hanging from the rock face, then resumed his climb.

"If he gets over that ridge, he'll be gone," I said hotly. "We gotta do something."

"Fuckin' calm down. He ain't getting over no ridge," Lester replied. Then he licked his fingertips and moistened his gun sight.

"You can't just shoot him in the back," I said.

"Suggestion box is open, Dudley Do Right, but you better make it fast." I couldn't come up with anything. The Cajun was almost at the top of the cliff as Lester carefully sighted down the barrel and slowly began to squeeze the trigger. It was a tough shot. Problem was I needed Lee Bob alive to make my case against Nash. I certainly didn't want this retired SIS gunfighter dropping him.

Without thinking, I lunged at Lester's gun hand, trying to throw off his aim. My speed and coordination were still way off. Lester saw my move coming and swung the Glock at me, slamming the barrel into my head. I fell sideways.

As I struggled to get up Lester barked, "Stay down," then retrained the 9mm on Lee Bob.

Batiste had just arrived at the top of the cliff face. He turned for a minute to look back at us. I could see him pointing a gun. A plume of dust kicked up a foot to the right of where we were. The sound was a bit slower and a second later we heard his distant gunshot.

"Adios, motherfucker," Lester said, and triggered off one shot.

Lee Bob was almost five hundred yards away and a hundred feet above us. Under optimum conditions it would have been a tricky shot. Out here, under moonlight, it was pretty much impossible.

As soon as the retort on the Glock sounded, Batiste straightened up from the impact. The bullet must have gone through him without hitting bone, because instead of blowing him backward, the recoil from the through-and-through shot tumbled him forward.

He took one hesitant step toward the ledge, as if to look down and check the height. Then he continued awkwardly forward, finally taking a swan dive off the top, waving his arms and yelling as he fell. His high-pitched scream cut the still night like a predator's cry. It was cut off abruptly as he thudded into the dirt.

"Not bad for a lousy three-inch barrel," Lester said.

When he looked over at me I saw the moonlight glint in gray eyes. No emotion, no feeling. Like Lee Bob's they displayed a remorseless soul. Shark eyes prowling in shallow water.

"Let's go spit on the carcass," Lester said.

He moved off, heading toward the place where Lee Bob fell. I got to my feet and followed.

Batiste's body was sprawled at an unnatural angle. His neck was broken, skull crushed. His orange hair was beginning to darken, turning red with matted blood.

He lay there in the dark, waiting for the loup-garou.

Chapter 50

"The friends of this charity deserve a huge standing ovation, so give it up for yourselves. Let's hear it!"

Nix Nash was onstage at a podium with signage that read FRIENDS OF THE CHILDREN'S CANCER FUND in the grand ballroom of the Beverly Hills Hotel. His eyes were shining happily as he stood in the spotlight gazing out at an audience of well-turned-out people and Hollywood celebrities who were now on their feet, applauding their own charity.

"You know, there's an important difference between love and friendship," Nash continued. "While the former delights in extreme opposites, the latter demands a high degree of quality. The Friends of the CCF display that quality daily as they give care and devotion to the children who desperately need this help."

I was standing in the wings at the edge of the stage in the large ballroom with two uniformed cops beside me. We had units from the Hollywood Division and the Beverly Hills PD deployed. I watched Nash from the side of the stage as he continued his pitch to raise money for children with cancer. Something must have alerted him to my presence. Some vibe—some predatory sense of danger. Maybe it was just the powerful hatred I was focusing at him.

He turned suddenly and saw me, then stopped mid-sentence and stared. I gave him an innocent little hand wave and then beckoned him toward me with one index finger.

He froze for a moment, the silk lapels of his beautifully tailored tux shining in a bright follow spot. Then he began to back away from the podium, still holding the hand mike. The audience sensed something was wrong and the room full of people at this five-hundred-dollar-a-plate dinner began to murmur. Nix turned quickly and bolted toward the curtain behind him, frantically pawing the fabric, looking for an opening.

There was nothing back there but a wall. I knew because I'd just checked it three minutes earlier.

Two uniformed officers moved out onto the stage from the other wing as two more teams came up the aisles toward the stage.

"Excuse me," Nash said, and threw down his microphone. Because six cops were closing in from the left, he turned and rushed offstage in my direction.

I grabbed him as he tried to push past.

"Hang on a minute, Nix. We've got a broken window to repair here."

"Let go!" he shrieked.

"I got this," I said to the two uniformed cops behind me who were moving in to assist. Then I spun Nix around and pushed him against a wall. I pulled out my cuffs and hooked his right wrist, but I was a little sloppy doing it, and before I could secure his left Nash pulled his hand free and threw a punch at me. It was a right cross and it was slow and ugly. He threw it from chest high and I easily knocked it aside; then I turned him away from the two startled cops.

"You don't want to do that, Nix," I said. "Just calm the fuck down."

But he was in a full panic and swung on me again.

I'd like to say that I didn't want to hit him and that this awkward hookup was simply the result of Lee Bob's drug overload, but that would have been a lie. I actually gave Nash the opening. I wanted the arrogant dirtbag to take his shot.

His second swing was a roundhouse left. Not much of a problem and I ducked under it easily as well.

My uppercut, on the other hand, was devastating. I heard his teeth chip as his jaws slammed together. His head went back. Blood spurted. I put everything I had into that shot. Every ounce of strength. I was hitting him for a lot of people, so it had to count. My punch was for every department that had lost credibility because of his dumb TV program. It was for Russ and Gloria Trumbull and their daughter, Hannah. I hit him for Hitch, who had a new hole in his leg courtesy of all this bullshit, and for Detectives Caleb Cole and Ronald Baron, who lost their jobs in Atlanta, as well as for Joffa Hill, aka Fuzzy, who was doing life in a Georgia prison on multiple murders he didn't commit. I hit Nash for Frank Palgrave, J. J. Blunt, and Marcia Breen, once good servants of the people who got confused and had sold out for Nash's version of success. But I especially hit him for Lita Mendez. She hated cops, but I was her final advocate. My job was to speak for the dead.

It sickened me that she gave up her life for six or eight points on the Nielsen ratings.

It was a helluva shot. Nash went out with a mouthful of ivory chips.

I didn't even feel it when the middle knuckle on my right hand broke. I was lost in the moment. That full of revenge.

Chapter 51

At the end of a case, you like things to be clean. Everything neat, every box on the arrest form checked. Unfortunately, on this one it didn't seem like that was going to happen.

Lee Bob was dead and couldn't turn State's evidence. Marcia didn't have anything but supposition on what Nix was doing, and I already knew most of what she had but couldn't prove it. Nix Nash was locked up in Metro Detention Center jail awaiting an indictment on the charges of kidnapping and conspiracy to commit murder. Marcia and I had been his victims, were eye-witnesses, and could swear to everything in court. Because we couldn't put him behind a direct murder charge, if Nix got the right lawyer he would probably end up getting twenty-five to life. With good time, he could be out in seventeen years. Not enough.

And I still didn't know who the hell had killed nurse Hannah Trumbull.

The next day, Hitch and I were back in our cubicle at Homicide Special, working that case into the evening. Hitch had a huge dressing on his thigh, and for the first time since I've known him he didn't look like a runway model. He was in baggy, oversized sweatpants and a sweater. I had a cast on my right hand to secure my broken knuckle. The plastic went all the way up my forearm. As far as Hannah Trumbull was concerned, we didn't have too much to go on, but Hitch and I had told her parents we would get some justice for their daughter and we were both determined to keep that promise. Problem was, the case was going nowhere.

At eight o'clock, as we were getting ready to leave, our phone rang.

"If that's my pizza order, tell the guy it's too late," Hitch said irritably as I nodded and picked up the joint line.

"Scully and Hitchens," I said.

"You guys are putting in long hours," a familiar voice said. It was Nix Nash, but he sounded different, like he was talking through a wired jaw, which he was. Nix was calling from the phone in the MDC.

"Whatta you want?"

"I want to make a deal."

316

"If you want to plead your case, take it up with the District Attorney."

"I don't want to plead it; I want to trade it."

"Just a minute." I put him on hold and looked over at Hitch. "This dirtbag is trying to give us somebody."

"Fuck him," Hitch said.

" 'Kay." I punched the phone up again. "Sorry, Nix. Take it up with the DA."

"I don't like the DA. Besides, you and I have simpatico and it's the Trumbull case I want to trade for. I understand you're working that now."

I sat there trying to deal with this.

"I know who killed Hannah Trumbull," he went on. "I had that case solved before I even picked it. It was going to be part of the show's finale. Got an eyewitness to the crime. It's direct testimony and will bring the killer to justice. I give that to you and in return you broker my deal with the DA for me."

"On my way," I said, and hung up.

"You're not actually thinking about dealing with that shit stick?" Hitch said, appalled.

"He says he can give us Hannah's murderer."

Hitch stood and followed me to the elevator.

After sitting vacant for over two years due to a city budget crisis, the gleeming new MDC where Nix Nash now resided had finally opened. This state-of-the-art facility was a much needed replacement to the decaying, over-crowded jail at Parker

Center. Hitch and I left our weapons in the gun locker and were buzzed back. We passed through automatic security doors and walked down a corridor wired with video cameras to an I-room where Nash was waiting. I told the jailor to activate the video equipment; then Hitch and I walked inside.

Gone were Nash's troublesome choices over wardrobe. He now only had one shade on his color wheel—jailhouse orange. His mouth was wired shut and he was chained to the wall, sitting at a low table on an attached metal stool.

Despite this huge change in his life circumstances, he seemed strangely happy and at ease. As if none of this really affected him. A total lack of emotion. Like Scott Peterson, he didn't seem to care. It was classic psychopathic behavior. I guess if you don't experience human emotion, everything is just in the moment.

"Make this good, Nix, 'cause if it starts coming off like bullshit, we're outta here."

"I know who killed Hannah Trumbull," he said again. "I have a witness. He never talked because he knew the killer and the man scared him. He didn't want to get involved."

"Keep going."

"If I give you this, what I'm going to need is a big reduction in charges."

"I can't make any deals."

"No, but you can take it to the DA and argue to support it."

"Who was the shooter, Nix?"

"Bring the DA over. Help me cut my deal. What I've got is provable. It's a slam-dunk murder one with a wit and a motive. When you hear what I have, you'll know it's too good to walk away from."

"I'll see what I can do."

We left the jail. Hitch and I walked across the quad toward the PAB.

"You believe him?" Hitch asked.

"Yeah," I said. "I don't think this guy bluffs."

We called Chase Beal, the county DA, and ran it past him. Chase set up a meeting for nine o'clock the next morning.

I went home. Alexa was cooking dinner. I told her what happened. She could see how bummed I was and gave me a long, tender embrace.

Later that evening we made love.

Afterwards we lay in each other's arms.

I didn't sleep worth a damn all night. I already knew who Nix was going to give us.

Chapter 52

A friend of mine in retail once told me that a job is 90 percent things you don't want to do, for 10 percent that you do. I remember thinking at the time those were pretty lousy percentages.

Police work can be ugly, emotionally draining, and yes, you do see the worst in the human condition. You meet and have to deal with serious predators like Nix Nash and Lee Bob Batiste. You see drive-by killers whose hate burns with the strong smell of sulfur. In amongst this human wreckage, you encounter tragic cases like the Persian rug and Fuzzy—so lost and passed over, their world is defined by their delusions.

Even with all this witnessed devastation, I've always felt the job was about much more. I hope this doesn't sound corny, but I believe it's about getting answers for the lost and dispossessed, about finding justice for victims and solutions for problems so ugly that you know in the end you have to make a difference. It's what keeps most cops going. But occasionally, you get a solution where you're the one feeling lost.

We arrived at the MDC at nine the next morning. Chase Beal didn't make it, but he assigned the duty to ADA Ferguson St. Claire, a big ex-linebacker who once played for UCLA and only missed the pros by three-tenths of a second in the forty. St. Claire had graduated law school and was one of the DA's brightest minds. Still huge and the color of polished mahogany, he was one of those guys who never smiled but always seemed to be slightly bemused. It was in his attitude, not his expression.

We filed into I-room four and met Nixon Nash.

He was strangely subdued this morning. He had an attorney named Timothy Rutland with him, but it was soon obvious that Rutland was just an ornament and that Nash wanted to handle the negotiation himself. Rutland settled into a seat beside his client, who sat on a stool chained to the wall. It seemed an unnecessary precaution, because I had already broken Nash's jaw and Fergie could have drop-kicked him over the dome in City Hall.

After the introductions, Fergie said, "Let's hear what you're trading."

"I can give you Hannah Trumbull's murderer," Nash said.

I had already prepped Fergie and he had Hannah's case file in his briefcase.

"Then do it," he said.

"I want a few reductions in charges."

"Show us your wares," Ferguson said.

"Here's what I'm looking for," Nash continued. "The double kidnapping needs to get kicked down to illegal restraint, the conspiracy to commit murder to involuntary manslaughter."

Ferguson had been writing in a notebook, but he stopped in the middle of this and looked up.

"You must be getting some pretty good drugs in here," he said.

"I'll give you the shooter now, just as a preamble, so you'll know how tasty this is. You will never be able to charge him without my witness. I think once you hear who the doer is you're going to change your mind on the disposition of charges."

Ferguson began tapping his pen on his notebook but finally nodded.

"Hannah Trumbull was shot and killed at her apartment in December of '06 by Lester Madrid, who was then a current member of SIS."

It was exactly what I thought Nash was going to say. This was complicated for me, because only two days ago Lester Madrid had saved Marcia Breen's life and mine.

"What was the motive?" Ferguson asked.

"Adulterous, love triangle," Nash replied. If his jaw hadn't been wired shut, he would have been smiling. "Lester was having an affair with Hannah Trumbull," he continued. "His wife suspected it, but couldn't prove it. She confronted Hannah at the hospital. They had words. After that, Hannah tried to convince Sergeant Madrid that since his wife already suspected the affair, he should just leave her. If he didn't, Hannah threatened to go to Stephanie herself. It's not healthy to threaten guys like Sergeant Madrid, so it didn't end well for poor Hannah."

"And you've got a witness to all this?" Fergie asked.

"Yep. A retired cop. He even dated Hannah once. She confided all this to him, looking for his help."

"That's hearsay," Fergie said. "You better do better than that."

"He saw Lester pull up in front of her house. She'd called him and asked him to look out for her. He was right outside her house, looking in the windows, when Lester dropped her. He saw Lester carry her out and put her in her car in the garage."

"And all these years later, he's finally developed a conscience?" I asked.

"He's in the final stages of bone and liver cancer," Nash said. "So this deal has a tight clock on it. He won't be around to testify or depose a month from now. I guess he doesn't want to try getting past Saint Peter with that much dirt on his shoes."

"I'll kick it down to first-degree murder with no death penalty," Fergie told Nash.

"Never happen."

"Then I guess you need to go back to your cell now," Fergie said. Nash's attorney called the guards and they led him out.

"Illegal restraint and involuntary manslaughter, that's gonna be less than ten years. How does this guy think he rates that?" Fergie groused.

"He doesn't," I said. "But the Trumbull murder is our case. We'd sure like to close it. And then there's a big murder case with a miscarriage of justice in Atlanta. We might be able to sign Nash up for a piece of that and get them to add a few years, maybe get him up over twenty."

323

"Instead of focusing on the charge, how about cutting a deal on the length of sentence?" Hitch suggested helpfully.

The rest of the day was spent negotiating with Nash and his attorney. The sentence the DA signed off on was for twenty years on two counts of conspiracy to commit murder.

Hitch and I stopped for a beer after work. We sat in a booth, drinking silently. It was a victory that felt like a loss.

Chapter 53

V-TV was immediately yanked off the air. A cheer went up in squad rooms all across America. The next week was spent gathering evidence and signing off on all our deals.

We got in touch with the Atlanta PD and told them about Joffa Hill aka Fuzzy's potential miscarriage of justice.

Our evidence techs collected beer bottles and coffee cups from the kitchen of Lee Bob's Airstream trailer. We sent them to Atlanta with a request that they scan the overcoat that Fuzzy had been wearing for a DNA match. It came back that some of Lee Bob's DNA was on the sleeve of that coat, which tied him to the murders in Piedmont Park. The Atlanta PD was so angry about the way the case had gone down with Nix Nash and *V-TV*, they were actually eager to reopen the investiga-tion. There was a pretty good chance they would be able to tie Nix Nash to Lee Bob in Atlanta. If they could, Nash would catch a piece of their prosecution, adding more years to the sentence he had agreed to here in L.A.

Hitch and I left the PAB in his Porsche at two thirty the day after the deal was cut with Nash. It was before any of this had hit the news.

It was one of those crystal-clear Santa Ana days when the wind blew out of the desert and L.A. seemed to sparkle. We drove over the hill to Studio City and parked in front of Russ and Gloria Trumbull's house, then sat in silence for a minute.

"This is why we do it," Hitch said.

"Yes," I said. "It is."

We got out of the car and walked up the steps to the front door. Hitch rang the bell. After a moment Mrs. Trumbull opened up. She was wearing pink shorts and a white jersey top over flats. She looked at us as if she couldn't quite remember who we were.

"Mrs. Trumbull, we're the detectives working on your daughter's murder case," I prompted.

"I know who you are," she said, and the anger in her voice confirmed it.

"Is Mr. Trumbull home?"

"He's taking a nap. Is this important?"

"Yes, ma'am," I said. "Could you please get him?"

"Come in."

She led us into the neat living room. We sat on the sofa, and as she left, Hitch and I locked gazes. He nodded at me and finally smiled.

Gloria Trumbull returned a few minutes later with her husband in tow. Russ was rubbing his eyes as he came across the room, wearing jeans and a sweater.

"Sorry, I was taking a nap," he said. "What is it? More questions?"

"Mr. and Mrs. Trumbull, we came here to tell you we've made an arrest in your daughter's case."

"An arrest?" Mrs. Trumbull said, her hands wandering up to hover near her mouth.

"Yes, ma'am," Hitch said. "It was a police officer. A sergeant named Lester Madrid. He'd been dating your daughter."

Then both of them sat down opposite us.

"A policeman," Gloria said.

"Yes," I replied.

Hitch and I told them what had happened, and when we were through they sat there in silence.

"You mean they actually caught him? He's in custody right now?" Russ finally asked.

"Yes, sir," I answered. "He was charged with the crime this afternoon. It's a solid case with a witness. The indictment will come down in a day or two."

They looked at each other. Gloria Trumbull started to mist up and then began to cry.

"We never thought this day would come," she said, through her tears.

"We just wanted to come over and tell you in person," I said. "We wanted you to hear it from us first."

Hitch and I stood. The Trumbulls walked us to the door. When we turned to leave, both Russ and Gloria reached out and stopped us.

"You kept your promise," Russ said. "Thank you, so very much. You can't know how much this means."

But I did know. It was on both their faces.

"We'll never be able to repay you," Gloria added.

Then she pulled us forward, gave us each a kiss on the cheek, and said, "God bless you."

We left them standing in the doorway, watching us as we walked away. We sat in the car for a long time. Then the Trumbulls closed their front door.

The San Gabriel Mountains were almost purple in the clear golden sunlight. The sky was so blue it seemed like a gift from God. I didn't have words for what I felt, but Hitch, the ersatz movie producer and bon vivant, who always seemed to be looking for a better gig, was able to sum it all up in just one sentence.

"Sometimes this job really kicks ass," he said.

Center Point Publishing
600 Brooks Road ● PO Box 1
Thorndike ME 04986-0001 USA

(207) 568-3717

US & Canada:
1 800 929-9108
www.centerpointlargeprint.com